EDUCATED BY THE EARL

Second Sons of London
Book One

Alexa Aston

Dragonblade Publishing, Inc. is an imprint of Kathryn Le Veque Novels, Inc.
P.O. Box 7968
La Verne CA 91750
ceo@dragonbladepublishing.com

Produced in the United States of America

First Edition February 2022
Trade Paperback Edition

ARE YOU SIGNED UP FOR DRAGONBLADE'S BLOG?

You'll get the latest news and information on exclusive giveaways, exclusive excerpts, coming releases, sales, free books, cover reveals and more.

Check out our complete list of authors, too!

No spam, no junk. That's a promise!

Sign Up Here

www.dragonbladepublishing.com

Dearest Reader;

Thank you for your support of a small press. At Dragonblade Publishing, we strive to bring you the highest quality Historical Romance from some of the best authors in the business. Without your support, there is no 'us', so we sincerely hope you adore these stories and find some new favorite authors along the way.

Happy Reading!

CEO, Dragonblade Publishing

Additional Dragonblade books by Author Alexa Aston

Second Sons of London Series
Educated by the Earl
Debating with the Duke

Dukes Done Wrong Series
Discouraging the Duke
Deflecting the Duke
Disrupting the Duke
Delighting the Duke
Destiny with a Duke

Dukes of Distinction Series
Duke of Renown
Duke of Charm
Duke of Disrepute
Duke of Arrogance
Duke of Honor

The St. Clairs Series
Devoted to the Duke
Midnight with the Marquess
Embracing the Earl
Defending the Duke
Suddenly a St. Clair
Starlight Night

Soldiers & Soulmates Series
To Heal an Earl
To Tame a Rogue
To Trust a Duke
To Save a Love

To Win a Widow

The Lyon's Den Connected World
The Lyon's Lady Love

King's Cousins Series
The Pawn
The Heir
The Bastard

Medieval Runaway Wives
Song of the Heart
A Promise of Tomorrow
Destined for Love

Knights of Honor Series
Word of Honor
Marked by Honor
Code of Honor
Journey to Honor
Heart of Honor
Bold in Honor
Love and Honor
Gift of Honor
Path to Honor
Return to Honor

Pirates of Britannia Series
God of the Seas

De Wolfe Pack: The Series
Rise of de Wolfe

The de Wolfes of Esterley Castle
Diana
Derek
Thea

PROLOGUE

The Shepton School, Kent—1793

S PENCER HADDOCK WAS terrified.
    And elated.

He glanced down as the carriage rumbled along the road toward The Shepton School. It was to be his new home for the coming term now that he was old enough to discard his tutor and go off to school as Wilford did each year. Of course, Wilford, being ten years Spencer's senior, had left The Shepton School several years ago and was now starting his last year at Eton. After that, he would be off to Cambridge, where all Haddock men went for seasoning and to complete their education.

Where Wilford was a terrible student, Spencer excelled at his studies. His tutor had called Spencer his finest student in all his years of private instruction. He couldn't help it—he loved learning. History. Mathematics. Languages. Everything about learning appealed to him. Wilford had laughed at him, calling him too eager. It was the only time his brother had spoken to him this summer.

His father hadn't spoken to him at all.

Spencer had hoped that the earl would actually go with him this first time to The Shepton School. After all, it was in Kent, where their family's country estate stood. It only took a little under two hours to reach it, according to the coachman who drove Spencer today. Instead, his father disappointed him today as he did every day in living memory, for all Spencer's seven years. He hadn't come up to the nursery while Spencer ate his last breakfast at Stoneridge. Nor had he bothered to step outside as the carriage pulled up.

He was used to it. As a second son, he was most often ignored. The Earl of Middlefield had his heir apparent in Wilford and wasn't interested in anyone else. Spencer wondered if his mother had paid him any attention. She had died in childbirth when he was two, along with the babe she delivered. He couldn't remember what she looked like. Only that she smelled faintly of lavender. If she would have lived, perhaps things might have been different.

It didn't matter. He was off to school. Excited to be gone from Stoneridge and the narrow world he inhabited there. Oh, his tutor had taken him out on the estate for studying nature and riding lessons but Spencer longed to see more of the world. The farthest he'd been from home before today was to Middleditch, the nearest village which was four miles from Stoneridge. That was why he was elated to actually be going somewhere.

Still, his excitement was mixed with a healthy dose of terror. He would know no one when he arrived. He didn't know how to make friends since he'd never been around boys his own age. His tutor had called Spencer an old soul. He wasn't certain if that was a compliment or not.

The carriage slowed a bit and he glanced out the window, seeing they turned and headed up toward an enormous building.

This was it. His new school. He swallowed, his mouth dry, as the vehicle turned into a circular drive. Moments later, a footman opened the door.

"We're here, Lord Spencer."

Climbing from the carriage, he glanced around and saw half a dozen other carriages nearby. Boys spilled from them, along with the adults who had escorted them. Trunks were being taken down. Greetings were shouted back and forth.

He was frightened out of his mind.

"Good morning, young man," a voice said. "I am Mr. Whittaker, headmaster of The Shepton School."

Spencer swallowed, standing straighter, and offered his hand as he said, "Good morning, Mr. Whittaker. I am Lord Spencer Haddock. I am a new pupil."

"You will be known as Mr. Haddock," the headmaster informed him. "Some boys here already claim a title. Some are scholarship students. We at The Shepton School try to look at all our students as equals."

"I like that," he said and then added, "I like to learn."

The older man chuckled. "Then you have come to the right place, Mr. Haddock." He consulted a page in his hand, telling Spencer his room assignment and directing the footman to take the trunk inside.

"I see you are alone today," the headmaster noted. "Your brother is Wilford and your father is the Earl of Middlefield. Is that correct?"

"Yes, sir."

Mr. Whittaker harrumphed. "It is good to have you here, Mr. Haddock. I hope you will prove to be a more engaged student than your brother."

"Oh, Wilford hates books and learning. We are opposites," he assured the headmaster.

"Go along, then. Follow your footman upstairs to your dormitory room," Mr. Whittaker urged.

Spencer hurried inside and found the servant heading up the stairs with his trunk. Other men, whom he decided were tutors at the school, were giving directions. Boys were calling out to one another. The air crackled with excitement.

They went down a long corridor and found Number Twelve, the dormitory room he had been assigned to, and went inside. Two older boys were already there, their trunks open as they unpacked.

"I am Georgie Putnam, your prefect," said the taller one. "I am in charge of this room and the boys within it."

He offered his hand and Spencer took it. "I am Spencer Haddock."

"You are over there," Georgie said and pointed to a cot on the opposite side of the room. "The last one. Have your servant leave the trunk. You are to unpack on your own. Boys at The Shepton School learn to do for themselves."

He nodded to his footman, who took the trunk and set it in front of the cot and gave him an encouraging smile.

"I hope you enjoy your new school, Lord Spencer. We'll be back to get you at the end of the term."

"Thank you."

He began unpacking as other boys entered. The prefect met them and pointed them toward their assigned cots.

Two boys entered together. Spencer had seen them climb from the same carriage, talking animatedly. Obviously, they knew each other. Whether they were friends or brothers, he couldn't say. Then he saw the two men accompanying them. The pair said a few words and shook hands with who Spencer assumed were their fathers. The adults left and the two boys came toward him, having been assigned the places nearest him by the prefect.

"Hullo," said the one who sat on the cot directly next to Spencer's. "I'm Owen Hasbury. This is Everett Wayland."

"I'm Spencer Haddock," he said neutrally, trying his best not to sound too eager.

The one called Everett smiled at him. "Good to meet you, Spencer Haddock." Then he looked to Owen, who had medium brown hair and dark brown eyes. "How did I do?"

Owen laughed, his brown eyes full of mischief. "Very well, Ev." Looking at Spencer, he added, "Ev and I are neighbors. Our fathers are friends. Our older brothers are best friends. We are friends, too. Ev is a little shy. I try to make him talk more."

"I can be a bit shy," Spencer shared.

Owen grinned. "Then we will have to liven you up a bit."

"I don't want to get into any trouble," he said quickly.

"There's fun—and then there's trouble," Owen said. "I know about both. I stay in trouble at home but I know when and how to behave. Ev's like you. Wants to always be good."

"There's nothing wrong with that," he said defensively.

"I agree," Everett said. "Is this your first year here?"

"It is." Spencer glanced around. "My brother went here. He's ten years older than I am so he is at Eton now."

"So are our brothers," Everett told him. "They are six years ahead of us and don't pay a bit of attention to either of us." He nodded at Owen. "We're second sons. The spares to the heirs."

"I am a second son, too," he shared and then confessed, "my father and brother pretty much ignore me, too."

"Same here," Owen said, as he lifted clothes from his trunk and set them out on his cot. "I don't care. I wouldn't want to be an earl. Too much to do."

"I never want to be a duke," Everett said, shuddering. "Mervyn can have the title."

"It means we get to be in the army," Owen said, his eyes lighting up.

"The army?" Spencer asked, puzzled.

"Don't you know?" Owen asked. "First sons are the heirs and get the title and money. Second sons go into the army. Or a few might enter the navy, I suppose. No Hasburys ever have. I will be happy to put on a red coat and serve the king when I am old enough to do so."

"Are you going into army, too?" Spencer asked Everett.

The boy shrugged. "It's like Owen says. First sons do their duty to their family by claiming the title. Second sons do their duty to their country and serve the king."

"I didn't know," he said, trying to adjust to the idea of being in the army. "I love to learn. I always thought I would be a tutor or perhaps a university don."

"No, it's the army for you," Owen declared. "That's how it's done."

"What if there is a third son?" he asked, curious.

"Third sons go into the church," Everett said solemnly. "I wish I would have been a third son. I'm not sure I want to fight and shoot guns."

"Well, I can't wait to shoot England's enemies," Owen said. "My father says with King Louis being guillotined in France this year, it will make for a mess. England has been at war with France off and on for centuries. Maybe by the time we are grown, we'll have another war!"

Owen looked far too gleeful for Spencer's tastes. He wasn't sure about making friends with this boy. Everett, who seemed far different from his friend, would make for a better companion. But with the two of them already being close friends for what must have been their entire lives, he doubted he could be friends with one and not the other.

"Listen up," Georgie said. "All those in our dormitory room have arrived. The Shepton School always mixes up students of different ages in each room so that boys get to know others beyond their form. The older boys are to look after the younger ones. I am in charge of everyone in this room—and everything that happens here," he said priggishly.

Spencer glanced over and saw Owen roll his eyes. Everett stared at his feet.

"We are to move downstairs for assembly," the prefect continued. "I expect you to be on your best behavior else I will have to call you out."

"Bloody awful," Owen murmured, loud enough for only Spencer and Everett to hear.

As they moved from the room and down the stairs, Owen slung his arm around Spencer's shoulders.

"We three should stick together," Owen told him. "Our brothers went here and both told us the older boys bully the younger ones. A lot."

"How?" Spencer asked.

"They do all kinds of mean things," Everett said. "Put stuff in your food and in your bedsheets. Call you horrible names. Even hit you."

"Hit you?" he echoed, appalled at the thought.

Owen looked serious for once. "You and I are tall. We need to let them know we won't allow them to bully us. Or Everett."

Spencer nodded. "All right."

Owen stopped and allowed the other boys to get ahead of them. Then he thrust out his hand. "We will be like brothers, the three of us. We will stay close and take care of one another."

He slipped his hand into his pocket and produced a pocket-knife. Unfolding it, Owen opened his palm. He dragged the knife across it, a thin line of blood welling up. Passing the knife to Everett, he did the same, though he looked a bit squeamish as he did so.

Finally, Everett handed it to Spencer, who took it and held it above his palm. He paused a moment, glancing up at Owen and then Everett. Realizing he was being tested—and at the same time given a choice—he chose these two boys. Sliding the tip of the blade across his palm, the blood bubbled up.

Owen claimed the pocketknife again and rubbed his palm against Everett's and then Spencer's, while Spencer and Everett did the same.

"Our blood has now mingled," Owen said solemnly. "We are now blood brothers. We will look after one another and stand strong together."

As each of them removed a handkerchief from their pockets and slipped it around the slice in their palms, Spencer believed he would always know—and come to love—these friends.

CHAPTER ONE

Oakley, Essex—February 1812

TESSA FOSTER FINISHED the chapter she read aloud and closed the book. She glanced up and saw her father's eyes now closed. She sighed. Another day at Oakley.

Where nothing ever changed.

Four years ago, she had been on the eve of her come-out. By now, she would have thought herself married, with at least one child and hopefully another on the way. Instead, her beloved mother had grown terribly ill. Tessa had put off her come-out to nurse Mama. A year later, her beloved mother passed, never getting any better. Tessa regretted her mother would never see her daughter march down the aisle, much less be able to become a loving grandmother.

Then Papa collapsed in the cemetery after the burial. And Tessa's world shrank even further.

Dr. Smith called it apoplexy, something she wasn't familiar with. He told Tessa her father could die within hours—or linger for years. They had gotten the earl home and put him to bed. In the days ahead, they had discovered Papa could no longer speak. That the right side of his body no longer functioned. He had a wild look in his eyes and one side of his face drooped. She had stayed at his bedside day and night for weeks until Dr. Smith told her Papa was out of the woods. That he would live.

But this wasn't living. It was barely existing.

Tessa spent a good portion of every day with her father. She helped his valet bathe him. She read to him. Talked with him. She had a small desk moved into his bedchambers and from there she handled her correspondence and wrote out menus. Almost every waking hour of the last three years was devoted to his care. Guilt filled her because she feared the situation could remain stagnant for years to come. Her youth was slipping away. She used to regularly visit her two cousins, Adalyn and Louisa, who were her best friends, but no visits had occurred in the last four years. She simply couldn't leave Papa to go see them in London or at their country estates.

Instead, she spent long hours in this bedchamber, worrying about her father's health and her own future.

Her uncle, who would inherit the title from his brother and become the next Earl of Paxton, had arrived two months after Papa fell ill. He now ran the estate, making the decisions the earl should make. He also went to town and stayed in the Paxton townhouse while there, attending the Season and living life as the earl in all but claiming the title itself. A lifelong bachelor who was in his late forties, he had wed at the end of last Season and brought home a child bride, Lady Beth, who was barely eighteen.

Tessa couldn't stand Lady Beth. She felt the girl was pure evil and referred to her in her head as Lady Macbeth, after Shakespeare's most famous female character. Lady Macbeth was possibly the most wicked person in literature—and Lady Beth came close to epitomizing evil incarnate. When she had arrived at Oakley last September, Lady Beth had made it known that once the current earl was gone, Tessa would also be leaving the house because it would then become the house of the next earl and countess.

She sighed, knowing her father's death would not only devastate her but quite possibly leave her homeless. She couldn't count on her uncle to stand up to his young wife because he was as greedy as she was. Tessa had never been comfortable in his presence, much less felt close to him. Even though he approached fifty, he seemed to have no mind of his own where his young wife was concerned. He would boot Tessa from Oakley without a second thought, merely to please Lady Macbeth.

If that happened, she hoped one of her two cousins' families would take her in. Oddly enough, neither Adalyn nor Louisa had wed. Adalyn was Tessa's age, while Louisa was a year younger. Both had made their come-outs and yet no weddings had occurred. The three women still wrote one another and from the letters, Adalyn revealed she was enjoying being in Polite Society too much to settle down with a boring lord. Louisa, whose mother had died when she was young, served as her father's hostess. Louisa's father worked in the War Office and held many dinners and affairs at his home that were business related. Louisa said her father needed her too much to manage his household and social affairs to allow her to wed. Louisa did write that when the war came to an end, she would seek a husband and allow her father to handle his own affairs.

Hopefully, one of her two uncles would allow Tessa to come and live with his family if the worst occurred. No, *when* the worst occurred. Tessa was certain Lady Macbeth would shove her out the door before her father's body cooled.

She picked up the book again, ready to continue Voltaire's interesting tale of *Candide*. She had no idea if her father really understood anything said to him or what she read but it helped her to pass the time. Tessa glanced at her father and saw his eyes were now open, that wild look in them that was so unsettling to her.

Standing, she closed the book and rested it on the table and leaned over.

"How are you, Papa?" she asked, smoothing his hair. "I was reading to you when you fell asleep."

He began making a guttural noise, which startled her. In the three years she had nursed him, no sound had ever emerged from him.

"What is it, Papa?" she asked eagerly. "Can you speak?"

Oh, if only things could go back to the way they were. Her father taking her riding on the property as they visited their tenants. Mama waiting for their return with a hearty tea in the drawing room. Plans for the dresses Tessa would wear and the events she would attend during her come-out being discussed.

The earl muttered something and then said, "Ov . . . oo."

Tessa thought a moment and brightened. "Love you? Is that what you are saying, Papa?"

"Ov . . . oo," he repeated.

She grasped his hands. "Oh, that is lovely, Papa. It is so good to hear you speak. Dr. Smith will be so impressed. And I love you, too."

Tessa bent and brushed her lips against his brow. When she rose and smiled at him, her heart stopped.

The frantic look remained in his eyes—but it was frozen.

"Papa," she cried, her heart lurching. "No, no, no."

She touched her fingers to where his pulse should be beating, as Dr. Smith had taught her. Nothing. She held a finger just under his nostrils. Again, nothing.

With great reluctance, she brushed the palm of her hand across his eyes, lowering the lids, forever hiding the disturbing look in them. Tessa perched on the bed, her hands taking his. Raising them to her lips, she kissed the knuckles tenderly.

"I love you, Papa. I always will."

Lowering them, she sat beside him for a few minutes, savoring the last moments she would have with him. Then acknowledging what must come next, she rose and went to her desk, writing two brief notes to the vicar and the doctor, informing them of Lord Paxton's death. Those were followed by two letters addressed to the Earl of Uxbridge, Adalyn's father, and Sir Edgar Goulding, Louisa's father. Both men were her mother's brothers. She informed them of her father's death and asked them to come to the funeral in three days' time.

Tessa sealed the notes and letters and left the bedchamber, not glancing at her father. She knew the body that lay in the bed was no longer the man she had known and loved. His soul had risen and gone to Heaven. She wouldn't torture herself further.

In her father's sitting room, next to the bedchamber, she rang for both the butler and valet. Both men arrived at the same time and she told the servants of the earl's passing.

"I trust the two of you to prepare Papa," she said. "I have written my uncles, as well as the vicar and Dr. Smith, and will send footmen to deliver those now." She paused, taking a cleansing breath. "I will also go and tell the new Lord Paxton what has occurred."

"I'm ever so sorry, my lady," the valet said. "The earl was such a good man and a good father to you."

"I can go with you while you speak to the earl and countess," their butler ventured. "You might need . . . support."

Tessa knew what he meant. "Thank you, but no. I'd rather you stay and make Papa presentable. He always loved gray. Perhaps that light gray waistcoat and the darker tailcoat would do."

Her father had lost a considerable amount weight since the apoplexy attack and she knew the clothes she mentioned would swallow him. She would leave it up to these two trusted servants to see that Lord Paxton looked the best he could.

Leaving the room, she made her way downstairs and found a footman. She instructed him regarding the notes and letters and he told her he would take care of it at once. Then she steeled herself and went up a flight of stairs to the drawing room, where she knew her uncle and his wife would be. Entering, she saw them sitting before the fire and crossed the room to them.

"Ah, Tessa," her uncle said. "You look tired, my dear."

"She always looks tired," Lady Macbeth said. "You really should take better care of yourself. Get out some. See people."

"Papa has passed," she said brusquely.

Her uncle rose and placed a hand on her shoulder. "I am

sorry to hear that. He was a good brother to me."

She wanted to ask if he was such a good brother, why hadn't her uncle gone to see him more? He had arrived at Oakley and entered the sickroom that first day—and never again. Her uncle went about the business of the estate and in London and never bothered sitting by his brother's side, trying to comfort him.

"He was the best of men. A wonderful husband and father and the best Earl of Paxton," she declared.

"Well, he isn't the earl any longer, is he?" Lady Macbeth said, rising. "A new Earl and Countess of Paxton are now in charge."

"You will plan Papa's funeral?" she asked quickly, panicked by that thought.

"No, my dear," her uncle assured her. "You know what he would have wanted."

"I will plan the reception after the funeral," Lady Macbeth proclaimed. "There will be all manner of people in attendance. I will get with Cook now and make certain it will be a memorable event!"

Lady Macbeth exited the drawing room and her uncle shook his head. "She is young," he told Tessa, as if that should excuse her outrageous behavior.

"She is old enough to know to offer me her sympathies," Tessa said bitterly. "Certainly old enough not to rub it in my face that there is a new earl and countess."

He shrugged. "She is eager to put her stamp on this household. It has been hard for her, being in limbo with these . . . circumstances."

Tessa wanted to argue that Lady Macbeth already ran the household the way she saw fit because Tessa had spent all her waking hours with her father. That nothing would ever excuse the girl's rudeness. She was too tired to argue, however.

"The vicar will be arriving soon. I sent word to him and Dr. Smith. I will work with him on the service. I will let you notify Papa's solicitor and any others you might wish to attend the funeral."

Wearily, Tessa left the drawing room, knowing the days ahead would be long ones.

TESSA WEARILY SAID goodbye to the last of the guests who had returned to Oakley after the funeral. Instead of being comforted by those in attendance, she had been the one to do the comforting. Her father had been much beloved by his tenants and the people who lived in the surrounding area. At least Papa was finally at peace.

She was grateful that her two uncles had brought her cousins with them. Usually, women did not attend funerals but Tessa had insisted upon seeing her father laid to rest. It was good to have Louisa and Adalyn with her when that occurred. She wondered how long her relatives would stay—or rather, how long Lady Macbeth would allow them to remain.

Their butler came toward her. "My lady, you are requested to join the others in the library for the reading of the will."

"Thank you," she said as her cousins joined her.

"We are going with you," Louisa said. "You shouldn't be alone."

"Especially with that monster, Lady Macbeth," Adalyn added. "Oh, I do like your nickname for her."

"I don't know if you will be allowed," she told her friends. "My uncle is the earl now."

Adalyn snorted. "Just let him try and toss us from the room." She linked her arm through Tessa's. "Come on."

Louisa did the same and they went to the library. Entering, she saw Mr. Ellsworth, Papa's solicitor, along with the new Lord and Lady Paxton. Relief swept through her as she saw both Uncle Uxbridge and Uncle Edgar also present.

"They aren't needed," the countess said, her nose crinkling in disdain at Louisa and Adalyn.

"They are my family," Tessa said. "I want them here for their support."

Lady Macbeth frowned and looked to her husband. He only shook his head, as if knowing this wasn't a battle he wished to fight.

Instead, Lord Paxton said, "Be seated."

Everyone took a place, with Tessa and her cousins sitting together on a large settee. She wasn't expecting any surprises and received none. As thought, her father had made small bequests to longtime servants, including his valet and their butler.

Then Mr. Ellsworth said, "Lady Tessa's dowry has remained intact and will now be under her control since she is of legal age." He smiled at her. "I do hope when the time comes for you to wed that you will seek my services—or that of another solicitor's—in regard to drawing up the settlements."

"Tessa has us to help her with this," Uncle Edgar said. "We will make certain she is taken care of where the marriage contracts are concerned."

Gratitude filled her, knowing that she had her mother's brothers looking out for her best interests.

"In addition to the dowry," Mr. Ellsworth continued, "Lady Tessa will receive an additional amount of one thousand pounds. These funds are to be used for creating the wardrobe for her come-out Season and any incidentals along the way."

"One thousand pounds?" said Lady Macbeth, not bothering to hide her astonishment. "Isn't that an excessive amount?" she said to no one in particular and then looking to her husband, she added, "wouldn't that be monies from the estate? Was it even his to give?"

"Let me assure you, Lady Paxton, that the sum belongs to Lady Tessa," the solicitor said. "It comes from monies brought into the marriage by Lady Tessa's mother and always designated for this. Surely, you wouldn't begrudge Lady Tessa a new wardrobe, especially seeing how long she has delayed her come-out in order to care for her parents?"

"It merely seems extravagant," Lady Macbeth said, slightly mollified that the sum wasn't part of her husband's estate.

Mr. Ellsworth began gathering up his papers and said, "I believe that is all. Should you have any questions, you may contact me at my London office. I need to leave now to return there for another business matter."

Tessa rose and smiled warmly at the man. "Thank you for all you have done, Mr. Ellsworth. Papa always enjoyed working with you."

"Lord Paxton was a gem among men, my lady. I am very sorry for your loss."

The solicitor left and Lady Macbeth said, "Do sit down. There are more things to discuss."

Tessa dreaded what was next because she knew what it would involve. Knowing how much Lady Macbeth despised her and wanted her gone, Tessa hoped she would be allowed to go to the dower house and do her year of mourning there.

Taking a seat, she steeled herself for whatever would come.

"It is difficult for my wife having my niece as a member of the household," the new Lord Paxton began.

"Why so?" Uncle Umbridge asked, his tone critical of the statement.

"I will tell you," Lady Macbeth said assertively. "She is unneeded and unwanted. She usurps me at every turn. Just look at how she rushed to Ellsworth and had to be the one to tell him goodbye. That should have been my role, being a gracious hostess to a departing guest."

Adalyn snorted and Tessa flashed her cousin a warning.

"I cannot change a rug or move a vase without the servants telling me I should be consulting Lady Tessa," Lady Macbeth complained. "They don't look upon me as their mistress."

"You weren't until Paxton's death," Uncle Edgar pointed out. "It says a lot that the servants remained loyal to Tessa and her father. Now, however, you are the new countess. They will—"

"They will behave in the same manner," Lady Macbeth interrupted. "The lot of them. They will always second-guess me and want her opinion. That is why she needs to be gone."

"I would happy to move to the dower house," Tessa offered.

"That isn't far enough," the countess said, her voice rising. "I want you gone. Spend that thousand pounds you wheedled from your father. You can rent something somewhere. Just make certain that is far from here." She placed her hand on her belly. "I will need peace and quiet—and totally loyalty from the servants—especially since I am now with child."

Tessa hadn't known about the baby but it didn't change matters. She only felt sorrow that the child would have such a viper as its mother. She saw her uncles exchange a glance and Uncle Uxbridge said, "That won't be necessary. Tessa can come live with us." He looked to her. "You might prefer to remain in the country when we head to town for the Season. I will leave it up to you."

Knowing from letters exchanged with Adalyn and Louisa, her friends would attend a whirlwind of events from April through August. If Tessa came to London, her cousins might neglect the invitations they received in order to stay home with her.

"Your suggestion that I remain in the country pleases me, Uncle," she said. "I would prefer to do my mourning in private."

"Then we will leave Oakley tomorrow morning," Uncle Uxbridge said. "You will come with us, Tessa."

"And know at any time you are always welcomed to stay with us," Uncle Edgar volunteered. "Though we stay year-round in London, due to my position at the War Office."

"I understand and I am grateful for your offer," she said, her eyes misting.

"Well, it is good that matter has been settled so amicably," Lord Paxton proclaimed. He rose and the others followed suit. "I shall see everyone in the drawing room at seven. We will have drinks and then go into dinner."

As the group moved toward the doors, Lady Macbeth said, "I would like a private word with Lady Tessa."

Louisa looked at Tessa. "Is that what you want? I will stay if you ask."

"Thank you. I can handle her. Go on."

The others left. Tessa remained standing in the same place, making Lady Macbeth come to her. She saw that displeased the young woman but she didn't care.

"You are never to come to Oakley again," Lady Macbeth began. "You will neither be invited nor welcomed if you turn up. Paxton and I wish to have nothing to do with you. Do not call on us in town, either. We will not be at home to you. If you see us at a ball or some other event, you may greet us politely but do not expect any prolonged conversation on our part."

"You certainly are full of yourself, Lady Macbeth," Tessa said. "Actually, your terms please me. I also prefer to have nothing to do with the both of you."

The girl's eyes narrowed. "What did you call me?"

"Oh, you mean Lady Macbeth? That is a famous character from a Shakespeare play. You remind me of her."

She bit back a smile, knowing the new countess had never read anything by Shakespeare and would have no clue what an insult the moniker truly was.

Lady Macbeth pursed her lips. "No matter. I am Lady Paxton now and you are to address me as such the few times our paths do cross."

"Of course, my lady," she said and turned away, leaving the library.

Tessa knew when she left tomorrow she would never return to Oakley. That the door to the first chapter of her life would close—and a new one would open.

She was eager to see what her future would hold.

CHAPTER TWO

London—March 1813

S PENCER THREW ON clothes and slipped from his London townhouse before the sun had peeked over the horizon. Usually, he would saddle Pilgrim and head to Rotten Row for a bit of exercise. Unfortunately, the horse had pulled up lame yesterday just as they had returned to Mayfair. He thought it better to give his mount another day to recover before taking him out again.

Instead, he would take to the streets this morning. He rarely saw anyone this time of day, save for a few grooms exercising horses.

And the woman from the townhouse across the street.

He had seen her every day since his arrival in town two weeks ago. She would emerge from the townhouse directly across from his, wearing a dark cloak, and set out on foot. He supposed she enjoyed the early morning quiet as much as he did. Spencer figured her to be the wife or daughter of the Earl of Uxbridge, who owned the residence. The earl had sent an invitation to dinner when Spencer first arrived at his London address but he had declined, not bothering to give a reason. He wasn't ready to be out and about in Polite Society just yet. That would come in three weeks with the start of the Season. Plenty of time for him to meet Uxbridge then.

No other tenants seemed to be on the square just yet. He supposed they would begin arriving as the Season drew near. For his part, Spencer liked that he was able to keep to himself for now as he set out at a brisk pace.

He had returned to England after he received word last September of his father's death from dropsy. Middlefield had died in July but it took a few months for the solicitor's letter to catch up to Spencer. Wellington's troops had been on the march after their success at the Battle of Salamanca and it surprised him that the letter had found him as quickly as it did. With regret, he resigned his commission and returned home. The army was his family. His chosen family. He hadn't even known he was destined for a military career until that first day at school when he'd met Owen and Everett, two second sons who'd informed Spencer of the career path they would all take in the future.

Those two had been constants in his life, along with two other men who were cousins, Percival Perry and Winston Cutler. The trio of friends had met the pair when they all arrived at Cambridge and the five had become fast friends. They had all joined His Majesty's army after university and, fortunately, were assigned to three regiments that were all under Wellington's command. It enabled them to continue living together, fighting alongside one another as they tried to end the menace of Bonaparte. Leaving the brothers of his heart had been done so reluctantly.

Spencer had become the heir apparent only a week into his military service when Wilford had died. It was never truly made clear to him what had happened, only that he was the new viscount and would succeed upon his father's death and become the Earl of Middlefield. His father had requested that Spencer resign his commission immediately and come home, the better to learn more about his future role.

He had refused.

Duty and honor meant everything to him. He wouldn't walk

away from a country that needed him, especially one in the midst of war. Spencer dedicated himself to his fellow officers and the men serving under him, patiently training them, supporting them, and leading them into battle. He never once used his viscount title in the army, preferring to be known as Lieutenant Haddock, then Captain Haddock, and most recently Major Haddock. He saw no need to race home when his father was in perfect health and could manage the estate and the responsibilities of the earldom.

It was a choice he celebrated over his years in the army. Spencer proved to be a strong leader, driven and confident. He enjoyed the discipline and camaraderie of the army and the chance to remain with those he cared for. Wilford, being ten years Spencer's senior, had never built any brotherly bonds with his younger brother. Their father had favored Wilford in everything and ignored Spencer his entire life—until the favorite son died and the younger one was needed. He told himself he would, in time, return to England and learn what he could from his father.

Until the letter came announcing the earl's death.

Spencer felt no sorrow at his father's passing. No remorse for having remained in the army. He did know that he must return to England and take up the mantle of the Earl of Middlefield. Bidding his fellow officers and friends farewell, he had returned to Stoneridge. The estate had excellent management. Pimmel, the Stoneridge steward, had been patient in teaching Spencer all he needed to know about the land and its people. Callender, the butler, and Mrs. Callender, the housekeeper, kept the household running effortlessly. It was thanks to their efforts that he was able to leave as soon as he had and make for London.

Here, he had found his townhouse incredibly large, along with a staff headed up by Marsh, his butler, and Mrs. Marsh, his housekeeper. The only servant to have accompanied him from Kent was Rigsby, his valet. Rigsby had served as valet to Wilford until his death and then traveled to Stoneridge, where he became the earl's new valet. Middlefield had recently pensioned off his own valet so the timing had been good. Since Spencer had no valet, Rigsby inherited that position. Though he didn't see the need for a valet, he knew it was imperative to have one. Polite Society would judge him to be uncivilized and uncouth without one.

He turned another corner, continuing his walk. Perhaps he should walk the streets more in order to become familiar with London. Usually, he was in his carriage and didn't pay much attention to his surroundings. That would soon change. He would be invited to balls and routs, card and garden parties, the opera and theatre. All because he was now a member of the *ton*.

In search of a wife.

It was only because Stoneridge was running so well that Spencer even deigned to come to town for the Season. He knew from talk that it was home to the Marriage Mart, where he would search for a bride. Thank goodness he had no illusions of finding something as ethereal as love. He wanted a basic *ton* marriage, one that would see a good-sized dowry arrive into his coffers so that he could make some improvements at Stoneridge. Love wasn't a part of unions in the *ton*. Marriages were made to increase wealth and social position.

His father had never showed him any attention, much less love. The same had been true of Wilford. Perhaps, long ago, his mother might have loved him. Spencer had no true memories of her. She had died in childbirth, along with the babe she delivered, when he was barely two. He wondered if things might have been different if she had survived.

What he did know was that getting an heir was critical. He believed his father foolish to never have remarried. What if Spencer had been killed while at war? Who would have inherited the Middlefield title and lands then? No, he was going to find a bride and get her with child as quickly as possible. He wanted to get as many children from her as he could. Though he had felt like an only child himself, he had always longed for siblings close in age to play with. He would see that his family was large and close-knit, spending time with both sons and daughters. Where servants had taught him how to ride and hunt, Spencer would teach his own children those things. He felt a deep sense of responsibility and would make certain his offspring spent time with him. Why, he might even grow to love one or more of them.

But never a wife. The idea of intimacy with a woman didn't appeal to him. He didn't want to pretend to love his countess. It would be enough if he respected her and she produced the children he required. Once she had, they could go their separate ways as most couples of Polite Society did. Spencer would pursue his own interests and his countess could do the same. If she died in childbirth, he would merely replace her with another woman if he thought more children were necessary. Thus, his reason for being in town for the Season.

He carried high hopes that he would find a bride quickly. If he did so, he could put a halt to attending society affairs, which he thought would be incredibly boring. Spending his days and nights with the same group of people—all strangers to him—terrified him. The quicker he could select a wife and wed her, the better. It would give him more time to devote to matters in the House of Lords, which he found fascinating. In fact, if he could wed and bed a bride and see her with child, she could return to the country for her confinement while he dealt with political matters in London. Naturally, he would return to Stoneridge for the birth of his first child. He would not make the same mistakes his own father had made. He was a better man than the earl had ever been and would certainly be a better father.

Making a last turn, he headed for home. He was beginning to enjoy having a comfortable bed to sleep in and regular meals to warm his belly. Though he had never complained about the rough life in camp, the luxuries at Stoneridge and his London townhouse were growing on him.

As he strode quickly along the pavement, he saw up ahead a

woman turn the corner and head in the same direction he did. Recognizing her by her cloak as his neighbor, Spencer decided to catch up to her and introduce himself. Walking along, he wondered if she was the countess or one of the daughters of the household. It would be convenient if she were a daughter and he came to know her even before the Season began. She might make for a good countess. Already, he knew she enjoyed daily exercise. She moved with purpose. If she were intelligent and could hold a decent conversation, his work would be done. He could offer for her before the Season even began and not have to go through all the motions of courting a woman, which had been explained to him in great detail by Rigsby. The valet had been a font of information, cluing Spencer in to many details he had limited knowledge about. He might enjoy picking up a book on history or economics but those did not contain the everyday essentials he needed to know to move successfully through Polite Society.

He had almost caught up to the woman when a figure stepped out, brandishing a knife. In the still of the morning, the thief's voice carried as he said, "Gimme your coin, my lady. Now."

Spencer started to run as the woman replied, "I have none with me but I live just ahead. Come eat something and we can talk."

Was she mad—asking a robber to dine with her?

He reached the pair and knocked the knife from the young thief's hand before soundly punching the bastard in the face. The boy crumpled to the ground.

Turning to the lady, expecting her gratitude, he was stunned when she slammed her palms into his chest, knocking him back. Spencer stumbled a moment and then regained his balance.

"What the bloody hell did you just do?" she demanded.

"Wh-what do you mean?" he sputtered. "I just saved you, Woman."

"Saved me?" Her bright blue eyes flashed in anger at him. "From this poor girl?"

Girl?

He glanced over as the woman rushed to the fallen figure and said, "There, there. Please don't worry. He isn't with me. I have never laid eyes upon him. Let me help you stand."

Spencer reached for the weapon still lying on the ground and the thief said, "My knife!"

As the woman pulled the thief to his—her—feet, Spencer saw that it was a girl. A young woman dressed as a man.

The woman glared at him. "Return the knife to her, my lord."

"Why the bloody hell would I do that?" he asked, puzzled by the events unfolding, knowing with certainty even if this woman were in search of a husband, she would be the last one he would want as his countess.

"Language, sir!" she chided before reaching out and snatching the knife from him, handing it back to her attacker.

Spencer didn't bother pointing out she had cursed at him first.

"Much thanks, my lady," the thief muttered.

"You are most welcome. Come, let us go."

The two started off and he loudly asked, "Where do you think you are going?"

Both women turned. The younger, bedraggled one had a look of fear on her face. The older one, however, raised her chin a notch, glaring at him and yet brimming with confidence. She appeared more like Boudica, queen of a Celtic tribe who led an uprising against the Romans in the first century. A lover of history, Spencer had always imagined Boudica to be an imposing figure, bowing to no man.

This woman, tall and lithe, with golden blond hair and piercing blue eyes, seemed even more impressive than the Boudica he had pictured.

"We are going to the Earl of Uxbridge's townhouse, my lord," she said, enunciating each syllable as if he would have trouble understanding their destination. "We are going to eat and get to know one another."

"But she tried to steal from you," he pointed out.

"Only because she had no choice." The woman turned to the thief. "Isn't that right?"

"Yes, my lady. I was hungry. Haven't eaten in three days," the girl admitted.

"Have you parents?" the woman asked kindly.

"No, my lady. Mum died two years ago. I never knew my father."

She stroked the girl's dirty cheek. "Things will get better. I am in need of a lady's maid. Perhaps you would be interested in the position."

"Lady's maid?" both Spencer and the girl questioned.

"Yes. I have been sharing a lady's maid with my cousin, Adalyn, but the Season will be starting soon. I will be in need of one of my own. Come along and we can discuss the position and your salary. What is your name?"

"Abra," the girl said, wide-eyed.

"How old are you, Abra?" the woman asked gently.

"Sixteen."

The woman cocked her head. "A bit young for a lady's maid but I know I can train you."

Tears welled in the girl's eyes. "Thank you, my lady."

They started off again and Spencer said, "You are seriously going to take home someone from the streets. Someone who brandished a knife at you. Someone who intended to take from you."

This time, the woman abandoned her new charge and stormed back to Spencer.

"Yes, I am, my lord. What business is it of yours? I have the coin to pay Abra. The position is open. I believe we will suit one another."

With that, she spun and returned to the dirty street child and slipped her arm through the girl's. They stepped away briskly.

Spencer followed at a distance, still not quite trusting young Abra and wanting to make certain the lady at least arrived without Abra slitting her throat.

When they reached the Earl of Umbridge's townhouse, he heard the street urchin ask her savior's name.

"I am Lady Tessa Foster. The earl is my uncle. He is quite kind. You will like him."

They disappeared inside the residence as he watched, the door closing.

Spencer wondered if Lady Tessa Foster was married. The thought shocked him. He had thought he wanted a pliant, complacent countess. One who would quietly do his bidding and see to his household.

Instead, he decided he needed his own Boudica, a woman of beauty and valor, who would stand up for herself and those she cherished.

He decided it was time to issue his own dinner invitation. To the earl and all members of his family.

And that it include the very interesting Lady Tessa Foster.

CHAPTER THREE

TESSA USHERED ABRA inside her uncle's townhouse. The sleepy footman on duty, slouched in a chair beside the door, immediately leaped to his feet.

"My lady," he greeted, his eyes flicking to Abra, and then turning back questioningly to her.

"This is Abra," she told him. "My new lady's maid. Come along, Abra."

They swept past the footman, whose jaw had dropped considerably, and went to the kitchens. Tessa did so each morning after her early walk, sitting with Cook and having a cup of tea to warm her before going upstairs and changing. She then joined Uncle Uxbridge in the breakfast room and they shared the meal together. Her aunt and cousin always ate in their rooms, neither liking to rise early.

"Good morning, Cook," Tessa said as she sailed into the kitchen. "Sit here," she instructed Abra, motioning to a small table.

"Who's that, my lady?" Cook asked, perplexed by their visitor.

"This is Abra, my new lady's maid."

The servant took at Abra and said, "Well, knock me down with a feather. You are one for surprises, my lady."

"Could we both get a cup of tea, Cook, and something hearty

for Abra? A cold compress, too. She'll also need a bath. Have the water sent up to my bedchamber if you would."

Cook's lips twitched in amusement. "Certainly, my lady."

Tessa joined Abra at the table as a scullery maid set down a pot of tea and two cups. Another placed a tray with cream and sugar next to the pot.

"How do you take your tea?" she asked, pouring a cup for Abra.

"Any way I can get it, my lady," the girl said in wonder as Tessa placed the delicate porcelain cup in front of her.

As she poured for herself, Tessa saw Abra added two lumps of sugar and a healthy splash of cream to her cup before stirring and sipping.

"Tell me about yourself," she encouraged, as another scullery maid brought the compress. Abra held it to her cheek with one hand and sipped her tea as she spoke.

"I told you Mum passed on two years ago. She worked at a tavern. I helped sweep up and did a bit of the cooking until I left."

"Why did you take to robbing people?"

Abra's head dipped. After a moment, she said, "It's not something I would really talk about with a lady."

Tessa reached out and took the girl's hand. "Did someone hurt you?"

Abra lifted her head and met Tessa's gaze as tears rolled down her cheeks. "Yes," she whispered.

"You are safe here," she promised. "We will send for your things."

Wiping the tears with the back of her hand, Abra said, "There are no things, my lady. I was living on the streets. I have the clothes on my back—and my knife."

Her heart ached for all this girl had gone through. With a cheery smile, she said, "Well, you will have new clothes and a bed. Hot meals. We'll make the best of it."

Abra smiled. "Thank you for your kindness, my lady."

Cook herself set a plate down in front of Abra. "Eat up.

You're too thin." To Tessa, she added, "I've told Mrs. Rainey about things."

"Good. Mrs. Rainey is the earl's housekeeper, Abra," she explained. "She runs a very efficient house."

Halfway through the meal, Mrs. Rainey joined them, introducing herself and saying, "I have found two uniforms for you." She glanced under the table. "Looks like you'll be needing shoes, as well."

Abra flushed. "How much will that be?"

"Nothing," the housekeeper assured. "His lordship will take care of it. When you finish eating, your bath should be ready by then."

"I'll take care of the uniforms, Mrs. Rainey," Abra promised. "And Lady Tessa."

"See that you do," Mrs. Rainey advised. "Lady Tessa is a generous soul. You would not want to disappoint her. She has given you a golden opportunity."

"I'll make the most of it. I'll sleep on the floor next to her. I'll see she has everything she needs."

"That won't be necessary," the housekeeper said. "You will be with Bridget. She has an extra bed in her room."

"Bridget is Lady Adalyn's lady's maid," Tessa explained. "I have been sharing her until now."

She thanked the housekeeper and watched Abra finish her breakfast before leading her up the back staircase.

"This is the one you will use, for the most part. All the servants do."

As they continued, Tessa said, "Your duties will include helping me to bathe and dress each day. When the Season arrives, I will be required to change gowns several times a day."

"What's that? The Season?"

"It is a whirl of social activities from spring through summer. It gives a chance for Polite Society to come together and for women like me to look for a husband."

"You ain't wed?" Abra looked shocked.

"No, I cared for my parents for the last several years. Both were very ill and they passed away. I have been in mourning for a year, living with my uncle and aunt, who were gracious enough to take me in when a new earl claimed my father's title."

"So, you were homeless, too?" Abra asked. "Like me?"

"I would have been except for Uncle Uxbridge's kindness," Tessa said. "So, I will be making my come-out to society much later than most. I hope by Season's end that I will be betrothed. I will leave it up to you, Abra, whether or not you will leave this household and come with me."

"Of course, I will come," Abra said, her eyes flashing, already displaying fierce loyalty to Tessa.

They reached her bedchamber and a maid was emptying the last can of water into the bath. She bobbed a curtsey to Tessa and left.

Abra gazed about the room. "It's so big."

"Yes, it is very nice."

"You'll wed a lord who has a nice house like your uncle's?"

"I hope so. At least the wed a nice lord part. I don't care if his house is big or small. It is who he is and how he treats me that will matter."

Abra thought a moment. "What about the one from this morning?"

Tessa thought of the too-handsome man who towered over both of them. He must have been two or three inches above six feet. His piercing green eyes and raven black hair had been as appealing as his muscular frame.

"Definitely not him," she said firmly.

"Why not? Do you know him?"

"I don't," she admitted.

"Then I'd consider him," Abra said. "He came to your rescue. A total stranger. That's a brave thing to do."

"But he struck you, Abra," Tessa pointed out. "I want to wed a man who is kind, not one who goes about punching others in the face."

"Well, on his behalf, he didn't know I was a female. And I was trying to rob you. Threatening you with a knife. Not that I would've used it."

"Of course, you wouldn't have," she said, soothing. "Let's get you undressed as we speak."

Abra pulled the shirt over her head. It was stained and smelled something terrible. Tessa took it and dropped it on the floor. She saw the strip of linen wound around Abra's breasts.

The girl said, "It flattens 'em when I do this. Easier to pass as a boy. I also lower my voice. Like this," she said gruffly, a good octave lower than her normal speaking voice. "I do think you should give him a chance. He risked himself to help you. I'd say that was brave and thoughtful, my lady. And he was certainly nice to look at."

Tessa laughed. "At least we can agree upon that. He did possess spectacular good looks."

"And impressive muscles," the girl added, stripping off her worn half-boots and baggy trousers.

She added the items to the pile and felt the hardness of the blade. Removing it from the trouser pocket, she said, "I will place your knife on the bureau. You may keep it in your room. I prefer you keep it there instead of wearing it. After all, you won't be living on the streets anymore."

"What if we go out? Do I go with you?" Abra asked as she stepped into the tub and gingerly sank into the hot water, sighing.

"Yes, you will accompany me if I wish to walk. Or if I go for a dress fitting. You will also act as my chaperone if I go somewhere."

"Well, I'll bring my knife if you insist on walking early in the mornings. There aren't many crooks about that time of morning. They've done their business for the night. But you never know. I'd rather be safe than sorry and carry it all the same."

"Then your weapon may come on our walks. I hope you don't mind being up so early."

"Not a bit," Abra proclaimed, sinking completely under the

water so that her hair got wet. She popped back up. "This is heavenly."

Tessa went to her dressing table and pick up a vial. Returning to the tub, she poured some of the liquid in.

"Stir this around," she instructed. "It's lavender oil."

The door flew open and Adalyn charged in, followed by Bridget and Mrs. Rainey.

"What on earth is going on?" her cousin questioned, marching straight to the tub.

Abra wrapped her arms about herself protectively. "Nothing, my lady."

Adalyn turned to Tessa. "This is your new lady's maid? Mrs. Rainey said you had hired one off the streets."

"I have," Tessa said, standing up to her cousin. "Abra is young and will be a fast learner. Between Bridget and me, she will learn her duties in no time."

Adalyn sniffed. "You may tell her your preferences, Tessa, but let Bridget teach the girl to learn what she needs to know. What's your name?" she demanded, her gaze falling to the tub.

"Abra. What's yours?" the girl countered.

Adalyn put fisted hands on her hips. "That is rather insolent."

Abra's chin rose. "I don't know what that means, my lady, but I do know it's a bit rude to burst in when someone is bathing."

Suddenly, Adalyn burst out laughing. "You are right, Abra. Forgive me. I am merely protective of my cousin."

"So am I," Abra said, her eyes burning bright.

Adalyn smiled. "I can see that. Forgive me. I think you will suit Lady Tessa quite well." She turned. "Bridget, you will teach Abra everything she needs to know, starting with how to bathe a lady. You can demonstrate on Abra."

"Yes, my lady," Bridget said.

"You'll only have to tell me something once," Abra told the lady's maid. "I have a good memory."

"Be glad you're starting in this position," Bridget said. "The life of a scullery maid or a house or parlor maid is far harder. I'm not saying you and I won't work hard—we will—but our tasks are more pleasant and we are considered upper servants."

Bridget knelt next tub and looked at Adalyn. "I have things in hand, my lady."

"Very well. I am going back to bed and will breakfast there." She sauntered from the room.

Mrs. Rainey said, "I brought the two uniforms for you. I'll place them on the chair. If they need a nip or tuck here or there, Bridget can help you alter them. That will be another good lesson you can learn."

"Thank you, Mrs. Rainey," Abra said.

The housekeeper left and Tessa said, "It is time for me to breakfast with my uncle. I will leave you in Bridget's hands."

Abra caught Tessa's wrist. "Thank you ever so much, my lady. I won't let you down."

"I don't expect you will. I am happy to have you as my maid, Abra."

Tessa left the bedchamber and went downstairs. Her uncle was already seated and she dropped a kiss upon his head before a footman seated her.

"I hear you have a new lady's maid," he said.

"News travels fast. I suppose you heard it from Rainey."

"Rainey got it from Mrs. Rainey," her uncle said. "Mrs. Rainey is always the best source of information in our household."

Her breakfast and tea were placed before her and Tessa dug into her food, always hungry after she had done her long walk.

"So I hear she's a street urchin. An orphan."

"She is. Her name is Abra. She's bright and clever and under the guidance of Bridget now."

"Egad, half the staff is afraid of Bridget and the other half in awe," the earl noted. "I hope it won't scare your Abra off."

Tessa chuckled. "I doubt Abra is one who frightens easily." As she buttered her toast point, she added, "I do need to ask you about how much I should pay her."

He looked surprised. "Why would you do that?"

"Because I must compensate her, Uncle. Giving her a place to live and providing her with meals isn't enough."

"I will merely tell my secretary to add her to the household staff. He will take care of things."

"But I have the money Papa left me. I can easily pay Abra from that."

Uncle Uxbridge patted her hand. "It is not necessary, my dear. When you find a man worthy enough to be your husband, you can take Abra with you. Then he can pay her. Save your money for other things you truly wish for."

"Thank you. You are so good to me."

"At least you are looking for a husband. I don't think Adalyn has any interest at all in one. Her mother encourages her in this."

She knew her cousin's unwed status bothered her uncle. "Adalyn hasn't found the right man to wed, Uncle. She is merely enjoying herself. When the perfect gentleman catches her attention, he will have to run because she will pursue him with a passion as she does everything else."

He barked a loud laugh. "Truer words have never been spoken. My daughter is strong-willed and does go after whatever she chooses. God bless the man who does draw her eye. His life will never be the same again."

The butler entered and brought a silver tray laden with letters. "The morning post, your lordship."

"Thank you, Rainey."

A footman entered the room and rushed over. "This just arrived, my lord." He handed it to Rainey, who set it atop the tray with the other letters.

"Set it down," Uncle Uxbridge instructed, lifting the recent arrival. He studied it a moment and then broke the seal, perusing it. "Hmm."

"What is it?" she asked.

"It seems that we have been invited to dine with the Earl of

Middlefield tomorrow evening."

"The one who declined your invitation?" she asked. "Without reason, if I recall correctly."

"The very one." He skimmed the note again. "The earl asks that all of my family members present in town be a part of the invitation, especially any family that might be guests in the household."

A sick feeling washed over Tessa.

"I gather he specifically wants you included, Tessa, else it wouldn't be worded in such a way. Have you met Lord Middlefield? I can't say that I have."

She swallowed. "It is possible I have, Uncle. When I was out walking this morning. I was talking with Abra when a tall man appeared and spoke to us briefly. He never introduced himself, nor did I, seeing as it wasn't really proper. I brought Abra home and supposed he might have followed us at a distance in order to see that we arrived safely."

Uncle Uxbridge chuckled. "It seems you made quite an impression upon him, Tessa. He refused my invitation but now is eager for my company—if it includes you."

"Are you going to accept?" she asked hesitantly.

"I most certainly will. He is a neighbor. I want to be on friendly terms with all my neighbors. Besides, I am curious about him. I knew his father and his older brother, who died some years ago. I also know the new earl was formerly in the army. I am interested to see the kind of man he is. Tell Adalyn of the invitation, if you will. I will tell your aunt."

They finished breakfasting and Tessa excused herself, returning upstairs to her cousin's bedchamber. She knocked and heard Adalyn call out.

Entering, she crossed the room and perched on the bed, seeing Adalyn had already finished eating.

"You look incredibly pale, Tessa," Adalyn commented. "Are you having second thoughts about hiring an orphan from the streets as your maid?"

"Not a single one," she said. "The family has received an invitation to dine tomorrow evening with Lord Middlefield."

Adalyn's' brows arched. "You mean the rude man who lives across the way? Papa wasn't pleased that his offer of friendship was slapped down without explanation. I wonder why the earl would invite us to dinner. Perhaps he regrets his previous behavior and this is the olive branch he offers."

"I think I met him this morning, Adalyn," Tessa confessed.

"What does he look like? I have yet to catch sight of him. Where were you?"

"He slammed his fist into Abra's face."

"He . . . what?"

"He thought she was attacking me," she said. "She was trying to rob me—"

"Are you joking, Tessa?"

She explained the situation and how the earl had charged up, knocking away Abra's knife and punching her.

Adalyn smiled. "I don't know whether to laugh at the incident or flutter my eyelashes at him. It's very romantic, Tessa. A hero emerging from the early morning mist, rescuing a damsel in distress."

"I wasn't in any sort of distress," Tessa said defensively.

"But Lord Middlefield did not know that," her cousin pointed out. "Oh, I think you may have already stolen his heart, Tessa. You will have a suitor before the Season even begins."

Adalyn began talking of which gown each of them should wear to tomorrow evening's dinner.

Tessa listened with half an ear, the image of the tall, broad-shouldered earl distracting her. She made up her mind not to like him. She didn't think him especially brave as the others seemed to believe. He was overbearing and uncivil and much too smug for her tastes. If she were a man, she might have challenged him to a fight at Gentleman Jack's.

"You haven't heard a word I have said," Adalyn pouted. Then her cousin grinned. "You are thinking of Lord Middlefield, aren't you?"

"Of course not!" Tessa denied, her cheeks growing hot.

"You think he is attractive."

She shrugged. "Others may find him so. Not I."

Adalyn tossed the bedclothes aside. "Then I will be the judge of that. I will also be able to tell if he is interested in you or not. I am good at that sort of thing. Others come to me for romantic advice."

"But you haven't even wed," Tessa protested.

"That may be the case but I have been out for a good while now. I am quite popular with the gentlemen of the *ton*, Tessa. I aim to make certain you, too, will be popular. I want you to have your choice of suitors." She paused. "I wonder how we can make Lord Middlefield jealous," she mused.

"Stop!" Tessa said. "I don't want him jealous. I don't want anything to do with him."

Adalyn's eyes gleamed. "We'll see."

Knowing her cousin as she did, Tessa knew to remain silent. The more she objected, the more Adalyn would dig in her heels to make a point. She better change the subject. Quickly.

Tessa smiled sweetly. "I have another dress fitting this afternoon. Would you like to go with me?"

As Adalyn chattered happily about their new gowns and the upcoming Season, Tessa hoped the subject was now closed.

At least until tomorrow dinner at the Earl of Middlefield's.

CHAPTER FOUR

S PENCER DID NOT want to stoop to gossip—but he was intrigued enough by Lady Tessa to see if he could find out anything further about her.

That meant a conversation with Rigsby.

It amazed him how much information the valet passed along to him in daily conversation as he shaved and dressed Spencer. Even though they had only come to town a few weeks ago, he knew Rigsby would know something about the Uxbridge household.

"I have invited Lord Uxbridge and his family to dinner tomorrow evening," he began, testing the waters.

"Oh, have you now, my lord?" Rigsby nodded in approval. "Hopefully, it will make up for things."

"What things?"

Rigsby's brows arched. "The fact that you turned down a perfectly good dinner invitation from the earl without providing any decent explanation as to why you did so."

Baffled, Spencer asked, "How do you know about that?"

The valet shrugged. "Servants talk, my lord. Especially ones in such close proximity. I know pretty much everything going on around this square. I can tell you who recently arrived. What family won't be attendance this Season due to a new baby's arrival. How long most families plan to remain in town. Which ones will host events for the upcoming Season."

"Wellington should have used you as a spy on the peninsula," he said.

Rigsby beamed at the compliment. "Just tell me what you wish to know, my lord. I will do my best to find out the information for you."

Though he felt like a gossiping girl, Spencer said, "Since I have invited the earl and his family to dinner, I should at least know how many guests are coming. To tell Cook how many to expect, of course."

Rigsby bit back a smile. "Certainly, my lord. Well, you have the earl himself. An affable fellow, by all accounts. His politics are a bit conservative. He usually votes how his younger brother tells him to when a vote in the House of Lords comes up."

"Who might Lord Uxbridge's brother be?"

"Sir Edgar something. He works in the War Office. The brothers are close."

"Who else?"

Rigsby scratched his chin. "Well, there is Lady Uxbridge. She's nice to her servants. A bit of a featherhead. Enjoys coming to the Season in order to visit with her friends. There's a daughter. Lady Adalyn. Now, she's well known in the *ton*. Pretty and vivacious. The earl's child."

When Rigsby fell silent, Spencer said, "So, it will be three for dinner then?"

"I would say four, my lord. Lord Uxbridge's niece, Lady Tessa, is here this year. Her father died and she went to live with Lord Uxbridge, her mother's brother. She's a favorite with the servants. Polite and friendly, she is. Doesn't cause much fuss."

Spencer refrained from chuckling, knowing Lady Tessa bringing home a street urchin to serve as her lady's maid would certainly cause a fuss.

"Then I will inform Cook it will be four for dinner tomorrow. You have been most helpful, Rigsby."

"Anytime, my lord. Especially during the Season."

"Why the Season?" he asked.

"Will you be looking for a bride?" the valet questioned.

If he was, sharing it with his valet wasn't what Spencer had in mind. "It remains to be seen," he said, not committing one way or the other.

"If you are considering a young lady, just let me know, my lord. I'll do my best to ferret out any information about her that might help you in making your decision."

Feeling he was stooping too low, he merely grunted. Let Rigsby take that however he chose.

"You might also want to start going to your club, my lord," the valet recommended.

"Why so?"

"Well, you being new to the title and all, it would be a place for you to make friends."

"You think I need friends?" he asked, anger simmering at the valet's suggestion.

"People will start arriving in droves during the next few weeks. Getting to know a few gentlemen at White's before the masses arrive might do you some good, my lord. I think it would be nice if going into a ballroom you could catch sight of a friendly face or two."

He had to admit Rigsby's advice was sound.

"I suppose I could do so now. Claim my membership. Where is White's located?"

The valet told him and said, "Your father and brother enjoyed going there."

"What on earth do you do at a club?" he wondered aloud.

"Read the newspapers. Talk politics. Drink coffee or tea if it's early. Brandy or whisky if it's later in the day. Some gentlemen even dine at their clubs on a regular basis."

"Very well. There are no sessions in Parliament today. I will venture to White's and see it for myself."

While he had been fascinated by the arguments he heard in the House of Lords, he had kept himself apart from others, feeling a bit shy and out of sorts at having taken his seat there. He decided meeting a few people in a more social setting might help him come forward in the House and other places, as well. After all, he had no friends in London since those he was closest to were all still out of the country fighting Bonaparte.

Spencer called for his carriage and directed his coachman to travel to St. James's Street. Once he descended from the carriage, he dismissed the driver, deciding he would walk back. Entering, he was greeted and explained it was his first time to visit the club. Immediately, he was thoroughly welcomed and given a tour of the place. He learned the table directly in front of the large bow window on the ground floor was reserved for the most socially influential members and that he should never sit there unless invited to do so.

What interested him most was a betting book, which he learned was quite famous in Polite Society. He was encouraged to peruse the entries and did so, seeing some of them involved sports but more revolved around political developments. Some were even social bets, where wagers were placed on which gentlemen would wed and to whom. He shuddered, hoping he would never see his name appear in regards to such a bet.

He did notice the name of one woman in the betting book. An Adalyn Goulding. Several pages were devoted to bets placed on whom and when she would wed. Unlike other entries, which were marked when a marriage occurred, it was obvious the lady in question still remained unwed. With such an unusual name, he guessed she must be the daughter of the Earl of Uxbridge and that he would meet her at dinner.

The place was only about a quarter full and he determined it was because of the Season not having started yet. He saw a group of chairs and decided to join the three men sitting there, hoping to introduce himself to at least a few people while here.

Approaching it, he saw one of the gentlemen intently reading a newspaper, while the other two were engaged in conversation.

"Might I join you?" he asked. "I am Lord Middlefield and I am new to White's and my title."

The pair halted their conversation and introduced themselves then immediately went back to speaking only to one another. Awkwardly, he sat and caught the third gentleman with graying temples looking at him intently.

Putting aside the newssheet, he said, "It is good to finally meet you, Lord Middlefield. I am your neighbor, Lord Uxbridge."

Spencer leaned over and offered his hand. "It is most wonderful to meet you, my lord."

The earl accepted it. "Thank you for your invitation to dine with you tomorrow evening."

"I hope you will accept it, Lord Uxbridge. I regret having turned down your invitation to do the same when I first arrived in London."

"We will be there. With no regrets."

"I must apologize," Spencer said. "I am new to all of this. A second son who knew from an early age I was destined for the military. I have come from the Continent, where I fought in a regiment associated with Wellington." He paused. "Joining Polite Society has made me a bit uncomfortable. I wasn't ready to do so when I received your invitation. I should have declined it with more grace."

Uxbridge nodded in a fatherly fashion. "You are here now, Middlefield. That is what counts."

"I first journeyed to Stoneridge, my father's country estate. I found much to do there. Thankfully, I have a wonderful steward who was a superior tutor and I was able to come to town, knowing things were well in hand under his care."

The two men talked of their tenants and various crops, along with discussing horses and dogs. Spencer grew more comfortable with the earl after an hour had passed and decided to ask him about his family although he already knew a bit about them from Rigsby.

"I came to town knowing no one but I hope we might become friends, my lord. I look forward to you and your family dining with me. Who might be coming?"

"My wife, naturally. Lady Uxbridge is charming and friendly. She is usually quiet but always seems to blossom whenever we come to town. She has many friends and looks forward to the Season each year. She knows absolutely everyone and is an excellent hostess. Perhaps we can host a small dinner party in your honor and allow you to meet a few others."

"That would be delightful."

"Adalyn, my daughter, will also be in attendance. She is our only child and probably a bit spoiled. I am prejudiced in her favor, naturally, but I think she is a beauty who is full of sparkling conversation."

"I look forward to meeting her, my lord."

"Don't let her break your heart, Middlefield."

"I beg your pardon?"

The earl sighed. "Adalyn has been out for five Seasons. She seems to have no interest in marriage or children. Each year, I have high hopes that a gentleman will come and sweep her off her feet." He paused. "Perhaps you will be that gentleman, Middlefield." Then he shook his head. "No, you are much too sedate for my Adalyn. She is far too adventurous for the likes of you."

"I still look forward to meeting your daughter, Lord Ux-bridge." He waited, hoping the earl would continue and when he didn't, he said, "I will be happy to entertain the three of you."

"No, no, there will be four," the earl corrected. "That is, if you don't mind my bringing my niece. I hope she would be included in your invitation."

"Of course. Whomever you choose to attend," Spencer en-couraged.

"Tessa is a sweet girl. Even though she is my Adalyn's age, Tessa will make her come-out this Season."

"Why the delay?" he asked, very curious now to glean infor-mation about her.

"Tessa stayed in the country when my sister—her mother—

grew quite ill. She nursed her mother for a good year or more. Then her father suffered an attack of apoplexy immediately after his wife's death." The earl shook his head sadly. "Poor Paxton was incapacitated. Couldn't even speak. Tessa stayed by his side, night and day, for the better part of three years. When he finally passed and she had nowhere to go, I asked her to come and stay with us."

"She was homeless? I am afraid I don't understand."

Uxbridge's face darkened in anger. "The new Lady Paxton didn't care much for Tessa. The chit is coldhearted and not yet even twenty. She demanded Tessa leave Oakley and never return. Tessa's uncle, now Lord Paxton, doesn't seem to have the desire to rein in his countess. If I were you, Middlefield, I would make certain I didn't find myself in the midst of the Paxtons' social circle."

"Have no fear of that, my lord. They wronged your niece greatly."

"Selfishly, I am grateful they did. Tessa has always been as a daughter to me, along with my brother's girl, Louisa. And Adalyn has always adored Tessa. We are happy for her to remain with us as long as she can. Of course, she is kind and beautiful. I hope she will have many suitors and choose to wed one of them at Season's end."

Spencer thought Lady Tessa to have been very selfless to have given up a good portion of her youth tending to her ill parents when she could have left that task to others while she came to London and found herself a husband. It spoke to her loyalty to family and decent character. Of course, he had also seen her in action recently, taking in an orphan off the street and helping give the girl a new life. That took bravery—and a bit of recklessness.

Lady Tessa was proving to be a very intriguing young woman. He eagerly looked forward to entertaining her at dinner.

CHAPTER FIVE

T ESSA LOOKED AT her image in the mirror and smiled. She turned and said, "You are a natural, Abra."

Her new lady's maid grinned broadly. "I think so, too, my lady."

It was hard to believe that Abra had only joined the household yesterday morning. After a day's tutelage from Bridget and becoming familiar with Tessa's wardrobe, the two servants had experimented with various hairstyles on both Tessa and Adalyn. Bridget would try something on her mistress and Abra would try to copy it with Tessa. Abra had caught on quickly and even seemed to surpass Bridget's skill with hair.

She stood. "That will be all. I will ring for you when we return from dinner."

The girl smiled. "I am liking this work, my lady." She smoothed the skirts of her uniform. "I like what I do and how I look. I didn't know I could be this happy."

Without warning, Abra threw her arms about Tessa and hugged her tightly. Rather than reprimanding her for inappropriate behavior, Tessa returned the hug.

Abra broke away. "I won't do that again. I promise." She rolled her eyes. "Bridget would have my hide for even thinking about hugging you. But I did want to show you how much I appreciate you."

Tears misted Tessa's eyes. "I think we are lucky to have one another."

As Abra left, Adalyn entered the room and said, "Oh, you should always wear that shade of light blue, Tessa. It truly brings out the color of your eyes. And your hair is marvelous. Perhaps I might steal Abra away from you and let you have Bridget."

She shook her head. "Don't let Bridget hear you say that. She is quite assertive and would probably take it out on poor Abra."

"Are you ready for your first foray into society tonight?" her cousin asked.

Tamping down her nerves, she replied, "It is only dinner. With one earl. It is not a true *ton* event."

Adalyn sniffed. "It may be an intimate gathering tonight but oftentimes a small dinner party includes a good twenty to thirty people."

"Are you joking?"

"Not a bit. This will be good practice for you, though. You never really dined out or with guests before now. Just family."

It was true. Her father enjoyed the peace of the country and they never had visitors beyond family when there. She had been on the brink of experiencing the world when her come-out was delayed. Now, five years later, she felt absolutely ancient and a bit terrified to attend social events. At least she would have Adalyn and Louisa by her side when the Season began.

As for tonight, she couldn't understand her nerves. It was just one meal with one man—and her family would be present.

"Bridget says the earl is quite good-looking."

"How would Bridget know?"

Adalyn grinned. "Abra told her so. She told Bridget that the earl must be smitten with you and that is why he extended an invitation to dinner to Papa. You, naturally, would be included in the family."

"Abra is making too much of this," Tessa protested. "Yes, Middlefield was rather nice-looking but he seemed quite overbearing. Not someone I would like to get to know at all. You are bolder than I, Adalyn. Perhaps the earl is meant for you."

Adalyn sighed. "I don't know what I am going to do. I have enjoyed my freedom and the fact I am not seeing any one gentleman exclusively. Half of the eligible bachelors are terrible rogues and would take too much work to tame. The other half are wishy-washy. They don't care to commit to anything and seem rather weak to me. They even seem afraid of me."

"I am sure they are. You are very strong in your beliefs and never one to keep quiet about anything. That's what I love about you. You will find the right man. I know it."

It surprised her when Adalyn teared up. "I am not at all certain that will ever happen. I have begun thinking about children. If I turn twenty-five and still haven't become betrothed, I am going to accept the first man that offers for me. I don't want to be placed upon the shelf. I want to live. To learn. To have children and pass along my zest for living to them."

"Who knows? Perhaps the Earl of Middlefield will catch your fancy."

Adalyn laughed. "I predict he will catch yours."

Tessa sensed her cheeks heat and turned away, picking up her gloves and putting them on.

"Shouldn't we be going downstairs?" she asked once her gloves were in place.

"Yes. Papa is a stickler for being on time. Why, I have never understood. No one in the *ton* cares about arriving on time. And Heaven help the man who arrives early at an event."

They went down the stairs, arm-in-arm, and it comforted Tessa to know she would have this wonderful friend by her side as she made her come-out. Having no experience with men put her a bit on edge. She remembered her mother's warnings of the rakes of the world and how they would try to take advantage of her. She had been told never to be alone with a man else she would find herself compromised—or worse—if the man in question refused to wed her.

She decided to look for someone like Papa. Steadfast. Loyal.

Quiet. Dependable. Most likely a man the exact opposite of the one Adalyn would eventually settle down with. Her cousin was so vivacious and energetic, she would need a husband of high spirits to match her own.

"There you are," her aunt said as they arrived in the foyer. "I was about to send a maid up to fetch you." She smiled. "You both look lovely, don't they, Uxbridge?"

Her uncle smiled. "They do. Middlefield will be struck dumb with their charm and beauty."

"I doubt that, Papa," Adalyn said. "I think—"

Tessa elbowed her cousin. "I think it is wonderful that he invited us to dine with him," believing her cousin would toss out her theory that Middlefield was already taken with Tessa and wanting to silence her.

"At least we don't need a carriage to simply walk across the square," Uncle Uxbridge said.

They set out for the short walk. The evening air was a bit cool and she wished she had brought her shawl. Hopefully, the earl's townhouse would be warmer.

A butler greeted them and escorted them to the drawing room, announcing them. Tessa saw the earl rise from the chair he sat in and was taken in for a moment by how handsome he was in his evening wear. He strode toward them, unsmiling, a serious look upon his face.

"Lord and Lady Uxbridge," he said, taking her aunt's hand and then shaking hands with her uncle. "I can't thank you enough for accepting my invitation to dinner."

"Wouldn't have missed it for the world," her uncle said. "May I introduce my daughter, Lady Adalyn?"

The earl took Adalyn's hand and kissed it. "A pleasure, my lady."

"And this is my niece, Lady Tessa Foster," her uncle added.

Middlefield turned his focus to her and her heart seemed to beat in double time. She gazed up at him, forgetting how tall he was, though she was very tall for a woman. His thick, black hair was swept away from his face. His eyes glittered like emeralds.

"Ah, yes," the earl said, taking her hand. "We have exchanged pleasantries if not names."

Pleasantries?

Tessa knew he was merely being polite. Their conversation hadn't been pleasant at all. In fact, she had been downright angry, while the earl had been overbearing. As her gaze met his, she saw a ghost of a smile and decided he knew exactly what she was thinking.

"When was this?" her aunt asked, curious.

Middlefield turned to Lady Uxbridge. "I ride very early each morning but my horse turned up lame so I chose to walk yesterday. Lady Tessa was also out for a walk and we spoke briefly."

Her aunt clucked her tongue. "Oh, Tessa, you are going to have to give up those early morning walks. These country hours you insist upon keeping simply won't do when the Season begins. Why, I do not see how you get up and walk before you even breakfast. It would be beyond me." She smiled coquettishly at the earl. "I never rise before eleven and, even then, I breakfast in my room."

"I admire Lady Tessa's commitment to walking," Middlefield said, surprising her. "I myself enjoy exercise, walking, in particular. It is not only good for the body but the soul."

"Why do you say that?" she asked, wondering what he meant.

He shrugged. "If I have troubles, I walk them away. If I encounter a problem I cannot solve, walking helps me think through it."

"I know what you mean," she said softly. "I also walk as much for my peace of mind as I do for the exercise."

Tessa looked at Middlefield with new eyes. He seemed to do the same with her for a long moment.

The butler appeared. "Dinner is served, my lord."

The spell seemed to be broken. She turned away, embar-

EDUCATED BY THE EARL

rassed at the blush that heated her cheeks.

"Might I escort you in to dinner, Lady Uxbridge?" the earl asked.

"Why, I would be delighted, my lord."

Her aunt took Middlefield's arm and they left the room.

Her uncle grinned. "I suppose I am left to escort the likes of you two." He raised both forearms and Tessa and Adalyn placed their hands upon them. "Let's see what the earl might serve us. I do hope something sweet."

She laughed aloud. Her uncle was famous for his sweet tooth and Adalyn had inherited it from him. She liked sweets but just as easily enjoyed savory fare.

They arrived in the dining room and Adalyn leaned across her father and said, "I saw how he looked at you."

"Stop," Tessa warned.

"Do as she says, Adalyn," Uxbridge agreed.

Her cousin pursed her lips. "It is a conspiracy against me," she said in a mocking tone.

The three of them joined the earl and her aunt at the far end of the table which seated twelve.

"I hope you don't mind that I asked for us all to be placed at this end. I see no point in shouting down the table at a guest. In my opinion, the distance keeps the conversation from flowing."

"That is very thoughtful of you, my lord," Adalyn said sweetly, her eyes then cutting to Tessa as she grinned.

Their host took the seat at the head of the table, with her uncle and aunt placed on his right. She and Adalyn were directed to sit to his left and her cousin quickly claimed the seat furthest from the earl, leaving Tessa to be seated directly at the earl's left hand. Gritting her teeth, she allowed a footman to seat her. After all, it was only one dinner. She could survive that.

And damn the man.

He was charming. A bit reserved but he opened up as the meal progressed, much as her father might have under similar circumstances. Lord Uxbridge urged their host to talk a bit about

ALEXA ASTON

his army career and he did so, downplaying the dangers of war
and making light of what occurred in camp.

"I was fortunate to be with several friends so it made a bad
situation better," Middlefield told his guests.

"Who were these friends?" she couldn't help but ask.

"Two, Owen and Everett, were from my earliest school days.
We met that first day. Or at least I met them. They were
neighbors and had known one another their entire lives. Everett
was quite shy, while Owen thinks it is his mission in life to
conquer the world." He chuckled. "He very well may do it
someday."

"It must have been a comfort to have familiar faces nearby,"
Tessa remarked.

"I also had two very close friends from our university days
with me. Percy and Win. Percy and I were officers in one
regiment. Owen in another. And Win and Everett in a third. All
were under Wellington's command. Being officers, we saw each
other frequently in meetings and worked together in training and
drilling the men under our command. Those four are as brothers
to me. Closer than brothers."

She heard the emotion in his voice. He reached for his wine
goblet and drank deeply before setting it down.

"How is it being the new earl?" Adalyn asked. "Of course, we
knew your father and brother, residing so close to one another in
town."

His brow furrowed. "I am learning, my lady. I wasn't brought
up to be an earl. I was meant for the military. The change has
been, to say the least, a little disarming."

"Was it hard to walk away from the career you had always
envisioned for yourself?" Tessa asked.

His gaze turned to her and the earl nodded. "Yes. Very much
so. My life was the army. I breathed duty and loyalty to my
country. My father wished for me to come home when my
brother, Wilford, died several years ago. I chose to remain on the
front. I believed myself more valuable there than home in

52

England. Father was in good health and I didn't question him running things. He did an excellent job until the bitter end. Now, I must pick up his mantle and try to do the best I can for my tenants."

"I know your steward to be excellent," her uncle said. "Middlefield told me enough times how pleased he was with the man."

"Yes, Mr. Pimmel is quite knowledgeable. He took me in hand the moment I arrived at Stoneridge and taught me a great deal. It was only because he is so capable that I felt comfortable coming to London for the Season."

"Have you ever been to it before?" Lady Uxbridge asked.

"No, my lady. I went straight from university into the army without a backward glance. I fear I have as much to learn about the *ton* and social affairs as I do matters at Stoneridge."

The countess smiled. "Adalyn will be an excellent guide for you. She knows all the young people and will be able to introduce you and Tessa around. There is no one more popular than our daughter."

"Don't bore the earl, Mama," warned Adalyn. To Middlefield, she said, "I will be happy to introduce you and my cousin around. Tessa is making her come-out this year. She has been in the country caring for her parents until recently."

Middlefield caught her eye. "That was very noble of you, my lady. Putting your own life aside while you tended to others."

"Those others were much beloved by me, my lord. It was no trial but a privilege."

"Will you be searching for a husband?" he asked.

She sensed the heat filling her cheeks. "That is a very personal question, my lord."

He shrugged. "It seems my manners are a bit rough around the edges. Time at war will do that to a man. Forgive me if I overstepped. I will say that I am looking for a bride. I was told that was what the Season is all about. It is the only reason I referenced it, my lady."

Her blush deepened. "The first rule of the *ton* is that everyone knows what is going on—and yet everyone talks around it," she said lightly. "While unmarried ladies and gentlemen might be seeking a betrothed, it is not commonly referred to. And when it happens, everyone acts totally surprised."

Middlefield laughed, rich and deep, causing her spine to tingle. "So, I am to look but pretend I am *not* looking for a wife. Do I have that correct?"

They all chuckled and Adalyn said, "That about sums it up, my lord."

He smiled, the first time he had done so, and Tessa caught her breath. His smile was like a lantern piercing the dark, lighting up everything around it.

A smile like that could be very dangerous.

Tessa decided she should avoid the man—and his winsome smile.

The rest of the dinner passed quickly, with the talk lively. When it came time for the men to sip on their port, the earl said, "I know it is customary for the men to have at their port. I would hate to neglect you ladies, though, and suggest we all adjourn to the drawing room."

"That is very thoughtful, my lord," her aunt said, approval in her eyes. "Perhaps the young ladies might entertain us."

"Not me," Adalyn said firmly. "I haven't touched the pianoforte's keys in months. Tessa is the one who should play. She practices daily and plays divinely."

They rose and Middlefield said, "Might I escort you to my pianoforte, Lady Tessa? I would enjoy hearing you play." He offered her his arm.

Her pulse quickened. Her belly flip-flopped. "Certainly, my lord," she said, hoping her words didn't sound as breathless to him as they did to her as she placed her hand on his sleeve. A giddiness filled her, unlike any feeling she had known. She swallowed hard, wanting to tamp down whatever was rumbling within her.

As they left the dining room, he asked, "Why do you practice so much?"

"Because I couldn't for many years," she replied. "As my cousin mentioned, my mother fell ill and then my father did. I spent most of my days and a good many hours each night in their sickrooms. I had no time for frivolity. Though I love music, it was no longer a priority."

"It is admirable for you to have nursed them as you did. Do you enjoy living with your aunt and uncle?"

"Very much so. Adalyn and I are more like sisters than cousins. Our other cousin, Louisa, is only a year younger than we are. We were extremely close growing up. Unfortunately, I did not get to see them for several years since I remained in the country. It is good to make up for lost time now."

They reached the drawing room and he took her to the pianoforte. He looked around a moment and said, "I know there is some sheet music here somewhere."

Before she could tell him she could play any number of pieces by heart, he said, "I am fond of Haydn and Beethoven. Perhaps you might play some of their work. Ah, here." He held up several sheets. "I know there must be something of theirs here. I can turn the pages for you."

Tessa sat on the bench and he joined her a moment later, placing the sheets in front of her. She had never sat so close to a man before who wasn't a relative. She felt the brush of his dark wool coat against her bare upper arm. Smelled the spice of his shaving soap. Felt the warmth emanating from him as his side pressed against hers. It all made her grow dizzy. She closed her eyes, inhaling deeply and blowing the breath out slowly to calm herself. It wouldn't do to be thinking of the man sitting next to her and having her fingers trip over themselves, especially after Adalyn had praised her so highly.

"Is this selection one you are familiar with?" he asked.

She glanced at the opening measures and recognized Haydn's work. "Yes, I can play this for you, my lord."

"Good." The one word was a rumble low in his chest, causing

the blood to rush to her ears, pounding so loudly she thought she might go deaf.

Another deep breath. In. Out. She laced her fingers together and cracked the knuckles, knowing her aunt would wince.

"Must you, Tessa, dear?" her aunt asked.

"It does help," she assured and then glanced at his lordship, whose lips turned up in a conspiratorial smile.

Placing her fingers on the keys, she began to play. It was a piece she knew by heart and she felt the music began to fill her soul. She was aware when the earl turned a page but it didn't throw her. Instead, she reveled in his very nearness and played for him alone. When she finished and lifted her hands from the keys, she heard his quick intake of breath.

"That was marvelous," he said, so low only she could hear. "You play beautifully." He smiled wryly and looked over his shoulder. "Lady Tessa is most talented. I am sorry the pianoforte is so out of tune."

Glancing back at her, he said, "I won't ask you to play again until I have had someone in to tune the instrument. I suppose no one has played it in a very long time."

Middlefield helped her rise and they returned to the others. "I never played but I enjoy music. My brother played for a short time and then quit. I have told Lady Tessa I will have the instrument tuned for her. Then I will invite you to return and we can hear her play again."

"You could always come to dinner and hear her on our piano-forte," Uncle Uxbridge said. "Say, next Tuesday?"

"I would be delighted to do so, my lord," the earl said, bowing his head in acknowledgement.

They spoke for a few minutes and then Adalyn said, "I don't suppose you are interested in lectures, Lord Middlefield."

"What kind of lectures, my lady?"

"Poetry. Science. Religion. Antiquities," Adalyn said loftily.

Tessa knew what was coming but could not nudge her cousin to make her stop without it seeming too obvious.

"Tessa is forever dragging me to all sorts of lectures, mostly at the British Museum. Might you care to accompany us sometime? In fact, there is one tomorrow," Adalyn mused. "What is the topic?" she asked Tessa.

"Egyptian antiquities," she said tersely, knowing perfectly well Adalyn knew the topic. "With a focus on the Rosetta Stone being the key to deciphering Egyptian hieroglyphs."

Adalyn sighed deeply. "See? Even hearing the topic bores me silly."

"I have wanted to see the British Museum since I came to town," Middlefield said. "I suppose this would be a good excuse to do so."

"We could go early and allow you to walk the museum and see this all-important stone before the lecture begins," Adalyn said. She turned to Tessa. "Isn't the lecture scheduled for one o'clock?"

"It is," she said reluctantly.

"Yes. We should plan on it," Middlefield said.

Tessa listened to the pair set a time and then her uncle said it was time to bid their host good evening.

"Thank you for your hospitality, Lord Middlefield. My family and I have enjoyed getting to know you."

"It has been a most pleasant way for me to pass my evening, as well, Lord Uxbridge." He looked to Tessa. "I will see you two ladies tomorrow morning."

"We look forward to it," Adalyn said demurely.

The earl accompanied them downstairs and they said good-night. The moment the door closed, Tessa linked her arm through Adalyn's and held her back as her aunt and uncle started across the square.

"Why are you playing matchmaker?" she demanded.

Adalyn grinned. "Because he is a very handsome man who couldn't seem to take his eyes off you the entire evening."

"Why did you invite him to come with us tomorrow?"

The grin widened. "Because I thought it would be a wonderful way for you to get to spend more time with him before the Season begins. Oh, don't be angry with me, Tessa. Lord Middlefield is suave and cultured. He's very well spoken. Mama liked him."

"For you. Not me," she said.

"Well, he doesn't suit me at all. He's a bit reserved. A little too bookish for my tastes."

"And you think that is what I want?"

"Admit it, Tessa. That he is the tiniest bit handsome. And intelligent."

Grudgingly, she nodded. "He is. Nice to look upon and intelligent enough."

"And he likes you."

"He does not," she protested, moving toward their townhouse, bringing Adalyn along with her.

"He does. He certainly sat close enough to you when you were playing at the pianoforte. And I know for a fact you didn't need him there to turn the pages for you. You play that piece all the time and know it by heart."

Her face grew warm at the thought of his side pressed against hers.

"See," her cousin said, her smile triumphant. "You have noticed his attention. I think you like him, too. At least a little bit."

"He is still overbearing."

"He wasn't tonight."

Tessa snorted. "He was on his best behavior tonight."

Adalyn halted. "If he is overbearing, then push back."

"You want me to physically push him?" she asked, her cheeks burning as she remembered having done that very thing. Her palms touching that broad chest. The hardened muscle beneath the elegant clothing.

"No. You are so clever. Verbally spar with him. That is a way to flirt."

She gasped. "Now, you want me to flirt with him?"

"Of course," her cousin said airily. "You might as well practice doing so on the earl. You'll be doing it with plenty of other men during the Season."

"I don't even know how to flirt," she admitted.

Adalyn studied her. "Then we'll go to my bedchamber now and I will give you your first lesson in the art of flirting."

CHAPTER SIX

S PENCER TOLD RIGSBY, "Make me shine today."
The valet cocked one eyebrow and solemnly nodded. "Of course, my lord. Though I believe I do so every day."

By the time he was ready, he wore a shirt whiter than snow with a pearl gray waistcoat and dark gray trousers and tailcoat. His cravat's knot was the most intricate Rigsby had attempted. To his credit, Spencer held perfectly still until the valet had finished.

"I have never seen you more patient, my lord," the valet praised. "Might this have anything to do with last night's dinner?"

He shrugged. "Possibly."

He probably should tell Rigsby about his plans because the servant was bound to learn through his vast network of sources.

"I am escorting Lady Tessa and Lady Adalyn to the British Museum today. To a lecture," he said, thinking himself clever not to give away which lady he was interested in.

"Ah, Lady Tessa quite enjoys the lectures there," Rigsby remarked.

Spencer's jaw dropped. "How do you know everything about our neighbors?" he demanded.

Rigsby grinned. "I might be stepping out with a certain Bridget in the earl's household."

"I see. Well, what else do you know about Lady Tessa? You

might as well tell me everything."

The valet mentioned a few things Spencer already knew, such as the deaths of Lady Tessa's parents and her coming to live with Lord and Lady Uxbridge. He did add that Lady Tessa had been a frequent visitor to the household during her youth, as well her cousin, a Miss Goulding.

"I do know Lady Tessa has hired a new lady's maid. Bridget didn't think she'd like the girl at all but says she is doing a credible job so far."

He thought of the street urchin turned lady's maid and thought the girl would be clever enough to pick up what she needed to know to stay in the household. He only hoped she wouldn't rob the earl blind and then disappear.

"Lady Adalyn is not one for the museums," Rigsby continued. "It is more to Lady Tessa and Miss Goulding's taste."

That was good to know. He had gathered Lady Adalyn wasn't a bit interested from last night's discussion but he didn't know if she was merely saying that in order to give him more time with Lady Tessa. In fact, it was Lady Adalyn who had planned today's outing. Lady Tessa had seemed reluctant to enter the conversation.

Spencer would need to change that reluctance.

He told himself not to gossip with the help anymore but he wouldn't turn down any additional information Rigsby forwarded to him regarding the golden-haired beauty.

Going downstairs, he called for his carriage to be readied. It was shortly after ten. With the traffic, they would make it to the museum by eleven, according to Lady Adalyn, giving them plenty of time to see a few exhibits before the lecture began two hours later.

He told his coachman they were headed to the British Museum and asked if he knew its location.

"I do, my lord. In Bloomsbury."

"Stop across the way at Lord Uxbridge's townhouse first," he instructed. "I will board the carriage there."

Strolling across the square, he went to the front door and knocked. The Uxbridge butler answered the door.

"Ah, good morning, my lord. The ladies should be joining you momentarily."

He heard them before he saw them, their voices carrying as they descended the staircase.

"You have to go, Adalyn. I cannot go alone with him," the first said, which he recognized as Lady Tessa's.

"You know it bores me to tears. I have absolutely no interest in going, Tessa. Besides, I sent for Abra. She can chaperone you. I have other things to do."

"What things?" Lady Tessa demanded as they rounded the corner. She stopped, seeing him in the foyer and composed her features.

"Ah, Lord Middlefield," Lady Adalyn said airily, continuing down the staircase. "How good to see you again. I was just telling my cousin that I had forgotten a prior engagement so I will not be able to accompany you to Montagu House today."

"I am sorry to hear we will be deprived of your company, my lady," he told her, secretly thrilled that he would enjoy having Lady Tessa to himself for the outing.

"I would like to know what engagement," Lady Tessa said testily, glaring at her cousin.

"Oh, I will tell you all about it at tea this afternoon." Lady Adalyn looked to him. "You must join us, my lord. By the time the lecture concludes and you make your way back to Mayfair, you will be desperate for a cup of tea. I will let my mother know you are coming. I will see the both of you later."

Lady Adalyn left, leaving him with a very unhappy Lady Tessa, who didn't bother to disguise her displeasure.

Then a servant came scurrying around the corner. "I'm here, my lady. Oh, hello, my lord. I'm Abra, in case you don't recognize me in my fine new uniform. I'm doing an excellent job, just ask Lady Tessa. She'll tell you."

He looked at her and asked, "Is it true? You have turned a

street orphan into an acceptable lady's maid in only a few days?"

A fierceness filled her eyes and Spencer saw Lady Tessa was still protective of Abra. "I don't believe I will ever have a finer lady's maid, Lord Middlefield. Abra has already learned so much and has taken to her new position with ease. She is most talented in putting ensembles together and has quite a way with styling hair."

"If she is responsible for how you are turned out this morning, my lady, then I would say she has done a very good thing. You look lovely."

Her cheeks pinkened. "Thank you," she said brusquely.

"Shall we?" he asked, waving his hand toward the door.

"I suppose so," she said, moving toward the door, Abra trailing her.

His footman opened the carriage door and helped them into the vehicle and Spencer followed, sitting opposite the two women.

As the carriage began to roll away, Abra said, "Bridget tells me I am to chaperone you today. What does that involve?"

"Who, exactly, is Bridget?" he asked, knowing that was who Rigsby was seeing.

"Oh, that's Lady Adalyn's maid. She's been teaching me about what to do and how to please Lady Tessa."

"I believe Bridget is friendly with my valet, Rigsby."

Abra nodded enthusiastically. "Oh, yes. She's told me all about him. Said he's a bit full of himself, being a valet to an earl and all, but she likes him all the same."

Spencer was a bit shocked at how chatty Abra was and the fact Lady Tessa didn't bother to rein her servant in. He wasn't going to correct her, however. He might actually learn something.

Unfortunately, Lady Tessa looked at her maid and Abra swallowed. "I suppose I should let the two of you talk. Don't mind me a bit. Think of me as a fly on the wall. I'll just be looking out the window, minding my own business."

As Abra turned and glanced out the window, he saw Lady Tessa's lips twitch in amusement. Then her gaze met his and he found himself grinning. Trying to grow sober, he asked, "Do you often go to the British Museum, my lady?"

"I spent a great deal of time in it as I was growing up. My father loved all its exhibits and passed along that love to me. When we came to London for the Season, it was always somewhere he and I frequented."

"But I thought you were only now going to make your come-out," he said, confused.

"My parents always came to town in the spring for the Season. From my earliest memories, I always accompanied them. The British Museum was a favorite of mine and Papa's. It was the world's first national public museum and has always had free entrance. In the old days, Papa would have to give his name to the porter. He would write it down in a book and give the book to the principal librarian, who issued tickets. The librarian would strike through our names after calling them aloud, assigning groups of five to an under-librarian. It would be he who led us up the great staircase and through all the upper rooms, telling us about the various exhibits before returning us to the ground floor."

"That sounds very organized."

"Oh, it was. They only allowed forty-five to enter at any given time, I believe. Actually, I started going long before I was supposed to. Children under ten were not allowed inside the museum. I was tall for my age, though, and when I turned eight, Papa said we could tell a small, white lie and tell the porter if he asked that I was ten. They never questioned us and I was allowed to go with Papa. There were times we went two or three times a week."

"Why?" he asked, as fascinated by what she was saying as watching how animated her features grew as she spoke.

"Because there is so much to see!" she exclaimed. "They have books and manuscripts which scholarly gentlemen peruse. Items of natural history and antiquities. I know we are going early for you to see the museum itself but if you have the slightest interest in things of this nature, it will take you many visits before you truly satisfy your curiosity."

He smiled. "I have always enjoyed history and mathematics, in particular."

"Then you will most likely return to the museum again and again."

"Do they present lectures often?"

She nodded. "Yes, usually once a week and sometimes more often when the Season begins and more people are in town. Those, too, are also free and open to the public. Last week, Adalyn and I heard one on Hinduism and Buddhism. They are Far Eastern religions. I found the topic fascinating."

Spencer found her fascinating.

He asked about other things within the museum and she spoke knowledgeably, proving to be a good conversationalist and allowing him to see she was quite bright. He had liked her looks and her spirit before. Now, he liked her even more. Being wed to Lady Tessa would never be boring. He still would keep those thoughts to himself. Though she had opened up to him in the carriage since she spoke about a topic she was passionate about, he had noted how reluctant she was to even go with him today. She didn't seem the type to be rushed. Though he was in a hurry to find a bride and marry, he realized Lady Tessa had never made her come-out. She would be curious about Polite Society and want to enjoy the various social events. He would let her. At least for a while.

Then he would speak to her and make his offer.

The carriage began slowing and Abra turned from the window. "I've never been in this part of town."

"You will enjoy the artifacts in the museum," Lady Tessa told her.

Abra frowned. "No, I won't."

"You must give it a chance," her employer urged.

"No. I'm not one for book learning, my lady. Give me the streets and the people on them. I'm people smart," the servant declared.

Before Lady Tessa could reply to that comment, Spencer interjected, "You might wish to walk about the area then while we are buried in antiquities and listening to the lecture."

"Yes!" Abra exclaimed at the same time Lady Tessa said, "No."

Both women looked at each other.

"You are to be my chaperone today, Abra. That means staying with me."

"I know," the girl said glumly. "Bridget told me I should walk several feet behind you and his lordship. But she also said nobody is here much before the Season begins. That last week when she came with you and Lady Adalyn, you didn't see a single guest, only the people who work there."

"That's true," Lady Tessa said. "Still, you could learn something."

"Why don't we let Abra come inside with us and she can go to the exhibits she finds interesting?" Spencer suggested.

"I can do that," the girl said, nodding in agreement.

The door opened and he climbed from the carriage, helping Lady Tessa and then Abra from the carriage.

Quietly, he said, "And if you find nothing of interest, you could always leave and come back after the lecture."

Abra grinned in response as if she knew he wished her to be out of sight.

Spencer stepped up and offered Lady Tessa his arm. Abra trailed behind them as they entered the building.

A portly man glanced up. "Ah, Lady Tessa. It is always good to see you."

"Good morning, Mr. Casher." She indicated Spencer. "This is Lord Middlefield. It is his first visit to the British Museum."

"Ah, you are in for a rare treat then, my lord." He chuckled. "Lady Tessa has been here so often she could serve as one of our guides. I think she knows more about the place than anyone on the staff does."

"Are you the porter we give our name to?" he asked.

"No, it is not done like that anymore," she said. "That was when I was coming with Papa. I learned on my first visit when I arrived in town a month ago that they have changed the process. No more giving of names and tickets with your entry spaced out."

"What happens instead?" he asked.

The porter smiled broadly. "You merely present yourself to me on Monday, Wednesday, or Friday any time between ten and two. If I judge you to be of decent appearance, you immediately gain entrance."

"Do I pass muster, Mr. Casher?" Spencer joked.

"I would say very much so, my lord. But I would have let you in even if you looked like a beggar, simply because you were with Lady Tessa. She is our favorite guest."

He saw how the porter's words pleased his companion.

"My maid, Abra, is also coming inside," Lady Tessa said, gesturing for Abra to come and join them.

Mr. Casher smiled. "I hope you all enjoy your visit. And don't forget the Egyptology lecture, my lady. It begins at one o'clock."

"We won't. It is the primary reason we came today."

They were given access and an elderly man with hair as white as snow smiled as they approached.

"Lady Tessa!" he cried out. "They told me you were back in the city. I have been away visiting my daughter and my three grandchildren."

"Mr. Smithson, it is wonderful to see you." She hugged the gentleman and turned to Spencer. "Mr. Smithson gave me my first guided tour through the museum many years ago. He was always mine and Papa's favorite guide."

The assistant librarian chuckled. "Probably because I let you in before you should have been allowed."

"You knew I wasn't ten?" she asked.

"Of course, I did, my lady. You were tall and mature for your age but I knew you were nowhere close to ten years of age."

"I never knew that," she said. "At least you came to the conclusion that I was no ruffian and would never damage anything on display."

"I did," Mr. Smithson said. "Lord Paxton had been coming for many years. I knew he would have passed his interest along to you." He turned to Spencer. "Lady Tessa could replace me. Even though she didn't visit us for a few years, she still knows more about this place than I believe I ever will."

He thought of her buried in the country, tending to her ill parents, watching them slowly slip away. Pity filled him.

"I am happily placing myself in Lady Tessa's hands," Spencer told the man. "It is my first visit here. She tells me I will want to make several more."

"I would listen to her, my lord," Smithson advised. "Do you need me today, my lady, or would you rather do the honors?"

He spoke up. "I would like to see the museum through your eyes, Lady Tessa."

"Very well." She glanced over her shoulder. "Come along, Abra."

As they moved toward a huge staircase, Spencer asked, "What will we see today?"

"We will be going upstairs since the lower floor is full of printed books. Upstairs there are works of art and treasures such as minerals, shells, and fossils. Even birds, insects, and snakes. We can save those for another time. I want you to see the gallery instead. It contains the Greek and Roman sculptures. The terra cottas. The Roman sepulchral antiquities." Her face lit up. "And the best of all—the Egyptian antiquities. Since that is the focus of today's lecture, I thought it would be best to start with the Egyptian section and then see other items in the gallery if we have time."

"I'm going to wander about a bit, my lady," Abra said. "See what I like and don't like."

"Very well, Abra," Lady Tessa said. "I hope you find something to your liking. The museum is full of wonders. Come along, my lord. This way."

He offered her his arm and glanced over his shoulder. Abra had the audacity to wink at Spencer and then she hurried away, heading back down the staircase. With no other visitors in sight, Spencer finally found himself alone with Lady Tessa.

Just as he'd hoped.

CHAPTER SEVEN

ESSA TRIED NOT to be upset that Abra had abandoned her. The girl was new in her position and really didn't understand that she shouldn't have left her mistress unchaperoned. If anyone saw Tessa alone with Lord Middlefield, even in a public place, it might cause gossip. Of course, the museum seemed as quiet as a tomb now. She supposed like last week, no one would be touring the exhibits at this hour. Closer to the lecture, however, might be a different story. She would make certain they were back downstairs and ready for the speaker, hopefully with Abra nearby.

They reached the section of Greek and Roman antiquities and the earl slowed until they came to a halt. She saw his gaze wandering the room, his eyes lighting up in delight at the treasures contained there. It would be interesting to view the displays through his eyes.

"There are so many items here. I don't even know where to begin to look." He took a few steps forward with her on his arm. "To see things I have read about and studied right before my very eyes. I am speechless."

He looked up at a statue and Tessa could tell he observed every detail of the artist's work.

"I am surprised since you have such an interest in history that your father did not bring you here when you were in town.

Unless he wasn't interested in history himself," she added, realizing not everyone shared their love for ancient items and the history behind them.

She sensed tension within him and wondered how she might have upset him.

"I have no idea what he was interested in," he said brusquely. "It certainly wasn't me."

His words shocked her. "I beg pardon?" she said, thinking she had misheard him.

He kept his focus on the statue as he said, "I spent my entire life being ignored. I have no memories of my mother. She died when I was two. I have no idea why. No one ever thought to tell me even after I was old enough to understand."

Tessa heard the hurt in his voice. Sympathy filled her.

"My brother, the heir apparent, was ten years my senior. I don't know if we had anything in common because I never really got to know him because of the age difference. Our father worshipped Wilford and invested all of his time and energy into that son. Sometimes I felt as if Wilford were his only child and I was a nobody. A leftover which he forgot about and therefore never thought to acknowledge."

"That is terrible," she said, outraged at the thought. "Your father should have showered you with love, especially after the death of your mother."

Middlefield turned his gaze upon her. "Families are diverse. Your father seems to have been a very different kind of man from mine."

Her eyes misted with tears. "Papa was generous with his time. I spent a good portion of my days with him from the time I was young. We called upon tenants together. Visited others in the neighborhood. When we came to London for the Season and Mama was busy with dress fittings, he would take me to this museum and to Hyde Park. We would walk along the Serpentine."

She smiled at the memories. "He taught me how to fold boats

from paper to float there. We also would go to the park to ride or fly a kite. I went with him to his tailor's shop, helping him pick out various materials for his coats. We were inseparable."

Tessa squeezed his arm. "I am sorry you experienced a different kind of childhood."

"It made me strong. In character." He paused. "It was part of the reason I didn't care to return to England when Wilford died. I had recently graduated from university and Father had purchased my military commission. I had just finished training and left for the Continent, commissioned as a lieutenant. I was with my two childhood friends and two more recent friends from university. I was eager to fight and honor my king and country. I especially felt a strong commitment to the men serving under me.

"Then I received news that Wilford had died and my father wished for me to come home."

"And you had no desire to do so."

"Not at all," he admitted. "My father was in good health. I decided I would continue to serve in the military until we defeated Bonaparte—or until I had to come home."

"When did you return to England?"

"Last autumn. Father died of dropsy and I knew I could no longer put off seeing to my duties back home. It was with great reluctance that I left my men and friends behind."

Trying to lighten the mood, Tessa said, "Well, you are here now. Your estate is thriving, thanks to a well-chosen steward. And here you are in London at the most wonderful museum in the world."

The earl looked out across the room, his features relaxing once more. "I could be lost here for days."

His words tugged at her heart.

"Then you will need to become a regular visitor," she told him. "This Greek and Roman section alone should have weeks devoted to it. For now, though, we should focus on Egyptian antiquities."

He sighed. "Lead the way. Do not let me become distracted."

"Eyes forward, my lord," Tessa said, laughingly. As they began walking, she said, "I rather like being a commanding officer."

"You would have made an excellent one," he said.

"Why do you say that?" she asked, curious about his words.

"You don't truly know me. We argued for a brief time one morning and then shared a dinner with others present."

Middlefield gazed down at her, causing her cheeks to heat. "I am a good judge of character, Lady Tessa. I have always been observant and carefully watched others. That talent, along with having to learn how to make instant decisions in the midst of battle, tells me you are intelligent, compassionate, and forthright—all qualities suitable for leadership within the ranks of the military."

"Thank you," she said softly. "For seeing me. It seems for so long no one really has. They have looked upon me and only seen the dutiful daughter. Or the grieving woman. While I love my uncle and his family, they seem to place me in either of those categories. I would like to be seen for myself. Past being a daughter. Past my grief."

His emerald eyes shone with intensity. "You are seen, Tessa. Have no fear of that."

She swallowed and looked away. She should correct him for having used her Christian name but she couldn't. It didn't seem right after what had passed between them.

They continued on until they reached the Egyptian wing. Excitement filled her. She couldn't wait to see what Lord Middlefield thought of the rooms devoted to such treasures, which were among her favorite within the museum.

"Let us make a quick pass around everything and then you may decide where we will start," he told her. "I merely want to familiarize myself with what is here."

They moved at a slow pace, not taking the time to read any of the information regarding the displays, but giving him time to at least view the many objects on display. When they had made an entire circle, he took a deep breath and exhaled loudly.

"So much wonder here," he declared. "You are right. This will be a place I will visit on a regular basis."

"Have you decided where you wish us to begin?"

"Why not at the Rosetta Stone itself since we will be hearing about it in detail today? Because no one is present now, we can admire it at length."

He led them to the stone and said, "Act as my guide and tell me about it."

Suddenly self-conscious, she said, "You are a student of history, my lord. Most likely, you know as much as I do about it—if not more."

A shadow crossed his face. "I have been at war for some time, Tessa. There was no time to talk about, much less think about, history."

Again, he had used her name. It seemed to come so naturally to him. She really should say something but found she liked hearing it come from his lips in that deep rumble he had.

"All right."

She turned to the Rosetta Stone, which stood almost four feet high and not quite two and a half feet wide. It was irregularly shaped and made of black granite. She had visited it often and knew its story well.

"The stone was found by a French officer. Some say his name was Pierre-Francois Bouchard, while others claim it was Boussard. This happened in 1799, during Napoleon's campaign in Egypt, near the town of Rosetta, north of Alexandria. Most likely it was carved during the Hellenistic period. Scholars believe it was used as building material while Fort Julien was being constructed in the Nile Delta."

She paused and watched as he studied the stone and then continued.

"It aroused excitement in the intellectual community since it is the first Ancient Egyptian text recovered in modern times. Lithographic copies and even plaster casts of it have circulated through various museums throughout Europe. Scholars believe it will eventually prove to be the key to deciphering Egyptian hieroglyphics."

"If the French discovered it, how did it wind up in the British Museum?" Lord Middlefield asked. "After all, we are at war with them."

Tessa didn't know if he asked merely to be polite and actually knew the answer or if he was truly interested. It didn't matter. This was a topic she loved and enjoyed talking about.

"Naturally, the British defeated the French in Egypt in 1801 when the two forces met."

"Naturally," the earl agreed, his smile again as heart-stopping as it had been last night. "Don't they always seem to be surrendering to us throughout history?"

"Well, they did indeed surrender and thanks to the Capitulation of Alexandria, the Rosetta Stone was placed in British hands. It was brought to London and awarded to the British Museum, really the only place for it, in my opinion. Ever since then, it has been on public display and is known as the most visited object within the museum."

"Anything else?" he asked cheekily.

Her hand remained tucked into the crook of his arm and she pinched him.

"Ow!"

"Behave," she reprimanded and then continued. "There are three versions of a decree issued on it, traced to the Ptolemaic dynasty. Two are Ancient Egyptian texts, one using hieroglyphics and the other a Demotic script, neither of which we can read in this day and age. However," she added, "the third version of the decree is in Greek. The first completed translation of this Greek text was published in 1803. To this day, scholars are studying the Greek text, comparing it to the other two. Many believe that using the Greek text, they will be able to decode the Egyptian writings, meaning that someday the Rosetta Stone will be the key to deciphering not only the decree chiseled upon it—but other

Egyptian hieroglyphs which are discovered."

"Do you believe we will see this in our lifetime?" he asked.

"Undoubtedly," she said with firm conviction. "Just think of how the Rosetta Stone will unlock other historical mysteries."

"You are quite knowledgeable about this stone. Are you certain you shouldn't be the one giving today's lecture?" he teased.

"A woman? Surely, you jest. I am not even allowed downstairs in the reading room to look at and study the various books and manuscripts. Papa did sometimes. He would make his request and a messenger would bring him his requested selection. Those were the times I would accompany Mr. Smithson on the tours he gave to others."

"That doesn't seem fair."

"Life isn't fair to females, my lord. Would I love to go to war as you did? Perhaps. But what I really would enjoy doing is traveling far and wide. I am fascinated by Egypt and wish I could view the pyramids in person. Feel the hot desert wind and sun on my cheeks."

"You might someday," he said encouragingly.

"No. That will never come to pass. I am an English lady. That means I am meant to wed and give birth to an heir and a spare, possibly a few daughters, as well. I will be subservient to my husband and support him in all he endeavors to do."

Lord Middlefield frowned. "You can wed and bear children but surely you wouldn't be subservient to your husband. You went about your father's estate from the time you were at his knee. Surely you learned a great deal about estate management and people from him."

"I did," she agreed. "But husbands aren't interested in their wives' opinions, my lord."

"Your father knew your worth. You are as intelligent as any man I have known. If you want to see the Egyptian pyramids, then go. With or without your husband."

She shook her head. "That is ridiculous. You still have much to learn about Polite Society, my lord. I couldn't go without a husband. Why, I even need a chaperone to go to a dress fitting or even to visit this museum." She snorted. "Of course, my chaperone today is nowhere to be found."

"You did tell her to follow her own interests. You should take your own advice and do the same, Tessa."

"As if I could find a husband who would gallivant around the world with me."

"Most women want to see Paris. Or perhaps Berlin," he said. "You could start there if this blasted war would ever end. I am certain you could talk your husband into going to either of those great cities. From there, you could urge him to be more adventurous and think of India or Egypt."

Tessa frowned. "Those seem like nice ideas, Lord Middlefield, but they will never come to pass. Even if I were to manage landing a husband who craved adventure as I do, why, he would merely find another adventurous male to accompany him and leave me at home with our growing brood of children."

She sighed. "Not that I think giving birth isn't a noble thing to do. It is. I am eager to wed and produce children of my own. Many, I hope. I despised being an only child. I know Mama could not help it. She tried for others. It just didn't come to pass."

Lord Middlefield's gaze pinned her. "You need to find a husband who will be a partner to you. You should not be a slave to him. You need to do what is right—and that means you must follow your heart."

Before Tessa could reply, he lowered his mouth to hers.

CHAPTER EIGHT

TESSA HAD NEVER been kissed before.

When she was twelve, she had once seen two servants in the stables kissing, their lips and bodies pressed together as they both made sounds she had never heard before. Quickly, she had fled, embarrassed by coming across them in such an intimate position. Afterward, she had talked about it with her cousins, all three girls wondering what a kiss would be like. She assumed since both Louisa and Adalyn were both out in society that they had at some point been kissed. Neither woman had mentioned it to her, however.

And now it was her turn.

She didn't know a man's lips could be so soft and yet firm at the same time. How she would not only feel his kiss on her lips but that his touch would cause ripples through her entire body. His hands clasped her shoulders, steadying her, as his mouth slanted over hers. Wonderful tingles ran through her, causing her body to heat. She was aware of the heat emanating from him. The spice of his cologne. The warmth of being so close to another.

Then his tongue—*his tongue!*—slid slowly along her lower lip, causing her to clench tightly between her legs. That place had awakened from a deep slumber and had begun to throb. As Middlefield lazily ran his tongue back and forth, the throbbing pulsated, causing her to gasp. That small gasp parted her lips.

And the earl took advantage of that.

His tongue slid inside her mouth, leisurely exploring it. Exploring her. Tessa had no idea tongues were involved in kissing but she quickly gave over to the notion. Tentatively, she moved hers against his. He made a low noise from deep within his throat, his hands tightening on her shoulders.

Oh, this was glorious!

Their tongues began a playful dance, one that set her sense on edge. Everything seemed more intense. His scent. His taste. His muscles. Oh, yes, her hands had gone to his broad chest, palms flattened against it, feeling the rock-hard plane there. Her body caught fire as one hand moved to her waist, anchoring her as his other hand slipped to her nape, holding her firmly in place.

She could have kissed him for hours.

Then a part of her brain slowly fired, a notion working its way through the haze of excitement.

They were in a public place.

In an embrace.

Kissing.

With tongues.

Panic seized her. Tessa pushed against the earl's chest and pulled her mouth from his.

"I cannot do this," she hissed.

Her knees buckled and the earl's hands quickly steadied her, holding her waist.

"I do not want to be compromised," she whispered, gazing into those emerald eyes, now burning with what she guessed was desire.

"I understand," he said, his voice quiet. "Can you stand?"

She nodded and he released her. Tessa swayed a moment but took a step back and locked her knees.

"If someone had seen us . . . if we . . ." Frustrated, she bit her lip, trying to gather her thoughts from the mush her brains had turned to.

She began again. "I do not want to ever be compromised. I would not want you to be forced to wed me. You don't even know me."

He smiled. "But I would like to know you, Tessa. Or more about you."

Blast him and his winning smile.

"You cannot call me by my name, Lord Middlefield. You can't be doing . . . any of this. We need to leave," she announced. "I must find Abra."

"She could be anywhere in the museum. Or perhaps she might have even left to explore the neighborhood," he pointed out.

How could he sound so reasonable and calm when her heart still pounded and the blood sounded so violently in her ears that she could barely hear him speak?

Lord Middlefield closed the distance between them. He took her arm.

"We should stay for the lecture. We both want to hear it. Come and finish telling me about the things that are here. I am sorry I ruined the outing for you."

She swallowed. "Are you sorry for the kiss?"

"No." He gave her a wry smile. "I am sorry for my behavior. For not asking if I could kiss you before I did so." Pausing, he added, "But I will never be sorry for kissing you, Tessa."

"Why did you?"

"Because I have wanted to ever since the morning we met," he admitted. "You were magnificent, coming to Abra's defense. Like Boudica boldly—"

"Boudica?"

He grinned. "Boudica. You would be a woman who would know who she is."

Tessa felt her face flame. "I do. But I am no Boudica."

"You are to me. And to Abra." He cleared his throat. "Again, I am sorry for having kissed you in a public place. I would not see you ruined. You should be given the choice as to the man you will marry.

"But I will tell you now, my lady, that I plan to woo you."

"Woo me?" she asked, breathless.

The earl smiled. "Yes. I am seeking a wife. You are seeking a husband. I think we should get to know one another better during the Season and see if we might suit."

Tessa grew lightheaded hearing his words. This handsome man, a powerful earl, was declaring his interest in her. She blinked rapidly several times.

"I plan to pursue you with a passion, Tessa," he added. "No other man will have a chance."

His arrogant words brought her back to reality.

"You thought you could tell me what to do from the moment we met, my lord," she told him, anger suddenly sizzling through her. "I will not be told what to do. I will not be pushed into a match by a high-handed lord. You aren't even the kind of man I am interested in wedding."

Lord Middlefield cocked his head and studied her a moment. "What, exactly, am I lacking? I would be interested to hear your opinion, Tessa."

"Stop calling me that," she demanded. "You are to address me as Lady Tessa. As for a husband, I am looking for someone who is steadfast and loyal. Patient. Kind. A man who will be a good father to our children."

He took a step closer, invading her space, yet she refused to step back. Instead, she glared up at him.

"I am those things. If my friends were here, they would tell you so. And I may not have had the good, kind parents you did but I know I want children and will treat them the way I always wished to be treated."

He brought his palm to her face, cradling her cheek. "You left out being a good husband, Tessa. You need a man who will be a good father and a good husband to you. One who will make you feel things you have never felt before. One who will introduce you to passion and pleasure."

Her face burned. "That . . . isn't necessary."

His thumb stroked her cheek. "I hope to show you it is very necessary," he said softly. "In the end, you will realize we are meant to be together."

She grasped his wrist and forced his hand away. "You are much too conceited for my tastes, my lord. You presume far too much. I am not interested in your suit. Find some young simpering debutante who will be impressed by your looks and title."

"Where there is anger, there is passion," Lord Middlefield said. "I have much I can teach you, Tessa."

"Someone should teach you some manners, my lord," she said coldly.

He shrugged. "I have already told you my time at war has left me rough around the edges."

The earl captured her wrist and placed it on his forearm. "Continue the tour. I promise to be a perfect gentleman. We will then attend the lecture and I will escort you to your uncle's house."

She seethed but felt she had no choice. With Abra nowhere to be seen, Tessa couldn't leave the museum and hire a hackney cab to take her back to Uncle Uxbridge's townhouse. She was stuck with the earl. Deciding he was right—for once—she wouldn't let him spoil the lecture for her. She would allow him to go with her and then see her home.

And she would never speak to him again.

SPENCER COULDN'T BELIEVE it.

He had kissed Lady Tessa.

Why he had done so was a mystery. Or perhaps not. He had been attracted to her from the beginning. The physical attraction had only grown since that first meeting. He had wanted to be alone with her, without others present, to truly see who she was. And he had liked everything about her. Abra abdicating her responsibilities of serving as a chaperone had only allowed him to do something his subconscious had yearned to do.

Kiss her.

So he did.

It was obvious from the first that she had never been kissed. That fact did not surprise him. Tessa had been buried in the country for years, away from Polite Society and the gentlemen who would have been interested in pursuing her. But the spark between them was undeniable. Their kiss had fanned the flame. So much that he had almost taken more liberties with her than he should have. It was already bad enough that he had kissed her in a public place, where anyone could have stumbled across them.

Discovered in an embrace would have been a disaster.

Not that Spencer wouldn't have offered for her immediately. He would have, as a gentleman should do. If that would have happened, though, it would have removed all choice from Tessa's hands—and he would never do that to her. Knowing how headstrong she was, it wouldn't have surprised him if she would have turned him down. He might not know much about the unwritten rules of the *ton* but common sense told him that move would have been catastrophic to her reputation. He had heard enough talk at school from fellow students with older brothers, some of them rogues, and how men seemed to be forgiven their discretions while women often suffered for transgressions not of their own making.

He wanted Tessa to go into marriage with him willingly, not because her hand was forced to do so. From their kiss, he knew they would be well suited in the bedroom and he could not wait to get her there and take liberties a husband could with his wife.

Still, he had acted far too rashly. His plan had been to allow her to enjoy the Season for several weeks before he made known his interest in her. That idea had been blown out of the water, like a cannon firing and leaving destruction everywhere.

Kissing her had been totally out of character for him. He was known for being methodical and thinking things through. True, in war, he'd had to weigh decisions quickly and act hastily sometimes, balancing the intelligence he had received against the men he had. More often than not, he had liked his chances and acted. Not rashly but perhaps a bit recklessly, though the recklessness was laced with courage and determination.

Perhaps this had been the same. He knew he wanted Tessa as his wife. She was not only fair of face but intelligent and spirited. She would be a commodity on the Marriage Mart that many bachelors would want to sample and eventually try to make their own. It was a good thing he had kissed her and told her of his interest. Guilt filled him, though, as he remembered his words. He had sounded rather arrogant, something that he saw definitely held no appeal for her. It would take time to win her favor and return to her good graces.

Could he do so before the Season began?

Spencer hoped so with all his heart.

He would need to draw up a battle plan, similar to what he had participated in on the Continent. This time, however, he was general and foot soldier rolled into one. The challenge of winning Tessa's hand would be next to impossible after the hole he had dug and placed himself in—but the reward of her becoming his countess would be incredibly sweet. He would have to think rationally about the moves he should make as he closed in on his prey.

Not something he could do at present.

She stood too close for him to think. True, she had removed her hand from his forearm in a very pointed manner. She had remained in the room, however, taking him from one exhibit to the next. Unfortunately, all animation had fled her face and her voice droned on in a monotonous tone, much like several tutors he had known, as she told him about various artifacts. He stood as close as he could to her merely to inhale the faint scent of lavender coming off her.

A scent he remembered from his mother.

When he had been old enough and recognized it when he smelled it again, he had asked what it was and had been told it was lavender. He couldn't recall his mother's image but he did remember associating that scent with her. Spencer wondered if fate had intervened, bringing him to a woman who also claimed the scent as her own.

He determined to show Tessa the man he was—and the one he could be with her.

"Lady Tessa," a voice called out, "the lecture will be starting in twenty minutes."

Spencer glanced to the doorway and saw Smithson, the museum guide.

"Thank you for alerting us, Mr. Smithson. I don't want to miss a minute of it."

Her voice had returned to normal as she spoke to the guide. Jealousy filled him. He wanted her to speak to him that way, not the boring monotone of the last hour.

"Shall we make our way to the presentation?" he asked, offering his arm. When she hesitated, he added, "Your mother taught you good manners, my lady. I would not think she would wish you to be churlish in public to an earl."

Reluctantly, she placed a hand on his sleeve.

"The lecture will be held in the hall downstairs," she told him.

As he led her from the room, Spencer said, "Thank you for sharing your time and information today. You know far more than most Cambridge dons."

He glanced down and saw she looked pleased at the compliment.

"If I had been born a man, I think I would have been drawn to an academic life," she said.

"My daughters will do whatever they wish in life," he proclaimed, causing her to come to a halt.

"That's a preposterous declaration, my lord."

"But one I believe in wholeheartedly. I never had a mother's love. I never knew any affection from my father. Oh, I thought if I could learn a great deal that he would be impressed. Reports from my tutor and school were always outstanding yet he never mentioned them. When I tried to engage him in conversation and show him how hard I worked at my studies, he would cut me off. He didn't care to converse with me, much less know me or anything about me."

"I am sorry your childhood was so bleak," she said, her tone softening.

"It made me self-reliant. I learned the value of depending upon myself. I grew in discipline and knowledge. And it allowed me to choose my own family instead of being a part of the one I was born into. My friends, first at school and then university, became my true brothers. Not Wilford, who was so much older and essentially a stranger to me."

Spencer began leading her toward the staircase as he continued.

"Because of that, I want to be a much different kind of father than the one whose blood runs through me. I know from my friends that second sons seem to be universally ignored in favor of their older brothers, who are the heirs apparent. My sons will be equals in my mind. Oh, I know I will treat some differently from others, based upon their interests and skills. But I will love them equally.

"The same goes for my daughters. Many peers see no value in daughters. They are mere pawns on the chessboard, given in marriage for political or economic reasons. I will teach my daughters the same things I do my sons. How to read and write. How to ride and hunt. How to be brave. How to stand up for what is right."

He paused and then said, "So if one of them wanted to pursue an academic career and become the first university don, she would most certainly have my support. I plan to love my children, Tessa. As much as my wife."

Spencer's words faded. And shook him to his core.

He knew instinctively that he wanted a large family and would love his children. But he had never given a thought to loving his wife. *Ton* marriages weren't built on love. It was as he had spoken. Betrothals signaled unions between families and were made for political or social gain. The idea of loving a woman—a wife—had never been a part of the equation.

Until now.

He believed he spoke so passionately about loving his children and his countess because things were changing within him.

All because of the woman before him.

CHAPTER NINE

A s THEY ENTERED the lecture hall, Tessa tried to focus on anything except Lord Middlefield.

She still reeled from his kiss. Still had the scent of his cologne in her nostrils. Had the taste of him on her tongue.

Mentally, she put her foot down. She wasn't having it. Any of it. He was conceited and haughty and far too sure of himself. Why, the man had boldly proclaimed that no other man would have a chance with her this Season. That he would be the one to teach her about passion and pleasure. Immediately, she sensed her cheeks reddening at that thought and pushed aside thinking about him. She had learned to place aside her feelings long ago during the long days and nights in the sickrooms of her parents. She would think about Lord Middlefield later.

Or not at all.

Instead, she drew on the well of good manners bred deeply within her and pasted on a social smile that would fool even the best gossips of the *ton*. She greeted everyone in her path, introducing them to Lord Middlefield and remaining silent while various gentlemen spoke to him.

"I've seen you in the House of Lords, Middlefield," an old friend of her father's said. "You must come and sit with me. I have a bill coming up soon and I would like to share its contents with you."

Other lords mentioned the same, having seen the earl in Parliament. One had spotted him at White's and said they must dine together soon. Another asked him to go riding the following morning in Rotten Row. She stood mutely, allowing herself to be ignored, happy to do so because it allowed her to get her feelings under control. By the time they reached a desirable area of seats, she felt distanced from the earl. She would remain polite now and continue to be polite—and indifferent—when they met up again at various social affairs. Tessa had no interest nor desire in furthering her acquaintance with Lord Middlefield. She would also warn Adalyn and Louisa about him and his outlandish declaration. Her cousins would help insulate her from the bullying earl.

They took their seats and her companion let out a long breath.

"I am glad that is over," he quietly remarked.

Turning to him, she asked, "What? The lecture hasn't even begun."

"All . . . those people," he said. "Talking to me. Asking me to do things. It's a bit overwhelming."

"You . . . were overwhelmed by a few peers introducing themselves? I don't understand, my lord."

His brow furrowed. "It is hard to explain. I have always been a bit reserved. I am comfortable with my closest friends but I have never really sought out the company of others. I believe the war also changed me in ways that I have yet to understand. Frankly, I have avoided contact with others since I returned to England. It was why I refused your uncle's dinner invitation. I didn't quite know how to act in the company of others, especially ones I didn't know."

He raked a hand through his hair, obviously frustrated. "Sometimes, all I long for is peace and quiet. London is far too loud for my tastes. I worry about how I will respond to walking into a ballroom full of strangers. That thought frightens me."

Tessa saw Lord Middlefield had let his guard down with this

confession. She couldn't help but empathize a bit—because she had held some of the same exact thoughts herself.

"I can claim no knowledge as to what it is like to be on a battlefield. The noise. The terror. But you are home now, my lord. Those men were merely being friendly to you."

"I understand that—and yet it doesn't keep me from wanting to flee the room," he admitted. He sighed. "I suppose you believe I am damaged goods. I will admit that I have many chinks in my armor."

"No, you are not damaged," she said carefully, believing she was walking on eggshells. "But perhaps you are not ready for the frivolity of the Season and the noise and size of London. It might do you good to return to your country estate and become more used to civilian life before you return and partake in the events of the Season."

He flashed her a quick smile, one which made her draw in a quick breath due to its beauty.

"You think you can get rid of me that easily, my lady?"

"I am not trying to get rid of you," she said testily. "Merely giving you advice on your return to polite company."

"Would I prefer to have a gun and bayonet in hand now?" he asked. "Of course. Would I rather be with my friends, leading my men against the enemy? Without question. But that part of my life is over and I am resigned to that fact. What lies ahead of me is a new life, one filled with new challenges." He clucked his tongue. "You aren't going to chase me off so easily. I am determined to stay the course."

"By that, you mean attend the Season."

"Yes," he said, determination plain on his face. "Contribute in Parliament. Meet people at social affairs. Claim my countess. And then return to Stoneridge."

"I wish you good fortune," she told him primly. "In all your endeavors."

Before he could reply, Mr. Smithson cleared his throat, asking that those in attendance be seated. He introduced the speaker and

Tessa applauded enthusiastically as the man took the stage.

Unfortunately, she didn't hear a word he said. Though she had looked forward to this lecture ever since she had seen it advertised in the newspapers, she lacked the concentration to follow along. Her thoughts kept returning to Lord Middlefield.

And their kiss.

Oh, it was so unfair that he was ruining this lecture for her. And he almost had ruined her life. She shuddered to think what would have been set in motion if anyone had discovered them in an embrace.

Especially since they were using tongues.

The idea that tongues were involved in kissing still startled her. She wondered how she could bring up the topic with Adalyn and Louisa since they had to have been kissed by now. But if she did, they would wonder how she even knew about it. It would come out that Lord Middlefield had kissed her that way and she would never hear the end of it.

What bothered her even more was how much she wanted to kiss him again.

Tessa also struggled with how his kiss made her feel. It had brought this incredible rush of giddiness, a lightness that possessed her. Those marvelous tingles, too, were an incredible surprise and felt so, so good. Worse, as she sat trying to forget everything about the kiss, it only made her remember how other parts of her body came alive. Her breasts had begun to ache. Where her legs joined pulsed so that she had wanted to touch there.

No, she had wanted Lord Middlefield to touch her there.

That would be an abomination.

Tessa tried to clear her mind of all thought. What was that called? It had been discussed during the lecture regarding Far Eastern religions. Meditation. That was the word. Those of certain faiths would engage their minds in a type of mental exercise. The lecturer had said an individual should concentrate on one's breathing or repeating a simple phrase. Doing so would bring about a sense of peace.

She tried it, gazing straight ahead and counting her breath as she drew it in and back out again. She did this several times and then began repeating the phrase *Forget him* in her mind, over and over. But the more she silently repeated it, the more she thought of who the him was.

Squeezing her eyes closed, she opened them again and looked to the speaker. She listened and found his lecture already done. He was now taking questions. Oh, she wished she had heard what he had to say. It was all the dreadful Lord Middlefield's fault for intruding on her thoughts. For kissing her without permission. For announcing to her that he was going to woo her. The audacity of the man was beyond the pale.

Applause began, drawing her from her reveries, and Tessa clapped politely. As it ended, others about them began rising and she and the earl did the same.

"He was fascinating," Lord Middlefield said. "I believe he's correct. That the Rosetta Stone will contain the key to breaking the code of hieroglyphics. If the Greek can be matched and translated to the other two decrees on the stone, it will unlock the entirety of hieroglyphics and a huge chunk of history to us."

Tessa saw the excitement on his face. Despite wanting to dislike him—actually, to have nothing to do with him—he looked boyishly appealing as he spoke.

"I agree with you. The Rosetta Stone holds the key to a largely unknown bit of history. When we can gain an accurate translation and apply our knowledge to other hieroglyphics, it will be a true discovery for the ages."

"I already want to see the stone again," he told her. "But I know too many who attended the lecture will go to see it now. I will come back soon." He looked at her hopefully. "Perhaps you might accompany me?"

"I don't believe that is a good idea, my lord. While I did not mind introducing you to the British Museum, it is something you will need to visit on your own."

"Even though you come here often," he pointed out. "And I could accompany you."

She firmed her resolve. "I don't mean to sound rude but I am not interested in you and do not wish for your company."

"Because of my declaration."

"Especially because of your declaration," she agreed. "You have noted that I am intelligent. I will make my own decision regarding the man I wish to wed. You are not that man, Lord Middlefield. I do hope you will find a lovely young woman to become your countess."

"Just not you."

"No. Definitely not me."

"Even though you kissed me back."

Tessa started. "What?"

"You kissed me back," he told her. "I kissed you first but you participated in the kiss, Tessa. And then you responded to it. You even took the initiative and began kissing me." He grinned. "Do I need to remind you how your tongue wound up in my mouth?"

"Bloody hell," she hissed.

His grinned broadened. "See. There's the passion I spoke about."

"It is not passion," she said, disagreeable. "It is my ire which is speaking."

"I would rather have your rage than your indifference. Come, let us return to the carriage. I am sure we will find the missing-in-action Abra."

Without asking, he took her hand and tucked it into the crook of his arm. Tessa fairly boiled over in anger but contained it. She would not make a public scene. She refused to draw attention to them. As it was, they were among the last to head up the stairs and exit the lecture hall.

Keeping silent, she allowed Lord Middlefield to escort her from the museum and to the waiting carriage outside. As expected, Abra stood next to the vehicle, her cheeks blooming.

"How was it, my lady? The lecture?"

"Fine," she said tersely, giving her hand to the waiting footman, who helped her into the carriage.

Abra followed and sat beside her, followed by the earl.

"I actually did like some of them things," Abra said. "The animals and the rocks. But I also walked about the neighborhood. Don't think I was trying to rob anyone, my lady. I'm proud to be your lady's maid. I've left that life behind."

"I need for you to do better at your position, Abra," Tessa said. "In the future when you are my chaperone, you are to remain in sight. No more traipsing off on your own. It isn't proper for me to be seen with Lord Middlefield—or any male—without you accompanying us. Do I make myself clear?" she asked sharply.

Abra's eyes grew larger. "Yes, my lady. I'm sorry." She glanced over to the earl and back to Tessa. "He didn't try anything, did he? Because if he did, I'll make him pay. He thinks he knows how to throw a punch?" She puffed up. "His lordship ain't seen nothing. Why, I'll box his ears and then slam my fist—"

"Enough, Abra," she said. "Lord Middlefield did nothing untoward," she lied. "I merely know that I should have had my chaperone with me at all times for propriety's sake. Is that understood?"

Her maid looked contrite. "Yes, my lady. Don't you worry. I will stick closer to you than you ever dreamed possible. As if someone glued me to you. You won't be able to sneeze without me knowing."

"Thank you," she said, turning her gaze out the window, not bothering to converse further with either Abra or Lord Middlefield.

They arrived in Mayfair and the earl exited the carriage, helping her and then Abra down.

She turned and said, "Thank you for escorting us to the lecture, my lord."

"It was my pleasure to have both your company and see the British Museum for the first time. I will plan on making regular visits to it now and in the coming years."

He offered his arm and she accepted it, allowing him to walk her to the door. It opened before she even knocked, Rainey himself ushering them inside. Tessa turned to tell the earl goodbye, ready to see him gone.

Then the butler said, "Lady Adalyn told me you were expected for tea, my lord. If you will follow me?"

Rainey started up the staircase. Tessa recalled her cousin inviting Lord Middlefield to tea this morning and gritted her teeth.

"Not rid of me yet, I see," he murmured so softly only she could hear.

"Bloody hell," she repeated back.

CHAPTER TEN

S PENCER KNEW TESSA was more than put out with him. She hadn't said a single word on the carriage ride from Blooms-bury to Mayfair. Abra had caught his eye and mouthed "What's wrong?" but he shook his head and turned away.

After her reaction now to him being invited to tea, he knew it would be more than an uphill battle.

It would be a bloody war.

He wondered if Tessa might be worth all the trouble he fore-saw in the coming weeks. After all, a myriad of young ladies would be making their come-out this Season. He was a wealthy earl with good looks to spare. Surely, it would be easier courting someone fresh on the scene. He might even find a woman even more beautiful and intelligent than Tessa.

But she was the one he wanted.

Tessa had captured his heart, which had knocked Spencer for a loop. Owen would never understand this. His friend played the field, fliting from woman to woman. Win, too, was much the same, chasing any female in a skirt. His other friends, Ev and Percy, would be more understanding. Percy was much like Spencer—reserved, dutiful, and one who very much stuck to the rules. Ev was downright shy, barely conversing unless he had known someone a long time and was comfortable in his company. His quieter companions would be men who sought only one woman and would understand how only one would do.

Spencer wanted Tessa as his countess because he wanted their children to have her determination and spirit. He still had much to learn about being an earl and a member of Polite Society and he could think of no one else he would want by his side more than the golden-haired beauty now simmering with rage as they moved down the corridor toward the drawing room.

The butler announced him and he and Tessa crossed the long room to an intimate seating of chairs with a teacart parked next to it. He greeted Lady Uxbridge and Lady Adalyn first and then shook hands with Lord Uxbridge.

"Please, have a seat," said the countess.

"Wouldn't we be more comfortable moving over there? It would give us much more room?" Tessa commented.

"It is only us, Tessa," her cousin admonished. "This is more appropriate for a small group."

That meant taking a seat on the only piece of furniture left, a small settee they would have to share. Spencer bit back a smile and allowed Tessa to seat herself first before joining her. Immediately, he understood her reluctance. He was a large man and because of that, the settee wasn't ideal to share. They were rather crowded together, their sides pressed against one another. Her lavender scent wafted toward him as he relished the warmth of her next to him.

She must be hating every minute of this.

His hostess poured out and they all placed various items on their plates.

"These scones are delicious," he remarked, which led to a discussion of their favorite dishes their cook made.

Excluding Tessa. She sat mute. And continued to do so throughout the tea unless a direct question was addressed to her.

"How did you enjoy your first visit to the British Museum?" Lady Adalyn asked brightly.

"I found it very pleasing," he shared. "The number of artifacts is astounding. Of course, Lady Tessa and I could not begin to scratch the surface during our visit. She suggested we concentrate on the rooms devoted to Egypt since today's lecture was on the Rosetta Stone."

"Ah, did you see the stone itself?" asked Uxbridge.

"We did. Lady Tessa proved to be an excellent tour guide and shared her extensive knowledge about the Rosetta Stone and other Egyptian antiquities."

"Tessa could run the museum," the earl proclaimed.

"She and Uncle Paxton were always going there when we were young," Lady Adalyn added. "And since we have been back in London, she has been several times."

"I plan to continue visiting it regularly," Spencer said. "I have a deep love for history. I am hoping Lady Tessa might accompany me on those trips and act as my guide again."

He glanced to her, seeing her face void of emotion.

"The British Museum has excellent guides, my lord," she said stiffly. "Mr. Smithson, in particular, would be the best one to introduce you to further exhibits there. I am afraid with the Season only two weeks away that I will be busy with dress fittings. And once it begins, I won't have time to visit the museum at all. There will be morning calls to make and others who will call upon us. Afternoon garden and tea parties. Events every night for months. I will be quite busy."

She smiled sweetly. "But don't let that stop you from going yourself, my lord."

"We should talk about the dinner party we want to host for you, my lord," his hostess said. "My husband told me you are available next Tuesday. I would like to invite those neighbors who live on our square and a few others."

"Whomever you invite is up to you, Lady Uxbridge. Just tell me what time to show up."

"Dinner will be served at eight o'clock but we will gather for drinks in the drawing room at seven-thirty," she said. "Why don't you come a quarter-hour before that in order to get settled?"

"I will do so. Again, my thanks for holding this dinner party in my honor."

"We are eager to help you get acquainted with others, Middlefield," Uxbridge said.

Spencer heard a clock chime and decided he should leave.

"I want to thank Lady Adalyn for inviting me for tea this afternoon," he began. "And I also wish to express my gratitude to Lady Tessa for introducing me to the treasures in the British Museum, as well. Overall, this has been the best day I have spent in London."

He rose and the others followed suit.

"I will walk you out, Lord Middlefield," Lady Adalyn said, surprising him.

He offered his arm to her and said goodbye to the others. Once they were in the hallway, she said, "Why was Tessa in such an awful mood, my lord? What could you possibly have done to make her so hostile in your company?"

He assessed the risks involved, knowing Lady Adalyn could be a powerful ally or even more powerful foe in his pursuit of Tessa—and decided to opt for honesty.

"I kissed her," he admitted.

Lady Adalyn laughed. "You seized the opportunity. Well done, my lord. Tessa had never been kissed before. I would know because she would have told Louisa and me if she had. Poor little love, buried in the country all these years, dutifully nursing her parents. She has such a good heart." She paused. "And if you break it, I will have to break you in two."

Spencer had no doubt Lady Adalyn would do just that.

"May I inquire how the kiss was?"

He decided she wouldn't do so if she weren't on his side and said, "Most pleasurable on both our parts. Your cousin was upset afterward because it occurred in a public place and we might have been observed."

"Oh, no one is at the museum this time of year. Attendance will actually pick up during the Season but I have been with Tessa three times now and only saw one other visitor."

"She was right, though. If we had been spied, she would have had no choice but to wed me."

They reached the foyer and Lady Adalyn stopped. "What of you, Lord Middlefield? What choice would you have made in that instance?"

"The honorable one, my lady. But I would never want Lady Tessa's own choice to be removed from her. She is vibrant and animated. She deserves to decide her own future and not having that future decided for her."

She eyed him intently. "That is very observant of you, my lord. And very generous. Yes, I think you will do."

"I will do?"

Lady Adalyn grinned. "You will make a fine husband for Tessa. I thought so from the moment she mentioned meeting you. Now that I have done so—and we have spoken honestly—my mind is made up. I have a bit of a reputation, you know, of playing matchmaker for couples in the *ton*."

"I did not know that," Spencer replied, thinking of the wagers regarding Adalyn Goulding in the betting book at White's and wondering why she matched others but did not choose to make a match herself.

"Well, I do. I think you and Tessa will make for a marvelous couple. And just think about how beautiful your babies will be."

He felt his face grow warm, thinking about how those babies would be made.

"I do like you, Middlefield. I can tell you now that my cousin is a most stubborn woman. She's already decided not to like you—even if she did like your kiss. I will be subtle at first in helping her try to change her mind about you. You must do the same."

He grimaced. "I am afraid I haven't been very subtle."

"Why? What did you say to her?" she demanded.

"I might have mentioned I was interested in her."

She chuckled. "There is nothing wrong in that. She would have to assume you were because you did kiss her."

"I also told her no other man would have a chance with her."

"Oh, dear," Lady Adalyn fretted. "That would certainly raise Tessa's hackles. She is sweet-natured but she has never liked being told what to do. That was not well played, my lord."

"I realize that now. I will do better in the future."

"You must if you are to win her hand—and her heart. Tessa hasn't told me she seeks a love match but I know her. It is what her heart will want." She paused, gazing deeply into Spencer's eyes. "Can you provide her with that, Lord Middlefield?"

He nodded. "Tessa has already claimed my heart."

She brightened. "I will think on things, my lord. You do the same. Together, we will make certain that Tessa becomes your countess."

Spencer left the townhouse and crossed to his own, his step light.

CHAPTER ELEVEN

Tessa braced herself, holding on to the bed's post while Abra tightened her stays. The hardest thing to get used to again had been wearing a corset. She had abandoned the practice during the long days in the sickroom with Mama and continued the practice when she nursed Papa after his apoplexy attack. It was easier to do so. She'd spent many hours with her parents, seeing no one else, often coming to bed in the wee hours of the morning. She hated to ring and awake a maid to help free her from her stays so she had simply stopped wearing them.

She had grown used to merely wearing her chemise and a gown atop it, tossing on a shawl when the weather grew chilly. Living with her uncle and his family, though, had changed all that. There was no way she could go about the country house, much less the Uxbridge townhouse in London, without donning the proper undergarments.

"Is that tight enough, my lady?" Abra asked, always in tune to Tessa's moods even after so short a while in service.

"Yes, it is perfect."

"Do you still wish to wear the gown we discussed?"

"I do."

She watched as Abra claimed the midnight blue gown, one of many she had made up for everyday wear and the upcoming Season. After four years in the country and never purchasing a single gown during that period, her wardrobe was sadly lacking. Everything needed updating. Her uncle refused to let her spend any of the money left to her by Papa for her new outfits, however. He told her she was as a daughter to him and the gowns would be his gift to her. She had kept her old gowns, intending to give them to the poor. Instead, she had passed them along to Abra, who was but an inch shy of Tessa's height and had a similar build. Both women had high, firm breasts and small waists.

Abra appreciated the gift of the gowns and had even, under Bridget's tutelage, added trims to some of them. She had decided to wear only a few of the gowns when she had her half-days off every other Sunday and take the others to a charity organization she said had been good to her while she lived on the streets. Tessa still couldn't believe Abra had survived as long as she had that way and was glad fate intervened and led them to one another. Tessa was pleased with her new lady's maid in every way.

Except her praise of Lord Middleton.

As Abra lifted the gown over Tessa's head and brought it down, she said, "It's a good thing the earl and countess are giving a dinner in the earl's honor. He's a little on the quiet side. Mind you, I don't think he's unfriendly but folks could perceive him to be that way. I think he's the kind that once he warms up to you, he's fine."

He'd certainly warmed up to Tessa. By kissing her.

Much as she had tried, she couldn't help but think of their kiss. How unexpected it was, both in the timing and the kiss itself. The kiss had made her feel powerful and feminine and yet weak and submissive. It had emboldened her and yet made her cower when she thought of it.

At least she had made her feelings known to him. He might think he wanted to pursue her but she had no intentions of being pursued. She hoped he would take her at her word and leave her alone because she did not want to be rude to him. She would, though, if he kept after her. Lord Middlefield was not the sort of man who would make for a good husband, despite everything he had said to her. Tessa believed him far too handsome. She didn't want to be a wife who always worried about her husband straying. Louisa had told her that husbands usually did that very thing once an heir had been provided. Lord Middlefield would attract far too much attention from other ladies.

Yet as she seated herself at her dressing table in order for Abra to style her hair, she thought of some of things he had told her. About his father and brother ignoring him. How he wanted a large family and would treat his sons and daughters equally. How he would love them.

And his wife.

With passion.

She glanced up and saw her cheeks flooding with color and quickly cast her eyes downward again, not wanting to draw Abra's attention. The girl now brushed Tessa's long, curly locks.

"You do have wonderful hair, my lady. It's nice not to have to use the curling tongs like Bridget does on Lady Adalyn."

"My hair's texture is good for some hairstyles but not other ones. Adalyn's hair, while straight, can also be curled. That allows her to wear a larger variety of styles."

"Your cousin is nice but I'm glad I am your maid."

She frowned. "Do you think Adalyn treats Bridget ill?"

"No, not at all," the servant assured her. "Bridget likes Lady Adalyn. So do I. I'm just glad you're the one who found me. It will be exciting going through your first Season with you. Finding you a husband. Like that nice Lord Middlefield."

"Abra," Tessa warned. "I have heard quite enough about the earl from you. I know your opinion of him. Mine is quite different, however. You see him as brave and dashing and handsome. I view him as arrogant and domineering. I seek a much gentler man."

"No, you don't," Abra corrected. "You are opinionated and strong-willed, Lady Tessa. Those are good things. But you don't want a milksop to boss around. You need a strong man—like

Lord Middlefield. I'm not saying it has to be him. But someone like him. Not a man who can be pushed around. One who can give as good as he gets. One who will stand up for you when needed because you'll be doing the same for him."

She did want a man who would stand up for her. Just not Lord Middlefield.

Then why couldn't she stop thinking about him?

And that kiss.

She fell silent, letting Abra work her magic. When finished, she exclaimed, "I believe this is the most flattering style you have created thus far, Abra."

The maid grinned. "You'll be the talk of the dinner table, my lady, what with your blue eyes and that dark blue gown and your golden hair making you look like an angel. Who knows? Maybe one of the gentlemen at dinner tonight might turn out to be your husband by this time next year."

In that moment, the idea of marriage became real to Tessa. Before, it had been an ethereal thing, a lofty goal, one that she would work toward as she met bachelors at various social affairs. Suddenly, she realized tonight was the first of many social affairs. A dinner party. Her first. She hadn't bothered asking her aunt who was on the guest list. If it contained any eligible men who might become a suitor to her.

Nerves flitted through her, causing her to wring her hands in her lap. Tonight was the true beginning of her being launched into society. She would attend many events such as this in the coming months. Abra was right. Each event would give her the chance to meet others, including men, one of whom might offer for her. She would need to be more aware of the behavior of others. Listen carefully to conversations. Glean what she could about those who interested her. And hope that by Season's end, she would find a man she could love.

One who could love her.

Tessa knew she was asking for the impossible. Her own parents hadn't been a love match. They had cared deeply for one another, though they often went about their separate lives, seeing their own friends and devoting themselves to their own particular interests.

She didn't want that. She wanted a man to love. To devote herself to. One who would challenge her and make her think. Laugh with her in the good times and hold her as she cried when things turned sour. Tessa had no idea how to go about finding a man to love, much less falling in love with him and he with her.

Could kissing help?

Though her own mother—and recently, her aunt—had held a conversation with her regarding rakes and how to avoid them, Lord Middlefield's kiss had certainly awakened desires within Tessa that she'd never known existed. It took her what seemed like hours to fall asleep each night because she lay awake thinking of places she wished he would touch. She would smash her hand into her pillow in exasperation, angry that the earl took up so many of her thoughts.

And made her think wicked thoughts about him.

Tessa rose. "That will be all, Abra. Why don't you take the book you were looking at earlier with you?"

"May I?" the servant asked, her eyes wide. "I don't know how to read. I just wanted to look at the pictures."

"You cannot read?" The thought saddened her as Abra shook her head.

"I never had time for schooling. Mum needed me too much. To help out and make money. But you know I'm a fast learner, my lady. Maybe I could learn how."

"I will teach you myself," she declared.

Abra shook her head. "No, I couldn't ask you to do that, my lady. You've got the Season coming up. You'll be busy night and day."

"Not so busy that I cannot devote an hour a day to teaching you. What do you say?"

The maid beamed. "How can I say no to your offer, my lady? Please, keep in mind when you do get busy—and you will—that we will put off these lessons until after you are married."

She blushed. "We don't know for sure if I will find a husband this Season, Abra. After all, look at my cousin. She has been out for several years and still hasn't found any man who pleases her."

Abra sniffed. "Lady Adalyn is having far too much fun to get married. That's what Bridget says."

"I believe she will find the right man. My heart tells me so. Adalyn is a wonderful person."

The maid snorted. "It will take a very powerful man to keep Lady Adalyn in line." She giggled. "But he would have fun doing so."

"Off with you," Tessa said.

The servant left and Tessa glanced into the mirror once again, seeing her cheeks filled with color and her eyes sparkling. She wondered if she would appeal to Lord Middlefield tonight.

"Drat!" she said aloud.

She didn't want to appeal to the man. She wanted to have nothing to do with him.

Except perhaps exchange one more kiss with him. Just to see if the first hadn't been a mistake. And to help her compare it in case she had the opportunity to try kissing another man.

A knock sounded on her bedchamber door and she answered it. Louisa stood there and she threw her arms about her cousin.

"It is so good to see you!" she exclaimed. "Come in."

"I did see you at tea several days ago," her cousin pointed out as she stepped inside. "But it's never enough. We have to make up for lost time."

"I hope to see you often once the Season begins."

"You will," Louisa promised. "We will go to many of the same events. Your introduction to society actually starts with tonight's dinner party. You weren't old enough to attend anything other than a family dinner the last time you were in London. Uncle Uxbridge told me there will be thirty-two for dinner this evening."

"That's so many people. I don't know how I will remember

all their names," Tessa said, worried.

"The ones to remember will be the bachelors," Louisa said. "The guest of honor is one. I know of two others who will be in attendance."

"I have no interest in Lord Middlefield," she declared.

"Why not? I met him before I came to see you. He had beautiful manners and was quite handsome."

"He is insufferable."

Louisa frowned. "Tessa, what is going on? How do you know Lord Middlefield? You wouldn't be saying such things if you didn't already know him."

"Remember how I told you I had hired a new lady's maid?"

"Yes. Abra was her name, I believe."

Tessa proceeded to tell her cousin about the entire encounter.

"Why, I think it brave and bold of his lordship," Louisa proclaimed. "He came to your aid even though he had no idea who you were. And a knife?" She shuddered. Then smiled. "I think it a bit romantic that he played the dashing hero."

"He is no hero to me. He is . . . that is . . . he . . ." Her voice trailed off.

"What did he do?" Louisa asked. "It wasn't merely hitting Abra."

"He kissed me! With his tongue!"

Louisa's eyes widened. "Lord Middlefield kissed you? When? Where? Tell me everything."

"It was in the British Museum. A public place, Louisa! Anyone could have come along and seen us together. Adalyn found out he hadn't visited the place and talked him into accompanying us to a lecture last week." Tessa sniffed. "Then she conveniently remembered she had another engagement, which I know for a fact she did not. I could not gracefully extricate myself from going with him. We were standing before the Rosetta Stone."

"When he kissed you."

"Yes."

"And how was it?"

Immediately, heat filled Tessa at the thought of the earl's mouth on hers. His tongue stroking hers. His strong fingers holding her.

"I don't know. Good, I suppose. I have never been kissed. Did I mention he used his tongue?"

Louisa chuckled. "You did. And some kisses involve that."

"Have you been kissed that way?" she demanded.

Her cousin nodded. "Twice."

"Did you like it?"

"Once. It was quite pleasant. The other time left me feeling distasteful. But how did you feel about it?"

"I liked it. Probably more than I should have," she admitted. "But he did it in a public place where discovery would have meant a scandal."

"I went with you to the museum two weeks ago. No one was there, Tessa. It seems Lord Middlefield assessed the risks and decided it was worth a shot to kiss you. He must be interested in you to have done so."

Her hackles rose. "Oh, he has told me of his interest. He said that no other man would have a chance with me with him around wooing me."

Louisa laughed aloud. "I'd say the earl is quite bold, making such a declaration."

"Well, I don't like it. I don't like him. I need a sedate man."

"You do not," Adalyn said.

Tessa turned. "I didn't hear you come in."

"You have led a sedate life, Tessa, especially the last several years, with your parents ill and then you in mourning." Adalyn gazed at her. "It is time you started living again, especially since we are on the cusp of the Season. It is a good thing Lord Middlefield is interested in you. Others will see that and it will pique their interests, as well. Men are odd creatures, Cousin. They see a man wanting something—and they decide they want it, too. And that includes women. It could be to your benefit."

"I don't know, Adalyn," she said, unsure of everything that

was happening.

"Let us go to the drawing room," Louisa suggested. "It is time we made an appearance. You can meet those invited and especially the two bachelors I spoke of, Lord Ellington and Lord Wethersby."

"Don't forget to enjoy yourself, Tessa," Adalyn admonished. "The Season is about fun. Getting to know others. Seeing and being seen." She gave Tessa a long look. "I have a feeling you will find a husband with ease. You are smart and beautiful and very kind."

Louisa tucked her arm into Tessa's. "Come along."

She did so, tamping down the nerves that filled her. Tessa told herself it was because she would be meeting so many new people tonight. But she knew she was lying to herself. She always looked forward to getting to know others. Her jitters had nothing to do with tonight's dinner party guests.

And everything to do with Lord Middlefield.

CHAPTER TWELVE

S PENCER WAS THOROUGHLY enjoying his discussion with Sir
Edgar Goulding, brother of the Earl of Uxbridge. Both men
favored one another in looks and were affable. He could tell,
however, that Sir Edgar's intellect far surpassed that of his
brother's.

Suddenly, his nape prickled with awareness. He knew Tessa
had entered the room. He glanced over Sir Edgar's shoulder and
saw her, accompanied by her two cousins.

He had met Miss Goulding a quarter-hour ago and found her
to be quite charming and beautiful. The same could be said for
Lady Adalyn.

Yet it was Tessa who had claimed Spencer's heart.

He hoped Lady Adalyn would prove to be the ally she said
she would be. Spencer thought it would be smart to include Miss
Goulding in his campaign for Tessa's heart. He wondered if he
should recruit her or if it would be better for Lady Adalyn to do
so.

He caught Lady Adalyn's eye and they nodded briefly at one
another before he turned his attention back to Sir Edgar. Still, he
tracked the trio's progress, seeing they came toward him.

"Papa, are you talking Lord Middlefield's ear off?" his daughter asked.

"Not at all, Louisa," Sir Edgar said jovially. "Before he

claimed his earldom, however, Lord Middlefield was Major Haddock. It is rare that I get to speak to someone with battlefield experience. It is imperative that the War Office understands exactly what is going on in the field."

"Tell us about the war, my lord," Lady Adalyn encouraged.

He cleared his throat. "I believe Sir Edgar and I have talked enough about war for now," he said lightly.

"Was it hard being away from home? Missing your family?" Miss Goulding asked.

"Lord Middlefield had good friends from his childhood with him," Tessa quickly said, saving Spencer from the embarrassment of having to say he missed no one and no one in his family had missed him during his time abroad.

"Oh, tell us about them," Lady Adalyn said.

"Two of them, Everett Wayland and Owen Hasbury, have been friends since my earliest school days. The three of us met Winston Cutler and Percival Perry at Cambridge. We were fortunate to be placed in regiments under Wellington's command so I saw all of them often. They are not just brothers-in-arms but brothers of my heart."

His gaze met Tessa's and she nodded encouraging at him.

"We are all second sons and knew from an early age that we were destined to enter the military. I have spent many hours in these men's company." He paused. "I hated leaving them—and my men—behind."

"You did for your country on the battlefield, Lord Middlefield," Sir Edgar said. "Now, you will continue to do the same as you sit in the House of Lords."

Before Spencer could reply, the Uxbridge butler announced the first of the dinner party guests.

"You should come stand by Mama and Papa, Lord Middlefield," Lady Adalyn said. "You are the guest of honor and they will want to introduce you to everyone upon first arrival." She glanced to her cousin. "You, too, Tessa. Come join the family."

"I am not truly a Goulding," Tessa protested.

Lady Adalyn's eyes narrowed and she took Tessa's hand. "You are—and Mama wants you to meet everyone since you truly know no one in London. Except for us and Lord Middlefield, of course. Come along."

Spencer followed the pair to where Lord and Lady Uxbridge stood. His host introduced him and Tessa to the first group which had entered and continued to do the same until all their guests had arrived. Footmen circulated with trays of drinks and he claimed one.

"You have met everyone invited, Lord Middlefield," Lady Uxbridge said. "Why don't you young people gather and speak before we go in to dinner?"

Lady Adalyn motioned and Spencer and Tessa followed her to where Miss Goulding stood with two men. One was blond and looked to be in his mid-twenties, while the other, with dark hair and eyes, appeared to be about thirty. He recalled the first was Lord Wethersby but couldn't remember the other fellow's name.

"Ah, here are my cousins and the guest of honor," Miss Goulding said, welcoming them to the circle. "This is Lord Wethersby and Lord Ellington," she continued, thoughtfully providing the men's names again.

"I hear from Miss Goulding that you are making your comeout, Lady Tessa," Lord Ellington said. "I think you will find London society to your liking."

"I hope so," Tessa said, looking poised.

Spencer had thought she might be a bit overwhelmed by meeting so many people but she wore an air of confidence which he thought would serve her well.

When she was his countess.

He didn't like the way either of these men looked at her, though. He knew he couldn't make a public proclamation regarding her, especially when she was already incensed at him, but he would keep a watchful eye on both men.

Especially Ellington. His gut told him the earl was not to be trusted around Tessa.

They spoke of a few of the early events which they had received invitations for and then Wethersby asked Spencer about his time at war. He told a few stories, sanitized versions of what happened, knowing that people who asked for them truly didn't want to hear about the atrocities of war.

"Are you interested in boxing, Middlefield?" Ellington asked. "I take lessons at Gentleman Jack's."

"I don't see why men need to take lessons in order to learn how to punch another man in the face," Miss Goulding said. "Boxing seems such a violent sport."

"Some men come by it naturally," Tessa remarked. "And need no lessons at all."

Spencer knew she spoke of him and his striking Abra.

"Well, if you are interested, I'd be happy to show you around," Ellington said.

"Do you know horses well?" Wethersby asked him.

"I know good horseflesh when I see it," he replied confidently.

"I could use your advice then. I'm in the market for some new horses. Would you care to accompany me to Tattersalls next Monday when they are open?"

He had wanted to see the famed place and decided to take Wethersby up on the offer.

"I would very much like to go, my lord," he told the viscount.

"What kind of horses?" Ellington inquired.

"Carriages horses," Wethersby said.

"I recently bought new horses for my phaeton," Ellington said. He turned to Tessa. "Have you ever ridden in a phaeton, Lady Tessa?"

"No. I am not certain exactly what that is," she admitted.

Ellington smiled winningly at her, causing Spencer to seethe inwardly.

"Phaetons are light, open-air carriages with a sporty, high perch," the earl explained. "No place for a coachman so they are driven by their owners. They travel quickly and take quite a bit of skill to handle. I would happy to introduce you to the vehicle, Lady Tessa. Perhaps I might call on you tomorrow afternoon at three and take you for a ride in Hyde Park if that is agreeable."

Spencer watched the blush stain her cheeks, willing her to tell Ellington no, but helpless to say anything.

"That would be most interesting, Lord Ellington. Yes, I will go." Tessa glanced to Lady Adalyn. "My cousin has encouraged me to get out more and try new things. I have spent many years in the country."

Ellington beamed at her. "Then we certainly need to let you see all the attractions of London."

The butler announced dinner.

Ellington said, "May I escort you in to dinner, Lady Tessa? I would love to tell you more about my phaeton." He offered his arm and she took it.

Spencer wanted to slam his fist into Ellington's perfect nose.

Instead, he turned to Miss Goulding. "May I escort you to dinner, my lady?"

"Yes, you may," she said, taking his arm.

As they crossed the drawing room, she said, "I heard you accompanied Tessa to the British Museum. And that you had a most interesting time at the Rosetta Stone."

He was taken aback for a moment, knowing exactly what she referred to.

"She told you about the kiss."

"She did," Miss Goulding said breezily. "You took a risk being seen."

"No one had come through there during our entire time," he said defensively.

"And if they had? Would you have offered for my cousin?" she inquired, her sapphire blue eyes boring into him.

"Absolutely. I have already told Lady Tessa I plan to woo her."

She chuckled. "I have heard. She is not eager for your suit."

"Lady Adalyn believes we are a good match. She has decided

to support my efforts." He paused. "I was hoping you might do the same."

Mischief lit her eyes. "Oh, dear. Poor Tessa. Everyone in league against her."

"But for a very good cause," he said smoothly and then added, "ask Lady Adalyn. She seems to be a good judge of character and she has told me of her success in matching other couples of the *ton*."

"I believe you, Lord Middlefield. I can see Adalyn championing your efforts. But tell me this—why are you interested in Tessa?"

As with Lady Adalyn, he knew total honesty would be important to this woman.

"Lady Tessa has more spirit and determination than any woman of my acquaintance. I think she would pass along those things to her children, both her sons and daughters."

Miss Goulding nodded. "Tessa would be an excellent mother. But what of her as a wife?"

"I think she has depths which need to be explored. I would want her as a partner. Not someone subordinate to me."

She bestowed a radiant smile upon him as they reached the dining room. "I think I shall support your cause, my lord."

"Thank you, Miss Goulding."

He helped her locate her place and seated her then looked around for his own seat. Spying his name on a card, he noticed he sat directly in the center of the table. He supposed Lady Uxbridge had placed him there so he would be able to converse with more people than if he had been seated at Lord Uxbridge's right hand, the spot usually reserved for an honored guest.

His heart sped up, though, when he took his seat.

Because Tessa was seated on his left.

WHAT HAD HER *aunt been thinking?*

Tessa realized it hadn't been her aunt at all. It had been Adalyn. She glanced down the table at her cousin, who smiled mysteriously at her. Why Adalyn had gotten into her mind to match Tessa with Lord Middlefield puzzled her.

She decided she would merely ignore him during dinner. Being seated in the center of the table, he would have access to a large number of people. It wasn't as if he would be stranded and lack for people to converse with.

Turning to her left, she spoke to the viscount who lived next door to her uncle. He had three children, one of whom was seated across from Lord Middlefield and had made her come-out last Season. When Tessa met Miss Allen, she had sensed some undercurrent that she couldn't explain. She had never disliked anyone on the spot—well, perhaps, Lord Middlefield—but Miss Allen would then be the second. Tessa had already decided to avoid her until she could ask Louisa and Adalyn about the young woman and her reputation.

The viscount only had thoughts for one topic. Horses. He droned on at length about them. She listened with half an ear, nodding occasionally, while her attention focused on Lord Middlefield and his conversation. She had to admit that he was socially adept for all his protests of being rough about the edges. Others asked him about his time at war and he readily had a few stories at hand. With ease, he would tell one and then turn the attention back to someone else, asking them a question and allowing them to speak at length about themselves or their opinions.

Finally, she grew weary of the topic of horses and said, "I have so enjoyed our conversation, my lord, but I have neglected Lord Middlefield. He is our guest of honor and I know my aunt wants me to make certain his lordship is comfortable."

Tessa turned and began listening to the others around her though she didn't immediately join in. She knew, however, that the earl realized she was more attuned. She couldn't say how or why, just that she felt she could read his mood.

"Since you are new to the title and have been at war, have you seen much of London, Lord Middlefield?" a guest asked.

"Not much. Lord Ellington has invited me to go to Gentleman Jack's with him and I believe I will take him up on it."

"We should spar together, Middlefield," the earl suggested eagerly.

"How about tomorrow morning?"

Lord Ellington smiled. "I look forward to it. I will have my carriage call at your townhouse. We can travel there together."

"I look forward to it."

Tessa saw the gleam in Lord Middlefield's eyes and thought Lord Ellington might be in for trouble. It wasn't her place to warn Ellington, however, even though she recalled the swiftness with which Lord Middlefield had struck Abra. Then a thought occurred to her.

Did Lord Middlefield wish to spar with Lord Ellington because the earl had asked Tessa to ride in the park with him?

Surely not.

Certainly not.

Unless he did.

"Where have you gone in London, my lord?" Miss Allen asked.

Lord Middlefield turned his attention across the table. "When I had tea with Lord and Lady Uxbridge last week, I learned their daughter and niece were attending a lecture at the British Museum. I invited myself along and we visited the museum for two hours before going to the lecture."

Tessa thought it gentlemanly of him not to mention that Adalyn had dropped out of the excursion and that only the two of them had gone together.

"Are you inclined to be bookish, my lord?" Miss Allen asked coquettishly.

"I do enjoy history," Lord Middlefield said. "I found the limited exhibits we visited fascinating."

"I believe there is another lecture being held there the day after tomorrow," Miss Allen said. "One I planned to attend."

Tessa highly doubted that and spoke up. "You are interested in Roman sepulchral antiquities?" she asked sweetly. "I know my cousins and I will be at this lecture."

She hadn't planned on going but hoped Adalyn and Louisa would vouch for her now.

"Oh, yes," Louisa said. "We are eager to attend. What is your special interest in this topic, Miss Allen?"

The young woman smiled brightly. "Why, the entire topic interests me, Miss Goulding." She glanced to the guest of honor. "Perhaps you would like to escort me to the lecture, my lord."

"I would be happy to," Lord Middlefield said affably. "And since we know of others' interest, we should go together." He turned to her. "Would you mind, Lady Tessa?"

"Not at all, my lord."

Tessa could feel Miss Allen's glare and avoided looking across the table.

"I say, I've never been to this museum," Lord Wethersby said. "Would you mind if I came along?"

"You would be most welcome, my lord," Tessa told the viscount. He had been very polite when she met him and he was also very charming.

"I don't want to be left out," Lord Ellington proclaimed. "Any objection to my coming along?" He smiled at Tessa.

"I think it's marvelous so many people are interested in Roman sepulchral antiquities," she declared with a straight face. "Of course, we would enjoy having you attend the lecture with us, Lord Ellington."

When dinner ended, the ladies rose to leave the men to their port and cigars. The group of over a dozen women retreated to the drawing room. Tessa refused a sherry offered by a footman, not particularly liking the taste of it and believing she needed to keep her wits about her.

Miss Allen approached her. "Would you care to take a turn about the room with me, Lady Tessa?"

Being in the woman's company was the last thing Tessa desired but good manners dictated she refrain from saying so.

"I'd be delighted to, Miss Allen."

CHAPTER THIRTEEN

M ISS ALLEN SLIPPED her arm into Tessa's and they began a slow parade about the edges of the room.

"I hear that you are making your come-out this Season," Miss Allen began. "Aren't you a bit long in the tooth to be doing so?"

Ignoring the rude statement, Tessa said, "My come-out was delayed by the ill health of my parents. They are gone now and I have completed my mourning period. I believe it is time I joined Polite Society."

"Are you looking for a husband?"

She demurred. "I think most women are. I would like to have children someday and that does involve marriage," she said lightly.

"I was very popular during my come-out last Season," Miss Allen boldly proclaimed.

"I am certain you were," she said, wondering where this conversation might be headed.

"I had several offers of marriage but wasn't quite ready to settle down. This Season will be different. I have found the man I am going to wed."

"Does he know this yet?" Tessa couldn't help but ask.

"No. But he will."

They continued strolling and then Miss Allen abruptly asked, "Are you interested in Lord Middlefield?"

"Why do you ask?" she replied, already knowing what now lay ahead.

"I asked you a question, Lady Tessa," Miss Allen said petulantly. "He seemed to pay special attention to you at dinner."

Tessa didn't believe that the case at all but decided this young woman saw her as a threat.

"Perhaps it is because I was one of the few present at the table that Lord Middlefield had previously met. My family accepted his dinner invitation last week and we also had him to tea. I am sure you heard him mention our trip which introduced him to the British Museum. My aunt placed me next to Lord Middlefield so that he would be comfortable. That is all."

"So you have no designs upon him? You don't wish to become Lady Middlefield?"

"Why would you ask such a thing, Miss Allen?" she countered. "Either Lord Middlefield and I will become better acquainted or we won't. Either our acquaintance will lead to something or it won't. It is no business of yours."

Miss Allen stopped them and turned to her, anger sparking in her eyes. "It is, actually. The earl is titled, wealthy, and quite handsome. I have decided that he will do as my husband. We will be wed by Season's end."

"Should Lord Middlefield have something to say about it?" she asked, digging in.

"He will offer for me. Mark my words," the woman said. "But I have to know that you are not interested in him."

Tessa wasn't—but she was not going to admit that to this harridan.

"I am merely eager to meet new people throughout the Season now that I am in London," she said. "Lord Middlefield is quite interesting."

She saw Miss Allen now fumed and began strolling again. The younger woman's fingers tightened on Tessa's arm.

"I won't have you trying to steal him away from me, Lady Tessa."

"I have never partaken in thievery, Miss Allen, and have no plans to do so now. Lord Middlefield is an intelligent man who can make up his own mind."

Miss Allen huffed and released Tessa's arm. Without a further word, she stormed across the room, rejoining her mother and two other women sipping sherry.

Immediately, Tessa found Louisa and Adalyn by her side.

"What is she in a snit about?" Louisa asked.

"She declared she was going to wed Lord Middlefield and believed I might be competition for her in that endeavor."

Adalyn snorted. "Miss Allen is deluded. Lord Middlefield is far too intelligent to become entangled with the likes of her."

"I agree," Louisa said. "In fact, I would venture to guess that is why he invited us to go along with them to the lecture. He couldn't publicly tell her he didn't want to accompany her. This way, there will be a buffer between them with the three of us."

"You don't mind going?" Tessa asked. "I know we hadn't planned on it."

"I am all for going," Adalyn declared. "I didn't like Miss Allen before and I certainly don't now."

"I thought her a tease during her come-out," Louisa added. "I don't think she has many friends though she does seem popular with the bachelors."

The men began joining them and Tessa saw Lord Middlefield entered the room. He made his way directly toward them. Tessa kept her face a blank though she wanted to gloat a bit.

"Since I am the guest of honor, I wonder if you might consider playing the pianoforte for us, Lady Tessa," the earl said. "I have also heard from Sir Edgar that Miss Goulding has quite the voice."

Louisa laughed. "Papa brags on me when he can. Singing is one of my few social accomplishments. Tessa usually plays for me." Her cousin turned toward her. "Would you do so now?"

"I would be happy to."

"And I will turn the pages for you," the earl said.

The trio headed toward the pianoforte and Tessa took a seat. Louisa reached into the basket containing sheet music and flipped through it, handing a few pages to Tessa.

"If I may have your attention?" Lord Middlefield called out. Conversation ceased and he said, "Miss Goulding has graciously offered to sing for us tonight and her cousin, Lady Tessa, will accompany her. My expertise involves page turning, no easy skill."

The guests chuckled as Lord Middlefield took a seat on the bench next to Tessa. Once again, she didn't truly need him turning the pages. The piece was one she had frequently played for Louisa.

But she wasn't going to ask him to get up and leave. Not when she glanced up and saw Miss Allen glaring daggers at her.

Turning to the earl, she smiled sweetly. "Thank you for offering to turn the pages."

He gave her a knowing look. "I didn't think you needed my services but I thought to offer since I think if I weren't seated here, I might be stalked."

"Ah, so you are aware of Miss Allen's interest in you, my lord?"

His lips twitched in amusement. "You better start playing, Tessa."

This time, she didn't correct him using her name. She glanced at Louisa, who nodded, and Tessa struck the first chord.

With pleasure.

>>>><<<<

SPENCER LOOKED FORWARD to rearranging Lord Ellington's pretty nose on his pretty face.

Sparring in a boxing ring would be the perfect excuse.

He thought the earl far too good-looking and much too confident. Especially when it came to Tessa. Not only had Ellington asked Tessa to drive with him in the park today but Spencer had watched him linger over her hand when Ellington said his goodbyes last night. As the honored guest, he had remained with the family and saw everyone off. Lord Ellington had held Tessa's hand far too long before lowering his lips to it and kissing her fingers.

He would think of that gesture when he smashed his fist into Ellington's face.

"I assume last night's dinner party was a success," said Rigsby.

"I believe so," he replied. "I met my neighbors who have arrived on the square and will be visiting Tattersalls next week with Lord Wethersby."

"And Lady Tessa?" inquired the valet.

"She was present. Looking lovely in midnight blue."

"Any plans today, my lord?"

"I am going to Gentleman Jack's establishment to spar this morning with Lord Ellington."

"I see."

Spencer waited a moment and then asked, "What exactly is it that you do see, Rigsby?"

"I shall merely suggest that you are most careful, my lord. Lord Ellington has a reputation of being quite skilled. Some say he could become a pugilist himself."

Interesting that the earl was good enough to be a professional.

"I will take that into consideration, Rigsby. Have faith that I will return to you in one piece."

"With perhaps a few bruises," the valet muttered.

No, Ellington would be the one sporting bruises. Spencer would make certain of that. He had high hopes of doing enough damage so that the earl would call off his outing with Tessa this afternoon.

He went downstairs to breakfast, making sure not to overeat. He didn't want to be full and sluggish during his bout with Ellington. After reading the newspapers, he retired to his study until Marsh summoned him with the news that Lord Ellington had arrived.

Leaving the correspondence on his desk, Spencer moved to the foyer, where he found Lord Ellington waiting.

"Ah, good morning, Lord Middlefield," the earl said pleasantly, his dark eyes assessing Spencer. "I hope you are eager for our match today."

"I am ready," he said, not wanting to tip his hand and let Ellington know that he was aware of the man's prowess in the ring.

"My carriage is waiting for us," Ellington said, leading Spencer outside and into the waiting vehicle.

As they settled into the carriage, Ellington said, "Do you know anything about Gentleman Jack?"

"Not much," he admitted, "other than he is John Jackson and was a former English heavyweight champion. He took the title when I was a boy."

"I was at that match," Ellington bragged. "I was thirteen and my father thought it important I witness it." He settled back into his seat. "It was held in Essex at Hornchurch. My father told me Jackson was the underdog by ten to one odds in the betting—but I knew a champion when I saw one. He was younger than Daniel Mendoza, the titleholder. Several inches taller and a good three stones heavier. Father said it was only the third time Jackson had fought professionally and that his lack of experience would show."

Ellington chuckled. "I still asked for ten pounds to bet with. Against Mendoza. I earned one hundred pounds that day."

Spencer didn't think Ellington had earned anything because he hadn't done any work. He despised gambling and gamblers but kept silent, letting the earl talk on.

"It took nine rounds before Mendoza was defeated. Jackson bullied his opponent into a corner of the ring. Grabbed his hair with one hand to steady him and battered Mendoza's head with a series of vicious uppercuts. The champion fought back but was knocked out a short while later, beaten into defeat. Mendoza challenged the hair-pulling but the two umpires ruled it to be legal."

The earl took off his hat and ran a hand through his dark waves. Grinning, he added, "Several pugilists after that bout shaved their heads to keep from having their opponents employ the same tactic." He replaced his hat. "Don't worry, Middlefield. I have no intention of yanking you around by your hair today."

"If you did, it would be your last day on earth."

Ellington looked startled at Spencer's words and then roared with laughter.

"You are a kidder, I see."

He wasn't kidding in the least.

"I've taken lessons with Gentleman Jack myself," the braggart continued. "He retired the year after he won the championship and now teaches three times a week at his academy during the Season. Though our government makes boxing illegal, it condones the practice as good exercise, as long as gentlemen of the *ton* are sparring under closed conditions."

"What have you learned through your lessons?" he asked, curious about what the former champion might have taught others.

"The Gentleman actually patterns himself after Daniel Mendoza's boxing style, believe it or not. Mendoza published a book, *The Art of Boxing*, almost twenty-five years ago. It's all about the stance. You must slightly bend your body, with your head and shoulders forward. Keep your knees slight bent and loose. Hold your fists up for self-defense. That position is called the guard. You keep opponents at bay with a left straight jab."

Spencer took in all that Ellington revealed. He was three inches over six feet and possessed a powerful, muscular build. His opponent was slightly over six feet and not as broad in the chest. He now knew how Ellington would defend himself and smiled broadly.

Because Spencer was left-handed.

He had only gotten into a few brawls during his school years. Being left-handed always came as a surprise to his challenger. It threw them off.

He hoped the same would be true when he tussled with Lord Ellington.

CHAPTER FOURTEEN

"AH, WE'RE HERE," Lord Ellington said. "Number Thirteen Bond Street in West London."

The carriage door opened and Ellington left the vehicle first. Spencer followed him, glancing about at his surroundings.

His companion motioned. "That building contains a fencing school run by Henry Angelo, a friend of Jackson's. Several men on the *ton* also take lessons from Angelo, as well."

Spencer had enjoyed fencing lessons at school and had been quick on his feet, an asset in fencing. Perhaps he might need to visit this Henry Angelo. That would be another day. Now, his focus was on his upcoming sparring match with Lord Ellington.

"Shall we?" he asked, heading toward the entrance of Jackson's gymnasium.

The two men entered and immediately he was assaulted with the smell of sweat and leather. He perused his surroundings, seeing men practicing on punching bags hanging from the ceiling and pairs sparring in marked off areas of eight feet squared.

Several called out Ellington's name and the earl said, "I will be back momentarily, Middlefield," striding off and getting a sound greeting from a group who gathered about him.

"They think he's as good as I once was," a voice to his right said softly.

Turning, Spencer saw a well-built man in his mid-forties.

"You are Gentleman Jack," he guessed.

"That I am. And who might you be, my lord?"

"Middlefield. Formerly Major Haddock."

The owner of the establishment nodded. "I have a soft spot for a military man. Your brother came here two or three times. Boxing didn't hold his interest for long."

"I didn't know him," Spencer shared. "He was a decade older and had nothing to do with me."

"Well, you're here now. And in Lord Ellington's company. Are you friends?"

"Acquaintances. We met at a dinner party last night and the earl offered to spar with me today."

The ex-boxer chuckled. "Pummel you is more like it. Lord Ellington is talented. He's taken my lessons to heart." He eyed Spencer a long moment. "Something tells me that he has no idea that you might be better than he is."

"I don't know that for a fact but I am fast on my feet and highly motivated."

"Ah. Sounds as if a lady is involved."

"You are very perceptive, Mr. Jackson."

"Come with me to the dressing rooms. We'll see you outfitted properly. Lord Ellington will be along shortly."

As they ventured past the other boxers and through a door to a back area where gentlemen could change, he said, "I was too young to know much about your career, Mr. Jackson, and have been away at war for a good number of years. Tell me about your best matches."

Gentleman Jack chuckled. "I was known as a remarkable amateur boxer before I became a paid pugilist, my lord. But I only fought three professional bouts."

"Three?" he asked, surprised.

"Yes. I was nineteen for the first. Defeated William Futrell in a bout that lasted a little more than an hour. Futrell was undefeated. Eighteen victories in all. He was so large that I nicknamed him Goliath in my head. I was younger though. Faster on my feet. It's all in the footwork, you know." He tapped his temple. "That and what's here. You have to know you can beat your opponent."

"What about your second match?"

Jackson shook his head. "A sour defeat, I'm afraid, fought nine months after the first one. I lost in five rounds to John Ingleston. It only took twenty minutes."

Spencer whistled. "What happened?"

"A broken leg about sums it up. Not an uncommon injury in boxing. It had been raining and the ground was rather slippery. I thought—and many who bet against Ingleston thought—that I would have won the bout if not for the broken limb. I could barely stand after it occurred and my opponent made quick work of me. I even announced my retirement afterward. I had a sleek physique and modeled frequently for sculptors and painters."

He looked at the former champion's long, sloping forehead and large ears that fanned out from the sides of his head and decided these artists must have only used the boxer's body and not his face in their work.

"I was still itching for the title, however, and returned six years into my retirement. That is the title bout that made me famous."

"Ellington told me of this fight with Daniel Mendoza."

"Mendoza was a good chap. He was the first English Jew to hold the boxing title. I decided I had met my goals and could only get hurt worse as time progressed so I called it quits again the next year and retired. That meant giving up my title. Thomas Owen was the champion who followed me. I settled in here. I have rooms above the boxing academy. Now, I charge an enormous amount of money to teach men of the *ton* how to box."

JACKSON FINISHED WINDING the long strips of leather around Spencer's hands as he finished speaking.

"You're set to go, my lord."

Lord Ellington entered the dressing room. "Good morning, Jack," he said breezily. "I see you are taking good care of my friend."

"Yes, Lord Middlefield is ready to warm up his muscles. I'll take him out on the floor and you can join us when you're ready, my lord."

As they left and returned to the academy, Jackson said, "He'll want the gloves to come off after you've sparred a bit. Only do so if you know you can take him, Lord Middlefield. Ellington is a clever man and a talented boxer. Do not underestimate him. And remember—bareknuckle boxing is all about the power of the punch."

"I understand."

They went to a punching bag and Spencer threw several punches at it. Jackson had him roll his shoulders, rotating them both forward and backward. He also had him stretch, touching his toes and pulling on Spencer's arms before allowing him back at the bag. As he struck it, he pictured Ellington's face.

"That's enough," Jackson said. "You don't want to waste all your efforts on a bag which can't fight back. Your acquaintance looks as if he's ready."

The two moved toward Lord Ellington, who danced from one foot to the other.

"Ready, Middlefield?"

"I am if you are," he said.

They went to one of the empty squares and when a man whom Spencer assumed was employed as an instructor or umpire came toward them, Gentleman Jack waved him off.

"I'll handle this," he said.

Spencer stepped into the designated area, along with Ellington. Several bystanders drifted their way in order to watch the two men spar. Gentleman Jack laid down a few basic rules and backed away, allowing the men to begin.

Immediately, Ellington assumed the guard position he had spoken of, his fists coming up, one arm slightly in front of the other. Then he began dancing about. It was obvious the earl had good balance and was comfortable. Spencer decided to make him more so.

By pretending his right hand was his dominant one.

It was a bit underhanded but by no means illegal. Spencer put up his hands as well, moving about in a similar fashion to Ellington. He had never used as much footwork before in his limited brawls and decided perhaps a few lessons with Jackson in the future might be wise.

They sparred for a good ten minutes, Ellington getting in more punches to Spencer than he would have liked. His opponent had good speed and used his hands well. Spencer thought his timing was better, though, and would be even more so once he lulled Ellington into complacency and then began using his dominant hand.

After another five minutes, Gentleman Jack called for a break. Each man, with help, guzzled down a mug of cider. Spencer wiped his mouth with his forearm since the boxing gloves prevented him from doing anything else.

"Would you consider taking off the gloves for a bit, Middlefield?" Lord Ellington asked affably.

"Why not?"

As Gentleman Jack unwound Spencer's gloves, more men began moving toward them, and he heard a few begin to call out wagers. One gentleman signaled to one of the academy's employees and a pencil and paper were produced. Bets were quickly written down.

"From the buzz, I gather it is not my name which is preferred," he said with a wry smile.

"No," Jackson agreed. "Everyone here has seen Lord Ellington box, both with and without his gloves. I told you, my lord, that Ellington is most capable."

Spencer met the man's gaze. "You also told me not to remove my gloves unless I thought I could take him." Determination filled him. "I can. And will."

"Just don't think of that pretty lady that has caused the animosity between you," the former boxer warned. "Visions of her dancing in your head will lead to a good bruising and possibly being knocked out."

"I have a trick up my sleeve," he promised. When he saw Jackson's look of consternation, he said, "Nothing illegal, I assure you. Your academy's reputation will remain spotless. Lord Ellington, however, will pay the price for underestimating me."

Jackson grinned broadly. "I look forward to it."

By now, every man present inside the academy had gathered around the boxing square. Spencer felt the charged air and caught a few sympathetic looks tossed his way. He also saw not only had Ellington removed his gloves but he had stripped to the waist. Immediately, Spencer did the same. He didn't need anything getting in his way or preventing him from giving Ellington a sound thrashing.

His shirt removed, he turned and faced his opponent. The earl's confident air gave him pause, as did the man's sleek physique. Ellington was no stranger to hard work, which had put the muscles on his athletic frame. Still, Spencer knew he had a definite advantage with more height and weight. His torso was even more muscled than his foe's. Lord Ellington might have more formal experience in a boxing square but Spencer had his years of war experience, which had honed his senses and given him the ability to think quickly on his feet.

That—and the shock of him leading with his left hand—would now come into play.

Gentleman Jack motioned for the two men to come to the center of the square and they did, each standing opposite one another, with Jackson's hands on both their shoulders.

"Broughton's rules, my lords," the former champion proclaimed. "Hitting a downed fighter is prohibited, as is grasping him below the waist. If a man goes down and cannot continue after I count to thirty, the match is over."

"How many rounds?" he asked, eyeing his opponent.

"Three—and they'll be three minutes each," Jackson informed him. "You are permitted to drop to a knee to end the round if you wish."

Ellington snorted. "It's unmanly to do so, Middlefield. If you are in trouble, own up to it and take your hits like a man."

"I won't be in trouble," Spencer said with no emotion, praying he could back up his words with swift action.

"What about biting, Jack?" a voice from the crowd called out.

Another added, "Or gouging?"

The academy owner glared out at the crowd. "I won't tolerate biting or gouging," he called out and looked at the two boxers. "And no hair-pulling."

"Understood," Spencer said and Ellington concurred.

"Good luck to you, gentlemen," the older man said.

He leaned in and tapped his knuckles against his opponent's and they both retreated to separate ends of the square.

A bell sounded and Spencer supposed that signaled the start of the first round. He moved to the center in order to meet Ellington. Both men's hands came up in the guard position. Within the first thirty seconds, they had traded half a dozen jabs between them. The punches left no open space for a counterattack. Spencer knew the importance of the jab. It helped to gauge distance between two fighters and also tested an opponent's defenses. A jab could also be used to set up a more powerful punch.

Already, he knew he could stand back slightly and still reach Ellington with his longer arm span. Spencer continued jabbing with his right hand and then threw in two blows in a row with his left. That wasn't unusual. Most boxers threw jabs with either hand as they learned about their foe.

Then without warning, Spencer threw a quick right jab, followed by a strong left cross to the earl's jaw, pushing his back shoulder forward and pivoting his body as he did so. The blow stunned Ellington and he staggered back. The shouts from the crowd intensified as Ellington regained his balance and met

Spencer's eyes. He saw the stunned look.

Ellington recovered quickly, however, moving forward and throwing a series of quick jabs, which Spencer defended. He blocked a cross from Ellington and delivered another powerful blow to the earl's chin with a second cross punch. Again, his opponent stumbled back, amazement clear on his face. The crowd began yelling all at once, some encouraging Ellington while others had turned on the earl and began shouting their support of Spencer.

A bell rang and he realized the round had ended. He retreated to his corner, where several men close by slapped him on the back or patted his shoulders. His knuckles were sore and bleeding from the numerous blows. Taking a towel handed to him, he wiped the sweat from his face and then dabbed the blood from his knuckles.

Before he could get another breath, it was time to go at it again and he joined his opponent in the center once more, both men exchanging brutal blows, holding nothing back. He was struck several times in his torso and face and returned the same, punishing blows to Ellington. He stunned the earl with another cross and Ellington stumbled backward. He bent a moment, his hands on his thighs, and Spencer took time himself to take several deep breaths.

Without warning, Ellington charged him and he quickly threw a hook, a semi-round punch aimed at the earl's head. It connected soundly.

The earl bent from the waist, his hands reaching out as he flailed. He never went down but Spencer moved back several steps in order to give Ellington some room. The older man swayed and Spencer held his breath, wondering if Ellington would drop to his knees and end the bout. He wished Ellington would. Already, his hands throbbed painfully, as did his chest and jaw.

The round ended and he retreated again to his corner. The crowd noise only grew during the brief respite, a cacophony of sound roaring in his head.

Then from across the square, Ellington smiled at him. As if he toyed with Spencer.

He couldn't afford to have the earl smile at Tessa. Renewed, he stood to his full height, waiting for the bell. When it rang, both men rushed at one another with a vengeance. A rain of blows came from Spencer's fists. He landed another hook to the side of the earl's hard head and a hard jab to his nose. Blood spurted everywhere and Gentleman Jack moved closer.

"Had enough, my lord?" he asked Ellington.

With a murderous look in his eyes, Ellington said, "I will kill him."

He came hard at Spencer and they traded several blows. Then he saw his window of opportunity and shifted his torso to the left, slightly bending his knees. His left fist rose vertically and he pushed his knees downward to give him more spring as his fist connected under Ellington's jaw in an uppercut punch. It lifted his foe's body, making Ellington off-balance as his head snapped back and then fell forward.

Spencer followed it with a right hook while Ellington was still vulnerable. The earl collapsed to the ground. Immediately, Spencer returned to his corner and Gentleman Jack began the thirty-second count. Twice, the earl tried to rise. The first time he made it to his feet and swayed, obviously dizzy, and dropped to his knees. He tried to push up a second time and was unable to rise this time. He twisted and sat on the ground as Jackson completed the count.

"The bout is over," Gentleman Jack announced to the crowd. "Lord Middlefield is the victor."

Though the horde had firmly been in Lord Ellington's corner at the beginning of the match, their allegiance had switched quickly to the predicted loser, now the winner. Cheers sounded throughout the academy.

Spencer acknowledged them with a quick nod of his head and then went to where Ellington sat. He offered a hand and the earl took it. Spencer raised his defeated opponent to his feet.

"You fought a decent match, my lord," he said, sticking out a hand, which the earl took reluctantly and shook.

"I should have noticed you were left-handed at dinner," he said. "I suppose I was too busy watching Lady Tessa to pick up on that." He touched his nose gingerly. "It would have saved me a broken nose."

"It might not be broken," Spencer told him. "Then again, it could be," he finished, unapologetically.

"You look a fright," Ellington said. "I can only imagine how I appear."

"Like something the cat dragged in. Only far worse."

The two laughed and Ellington winced. "I must see to my nose."

"Of course." He retrieved his shirt.

Both men made their way through the crowd, now openly supporting Spencer. They returned to the dressing area, Gentleman Jack following them.

"Let me fix your nose, my lord." Jackson stepped close and examined it a moment. Then placing his hands on Ellington's face, he jerked quickly.

Spencer had to look away as the injured Ellington roared.

"That'll do the trick," Jackson said. "Towels and washbasins are over there."

In silence, the two men washed away the blood and dressed in silence. Spencer held his hands out, looking at the bruised knuckles.

And decided Tessa was worth every scrape.

CHAPTER FIFTEEN

T ESSA DECIDED TO go downstairs and play the pianoforte for a while. The group going to the lecture at the British Museum was set to meet outside her uncle's townhouse in an hour. Already jittery, she hoped playing a soothing piece would calm her nerves.

Adalyn had gone with her mother to a final fitting at the dressmaker's shop. Since it was so close to the beginning of the Season, the appointment could not be canceled or delayed because of the impromptu outing. Adalyn said she would be finished in time for the carriage to drop her at the museum so she could meet up with their party.

As she reached the drawing room and took a seat in front of the instrument, she thought about the note she had received from Lord Ellington canceling yesterday's outing in Hyde Park, an outing which she had looked forward to. The earl had profusely apologized, saying unexpected business had come up at his country estate and he needed to return there and see it resolved before the Season began. In it, he not only asked Tessa's forgiveness for missing their drive in his phaeton but he also asked that she reserve the first dance at the Healeys' ball with him, the first affair opening the Season.

Adalyn had told Tessa it was not necessary for her to reply to the earl's note. That doing so wasn't acceptable. She was never to write a gentleman who was not related to her. Word from Lord Ellington's footman that the note had been delivered to her would be answer enough. She hoped the business wasn't difficult and could be concluded in time for him to return to London. She thought the earl quite handsome even if he seemed a bit forward, holding her hand too long when he departed from dinner the other night.

She decided to play a lively number by Bach, hoping it would keep her mind off Lord Middlefield, who constantly invaded her thoughts. Drat him and his drugging kiss. She hadn't had a moment's peace ever since that had occurred. She didn't think she would ever be able to stand before the Rosetta Stone again without remembering what they had done before it.

Sensing the door open, she glanced up and saw Rainey coming toward her. She lifted her fingers from the ivory keys.

"Lord Middlefield is here, my lady," the butler informed her.

"But . . . he is very early," she protested.

His arrival put her in a dilemma. With her aunt and cousin at the modiste's and her uncle at his club, Tessa had no one to chaperone her. She hesitated a moment and then decided they were inside the house. No prying eyes of Polite Society would know if they were in a room together alone for a brief spell.

"Show him in, Rainey. And leave the doors open if you would, please."

"Yes, my lady."

Rising, she gripped her hands in front of her, forcing herself not to wring them and give away her discomfort.

"Lord Middlefield," Rainey announced and the earl entered the room, meaning he had been waiting in the corridor.

As he came toward her, Tessa saw he sported a black eye and swollen jaw and she asked, "What on earth happened to you?"

Ignoring her question, he said, "I couldn't help but hear you playing. I have had my own pianoforte tuned recently. You are welcomed any time to come and play it."

"I asked what happened to you, my lord."

Then she recalled he and Lord Ellington were supposed to go to Gentleman Jack's to spar.

"You and Lord Ellington went at it," she accused.

"Yes," he said agreeably. "Without gloves. They call them gloves but they are little more than leather strips wound about a man's fist. Taking them off does make a difference, however."

Without thinking, Tessa grabbed his wrist and lifted it, seeing his knuckles battered and still raw. She quickly released him.

"I cannot understand why men think pummeling one another is a good idea. I find it uncouth and uncivilized. Why on earth would you and Lord Ellington attempt to do this without gloves?"

"I found out he is a skilled pugilist and needed to put him in his place. On my behalf, he is the one who asked that the gloves come off."

She frowned. "Whyever would you wish to put him in his place?"

He grinned. "Why, over you, of course. Men can tell when another man is interested in a woman. We both are interested in you, Tessa."

"You told him that?" she accused.

"No. I didn't have to. Women have their intuition. Men have their gut feeling. We sniffed one another out and it was obvious."

"If you look like this, what does he look like?"

"Worse," Lord Middlefield admitted. "I suppose you haven't seen him."

"He canceled our drive. Actually, he said it was postponed due to unforeseen business that needed attending to at his country estate."

"Good," the earl declared. "You didn't need to be off driving in his phaeton with him anyway. And I seriously doubt his lordship adjourned to the country. He is probably at home licking his wounds after being embarrassed."

"What do you mean?"

He shrugged. "Everyone at Gentleman Jack's came to watch

our bout. Several already watched us as we sparred. When Ellington suggested our gloves come off, all activity inside the academy ceased and dozens of men gathered around us—all betting against me."

"Why would they?" she asked, puzzled. "You are taller and much broader. You have been to war and know how to fight. Lord Ellington is just a gentleman of the *ton*."

A slow smile spread across his handsome face and her face grew hot. She realized she never should have acknowledged that she had noticed his physique.

"I taught him not to take advantage of someone he thought he could," Lord Middlefield explained. "You believe I am arrogant but Lord Ellington is much more so. He needed to be taken down a notch or two."

"You sound so uncouth. You shouldn't participate in such a barbaric practice."

"It is good exercise," he told her.

"But it left you looking like this? And poor Lord Ellington."

Lord Middlefield snorted. "There is nothing poor about him. He kept from me his reputation. I could truly have been hurt in our match if I hadn't been forewarned regarding his prowess."

"You are impossible," she proclaimed, angrily pushing her palm against his chest.

He winced.

"What's wrong?" she asked worriedly.

He smiled ruefully. "It is not only my eye which is blackened and my jaw which is sore and swollen. My torso is battered and bruised. I didn't get away from our encounter scot-free."

Sympathy sprang quickly within her. She raised a palm and placed it against his cheek. It was warm to her touch and flooded her with a strange feeling.

Gazing down at her, he softly said, "I would do it again for a simple touch from you."

She wet her lips nervously, drawing his attention to them. Knowing what was coming, she still remained in place.

He lowered his lips to hers. Her other hand came up to frame his face. He brushed his lips softly against hers at first, over and over, causing a ripple down her spine. His hands grasped her waist, anchoring her, and he pressed his mouth more firmly against hers. This time, she knew what was coming.

And was eager to participate.

His tongue glided along the seam of her mouth and she opened to him. Her tongue waited for his, playing with it. He groaned, low and deep, his hands tightening on her waist, making her feel powerful again in her femininity. His tongue grew bolder, stroking hers, trying to dominate her. Tessa pushed her fingers into his thick, raven waves and clutched them.

The kiss went on and finally he broke it. Resting his forehead against hers, his lips hovered.

"I could do that all day," he murmured as she let her fingers fall.

She could, too, but she had no idea how much time had passed. Louisa would arrive any minute and Tessa couldn't allow her cousin to catch her kissing the earl like this.

She tried to pull away but he kissed her again and she was powerless to keep from giving in to it again. The kiss was hard. Demanding. Uncompromising. It told her he wanted her.

Worse, she knew she wanted him.

Again, he was the first to pull away, releasing her and taking a step back "Will you play for me? It soothes me."

"I will if you sit over there."

Lord Middlefield chuckled and moved to the chair she indicated. She remembered he mentioned liking Beethoven and she sat at the pianoforte, taking a deep breath to compose herself before beginning to play. She avoided looking at him but could feel his intense gaze burning into her.

Near the end of the piece, Tessa sensed another presence and glanced up, seeing Louisa had arrived. She remained near the doorway until Tessa finished playing and then made her way toward them.

"I am always astounded at your talent," her cousin said, kissing Tessa's cheek and then greeting the earl.

"I hope the other fellow looks worse, my lord," she teased. "I assume that would be Lord Ellington."

"Yes, I sparred with Ellington."

"I would say more than sparred. I should have warned you of his reputation when I heard you making plans to go to Gentleman Jack's academy with him." Louisa smiled at him. "But I thought you could handle yourself."

Something slammed into Tessa, almost knocking her off-balance.

Jealousy.

She felt ridiculous. If Louisa liked Lord Middlefield, they might be a good match. Just because Tessa herself found him irritating and arrogant did not mean her cousin wouldn't suit with the earl. Louisa had been out in society for a long time and had never written to Tessa of feeling any man was special. She decided she would encourage Louisa's attention in Lord Middlefield.

Even if it killed her.

"It is close to our time to depart," her cousin said. "I saw Lord Middlefield's carriage waiting outside and know the others should arrive momentarily."

"Then we should go downstairs," Tessa told the pair.

They went to the foyer and Abra awaited, holding Tessa's spencer, bonnet, and reticule in hand. Her maid helped her into them and she turned, ready to go.

The three stepped outside as Tessa told Louisa that Lord Ellington would not be joining them today and that Adalyn would come straight from a fitting.

Lord Wethersby rode up and dismounted, giving his reins to a nearby footman, who led the horse away. He joined them and Tessa repeated her news about Adalyn and Lord Ellington.

"I figured Ellington wouldn't be here after hearing of his match with you, my lord," the viscount said. "It was the talk of

White's and Brooks' both."

"And how many pretended they bet on me?" Lord Middlefield asked.

Lord Wethersby laughed. "A good many. Though I can't imagine anyone placing a wager against Ellington before the match began. He is known for his pugilistic skills. Now, however, I doubt anyone would dare bet against you, Middlefield."

"Where is Miss Allen?" Louisa asked. "She only lives next door."

"I suppose I should be the one to call for her," the earl said, sounding resigned to his fate. "After all, this outing originally began when she asked me to escort her to the lecture."

Tessa recalled how certain Miss Allen was that she would nab Lord Middlefield as her husband and spoke up.

"I will go with you, my lord," she said pleasantly, tucking her hand through his arm. "Why don't the two of you step inside the carriage?"

Louisa let out a slight giggle while the viscount bit back a smile.

"Let me help you, Miss Goulding," Lord Wethersby said.

"Come along, my lord," Tessa said, hoping she sounded braver than she felt.

As they walked down the pavement, she said, "I am sorry everyone seemed to know Lord Ellington was such an excellent boxer and yet no one warned you of the fact."

"Well, Gentleman Jack did just before I went into the boxing square."

"Still," she said, "I will warn you now. Miss Allen announced to me after dinner the other night that she has decided you are to be her husband."

"She what?" he roared.

"Quiet, my lord," Tessa warned. "I am sharing this in confidence."

"What, exactly, did she say?" he asked as they approached the door.

"She wanted to make certain I was not interested in you and informed me that she would be your betrothed by Season's end."

He looked amused. "What might you have told her, Tessa?"

She shrugged and nonchalantly said, "I told her we either would further our acquaintance and see if we might suit or we wouldn't. That it was no business of hers."

"It isn't her business and never will be. I find Miss Allen remarkably tiresome." He paused. "I only hope you meant what you told her. That you will give me a chance to get to know you better."

"I have no plans to do so, Lord Middlefield. I merely thought Miss Allen overstepped her bounds. You may get to know whomever you wish. I have told you I have no interest in you."

He gave her a long look. "And yet we have now kissed twice. I have found both times extremely enjoyable."

She huffed, "What if we did? I have now been kissed and know what to expect. I will have your kiss to compare to others and theirs."

She saw anger spark in his eyes but he coolly said, "What we have is special, Tessa. You will come to believe that."

"What I believe is that you think much too much of yourself, my lord."

With that, she rapped on the door.

CHAPTER SIXTEEN

S PENCER TAMPED DOWN the hope that sprang within him. Tessa had not told Miss Allen that she was uninterested in him.

That was progress.

She could have immediately told the younger woman she had no claims on Spencer. No desire for his company. She had told him enough times. Yet she had wasted the chance to do the same with Miss Allen.

He grinned.

She was softening toward him. Kissing certainly helped. He thought of her palm against his cheek. Her fingers pushed into his hair. Desire flickered through him as the door opened and a butler appeared.

"We are here for Miss Allen," he said crisply. "Lord Middlefield and Lady Tessa."

The butler looked momentarily confused. "I do know Lord Middlefield was expected. Miss Allen requested that you come to the winter parlor when you arrived."

"We have no time for that. We are due to leave for the British Museum. Miss Goulding and Lord Wethersby are already outside in the carriage and awaiting us. Please send for Miss Allen. We will meet her outside."

His carriage pulled up as he finished speaking and Spencer

said, "Here it is. Come, my lady."

He led Tessa away from the door, which the befuddled butler closed.

"She will be furious," Tessa pointed out as he escorted her to the carriage.

"She will," he agreed. "Shall we see if her good manners prevail and she hides her anger?"

Spencer handed her up and she entered the carriage with him following. Tessa sat on the empty bench across from her cousin and Lord Wethersby. He took a seat beside her.

"Well?" Miss Goulding asked.

"She is coming," he said.

Miss Goulding clucked her tongue. "Oh, this won't be good at all," she said.

"Am I missing out on something?" the viscount asked, concerned.

"Storm clouds on the horizon," Spencer said to a still-perplexed Wethersby.

"Miss Allen will perhaps be upset when she joins us," Tessa said.

"Why?" Wethersby asked.

"Because she has designs on Lord Middlefield and may feel thwarted by my cousin's and my presence."

"Oh," Wethersby said, nodding his head. "Oh," he repeated, glancing to Spencer.

"I have no interest in the chit, my lord," he told the other man. "If you do, please let her know."

The viscount grinned. "I only came into my title eight months ago," he shared. "I am not looking for a bride. Just a bit of fun."

The carriage door opened and Miss Allen appeared in the doorway, dressed in light blue. A footman helped her inside the coach and she glanced about, her gaze landing upon Spencer. Despite his decision to have nothing to do with her, he grew warm under her stare and wished he could loosen his cravat.

"Where to sit?" she said, moving toward him and Tessa.

Before Spencer could slide over, Miss Allen stepped between his and Tessa's feet and turned. As she lowered herself, he saw she might very well land in his lap if he didn't act quickly and so he pushed himself out of her way and she plopped between him and Tessa.

An awkward silence filled the carriage and then Tessa said, "It is good to see you again, Miss Allen. Our party is now complete."

Spencer took that as a hint and rapped on the roof. The carriage began to roll.

"Where are the others?" Miss Allen demanded.

"My cousin, Lady Adalyn, is at a dress fitting. She will join us at the museum when it is completed. Lord Ellington had estate business which claimed his attention."

"I see," Miss Allen said dismissively.

Wethersby glanced to Tessa. "You seem to be a frequent visitor to the museum, my lady. Can you tell us more about it?"

"With pleasure, my lord," Tessa replied and launched into an explanation of the museum.

Spencer could tell her words bored Miss Allen and the woman turned toward him.

"How are you today, Lord Middlefield? I was hoping you would come inside and allow us to visit for a bit."

"Everyone coming today had already arrived, Miss Allen. I thought it best we not tarry. You never know with London traffic how long it might take to reach somewhere. I know you will want to claim a good seat at the lecture, especially since you were so keen on attending it."

She gave him a deliberate pout. Spencer supposed there were men who might find it—and her—attractive. However, Miss Allen did not hold a candle to Tessa.

"I will admit that I was mixed up on my days, my lord," she said, batting her eyelashes at him. "I am not that interested in today's topic, after all."

"You shouldn't have come then," he stated.

Her pretty pout turned sour. "But I wanted to see you," she explained.

He could think of no witty response that would keep her at bay and put her in her place at the same time so he said nothing.

Instead, he asked Tessa a question and looked across Miss Allen, joining in on the others' lively conversation. Lord Wethersby had an interest in the Greeks and Romans and was looking forward to today's speaker. Spencer began telling the viscount about some of the statues he had viewed on his trip to the museum and the two men chatted affably. All the while, though, he could tell Miss Allen brooded.

They arrived and after everyone had exited the vehicle, he found Miss Goulding had taken Wethersby's arm. Spencer hoped Tessa wouldn't do the same and looked to the two women.

"It looks as if I am fortunate enough to escort both of you lovely ladies inside."

Tessa stepped to one side and took his arm, leaving Miss Allen to join him on the other side. They followed the other two inside, where Tessa was greeted personally even though it was growing crowded.

"I had no idea sepulchral antiquities were quite so popular," he quipped.

"Mr. Pilson is extremely well known in the field. He is an expert on anything Roman in nature," Tessa said. "Ah, there is Mr. Smithson. We must say hello."

They ventured toward the museum employee and he greeted Tessa and Miss Goulding by name. Turning, he added, "And it is good to see you again, Lord Middlefield, shiner and all."

"I am looking forward to hearing today's speaker. This is Miss Allen and Lord Wethersby. Mr. Smithson gives guided tours at the museum."

Wethersby began a conversation with Smithson and Tessa said, "We should go and find seats. We can save some for the others."

They moved toward the lecture hall but were stopped several

times, all by gentlemen congratulating him on his victory over Lord Ellington yesterday. He didn't know which of them had seen him box in person and which had merely heard of his pairing with Ellington. He briskly thanked all of them and continued steering his two companions toward the lecture hall.

Entering, Tessa pulled on his arm. "Over here, I think. I see more objects on display on this side of the room."

She moved down a row, leaving the three seats against the wall empty, while sitting in the one next to them. Immediately, Miss Allen muscled through and sat next to Tessa, leaving Spencer to sit to Miss Allen's left. He paused a moment, thinking Tessa might say something that would allow him to sit in-between the two women.

She didn't. She merely smiled at him.

He sat.

Miss Allen began talking his ear off, gossiping about people he didn't know and upcoming events that he had no idea if he was attending or not. He knew he had received a myriad of invitations but hadn't responded to any. He better, especially if he wanted to pursue Tessa during the Season. He couldn't do so by sitting alone at home.

Miss Goulding and Lord Wethersby appeared, along with Lady Adalyn. Spencer rose.

"Don't come past us. It is a tight fit. Lady Tessa, you should move down. Here, let me help you."

He moved past Miss Allen and took Tessa's elbow, guiding her to the far seat—and then sitting down beside her. Turning, he smiled at Miss Allen.

"Please do move down, Miss Allen. That will allow the others to claim their seats."

She did, fuming.

Spencer bit the inside of his cheek to keep from erupting in laughter.

Tessa turned away and faced the wall, her body shaking with silent laughter.

Graciously, he said, "You were talking about a ball, Miss Allen?"

Happy to have his full attention once more, the chit began babbling again. He didn't listen to a word she said. Instead, he was aware of Tessa on his other side. He had smelled the lavender scent on her in the carriage and again caught a whiff of it.

God, how he wanted to kiss her again.

Thank goodness Mr. Smithson appeared at the front of the room. The crowd, which had been murmuring, now fell silent.

"It is my great honor today to welcome to the British Museum a scholar of notable fame."

Smithson went on, elaborating on the qualifications of Pilson, whom Spencer spied standing off to the side. When the lengthy introduction finished, a sound round of applause was heard as Pilson took the stage.

"Thank you for that warm greeting," the man of slight stature said. "And thank you for the warm welcome. Roman antiquities gained my attention many years ago when I was boy fascinated by both the Greeks and especially the Romans."

As Pilson began to speak about sepulchral antiquities, Spencer felt a nudge against his boot. Coming from Miss Allen. He dared not look at her because if he did so, it might encourage her. Besides, he was a large man and had really nowhere to move to. If he leaned to his right, he would be infringing upon Tessa's space. Not that he would have minded that, but she certainly would have harsh words for him afterward if he did. Or worse.

She might say something right now.

Though he didn't think she would draw attention to them, considering she, her cousins, and Miss Allen were the only ladies present in the room, full of over one hundred gentlemen.

He thought he heard a noise coming from Tessa. Miss Allen's slipper nudged him again and he shifted in his seat, still having nowhere to put his booted feet except directly in front of him. Spencer did his best to focus on Pilson's lecture. The scholar was well-informed and presented many details that Spencer found fascinating.

Then the chit did it again.

This time, her hands, which had been folded demurely in her lap, were unfolded. She allowed the right one to slip from her thigh and rest in-between her leg and his, pressing against his leg in a most unseemly fashion. Now, he was in a true dilemma. He didn't want his hand anywhere near hers. Especially in a room full of gentlemen representing Polite Society. As he debated on what to do, Tessa snickered.

Snickered.

Spencer eased his arms up until they were crossed over his broad chest. They would remain there until the end of the lecture.

He turned his head slightly, tilting it downward, and said, "Snickers, Tessa?"

She glanced at him, mischief in her eyes, and bit her lower lip to keep from laughing aloud. The gesture kept her quiet but it caused a frisson of desire to ripple through him.

He wanted to be the one biting into that soft, plump lip.

He would do so soon. He had taken an opportunity earlier while they were in Lord Uxbridge's drawing room. A calculated risk because the door had been left open since she had no chaperone. He figured Lady Adalyn and Lady Uxbridge must not be at home because Tessa would have sent for them promptly to act as chaperones when he arrived.

After their kiss, Tessa could not deny what was between them. She was stubborn, however, and he could only do so much to point out to her what lay between them. Spencer would have to continue to do whatever he could manage in order to persuade Tessa that she was destined to be his countess.

He turned his attention back to Mr. Pilson, glad that Miss Allen made no further, unwelcomed moves upon his person. When the lecture ended, the scholar opened it up for questions. Several men asked him various things and Pilson had quick answers for them. Then it surprised him when Tessa raised her hand.

It must have surprised the speaker as well because he looked in her direction and blinked rapidly, as if he didn't know women could think, much less speak.

"Yes," Pilson asked hesitantly. "You . . . have a question, my lady?"

"I do," Tessa said confidently.

Then she asked him about burial customs and the differences in items carved upon tombs when it came to men and women. She referenced several instances, one from a previous lecture he had given and others in regard to various antiquities on display in the British Museum itself.

Spencer was surprised at the depth of Tessa's knowledge but he shouldn't have been. She had proven herself to be bright and inquisitive. He actually was a bit proud of her as gentlemen throughout the room murmured, discussing her question amongst themselves as Pilson took a moment to collect his thoughts.

Then the scholar answered her at length and concluded with, "I am used to questions, my lady, but not one so thoughtful. I would like to speak to you when this session concludes."

"Of course, Mr. Pilson," Tessa said brightly.

Only two other gentlemen asked a question afterward and, soon, Mr. Smithson appeared again, thanking both the speaker and the audience for their time, encouraging everyone to visit the Roman wing of the British Museum and see examples of the objects Mr. Pilson had discussed with them.

Applause erupted again and Pilson nodded bashfully. Then audience members rose and began making their way from the lecture hall.

Lady Adalyn leaned out and said, "Tessa, a remarkable question. It even interested me and you know I find everything in this museum to be dull."

"I am just glad that you were able to make the lecture," Tessa told her cousin. "I was worried you would not arrive in time."

Tessa rose, as did Adalyn, and the others followed suit, all filing from the row in which that sat.

"How did the dress fitting go?" asked Tessa.

Lady Adalyn said, "I am very pleased and the remainder of my gowns will be delivered by tomorrow. Not only mine but the last of yours, as well. I am glad we will have received our entire wardrobe before the Season begins."

Miss Allen said, "What? You have *every* gown you have commissioned?"

Lady Adalyn gave the younger woman a superior smile. "Yes, of course. Louisa and I always have all our gowns readied by Season's start. It took a bit longer this year simply because Tessa was also part of the order of Madame Chevalier."

"Madame Chevalier!" Miss Allen exclaimed. "Why, she is the most sought after modiste in all of London." She turned to Tessa. "How did you, a nobody from the country, wind up becoming one of Madame Chevalier's exclusive clients?"

The chit's words riled Spencer but he decided this was a battle Tessa could fight adequately with both hands tied behind her back.

As expected, Tessa smiled sweetly and said, "It was nothing of my doing. My mother was a client of Madame Chevalier's, going back to her own come-out. Madame was more than happy to take me on because she had enjoyed working so much with Mama all those years ago and throughout her marriage. Until her passing." She paused. "I did need a good amount of everything, especially since I had no gowns created for me for several years. My wardrobe was sadly lacking."

Miss Allen had no response and merely huffed her displeasure. She looked to Spencer and said, "It is time we leave, my lord," and possessively slipped her arm through his.

"We must wait first for Lady Tessa to have a word with Mr. Pilson as he requested."

The group spoke of the upcoming ball hosted by Lord and

Lady Healey, which would open the Season, and then Mr. Pilson appeared.

"Might I know your name, my lady?" he asked.

"I am Lady Tessa Foster. My father was Lord Paxton and he brought me to the British Museum from the time I was quite young."

"Ah, that tells me why you were so interested in Roman antiquities and displayed a vast knowledge of them. I used to correspond with Lord Paxton for several years regarding archeological artifacts." The scholar frowned. "He never answered my final letter and I heard that he had suffered an attack of apoplexy. Is he still with us, my lady?"

Tessa shook her head sadly. "No, Mr. Pilson. He has gone to join my mother in Heaven."

"My sympathies, Lady Tessa. Perhaps you and I could take up where your father and I left off and continue the discussions."

Tessa smiled warmly at the man. "I would be happy to correspond with you, Mr. Pilson. It will be an honor. In fact, why don't you come to tea tomorrow? You can meet my aunt and uncle and we can talk about how you knew my father."

"I would be delighted to do so, my lady."

Tessa gave the scholar Lord Uxbridge's address in Mayfair and Spencer, who had done his best to keep from squirming uncomfortably because of Miss Allen glued to his side, now offered Tessa his arm.

"Shall we return to my carriage?" he asked.

"Thank you," she said, taking his arm.

The group returned to Spencer's coach and everyone but Miss Allen contributed to the conversation on their way home. His carriage pulled up in front of Lord Uxbridge's townhouse and they began spilling from it. Miss Allen was the last to depart the vehicle and she smiled up at Spencer.

"My lord, would you like to come in for tea?" she asked softly so that the others could not overhear the invitation.

Somehow, Tessa did, though, and flashed him a smile. Ignoring what Miss Allen said, Tessa said brightly, "Thank you again for accepting my uncle's invitation to tea today, Lord Middlefield. I know Uncle is looking forward to just the two of you discussing crop rotation."

He couldn't help but smile at her quick thinking. "Yes, Lord Uxbridge has some very specific ideas that he wishes to share with me regarding not only crop rotation but a new method of harvesting."

He glanced back to Miss Allen and said, "I am sorry. I have a prior engagement. Perhaps another time."

Before she could name another time, putting him on the spot, Spencer added, "Lord Wethersby, would you escort Miss Allen back to her father's house since I am to have tea with Lord Uxbridge now?"

Wethersby nodded agreeably. "It would be my privilege to do so, Miss Allen."

The viscount said goodbye to the others and Spencer saw Miss Allen takes Wethersby's arm. He thought she would be wearing a sour look on her face but, instead, she beamed at Lord Wethersby. Spencer supposed she thought to make him jealous. He hoped Wethersby was smart enough to stay far away from Miss Allen now—and in the future.

Lady Adalyn and Miss Goulding moved toward the town-house, leaving Spencer alone with Tessa for a moment.

"Thank you for coming to my rescue, Tessa. Might I ask why you did so?"

She chuckled. "It was the least I could do, my lord. Miss Allen is simply awful to be around. It was bad enough that I wasn't able to sit between the two of you during the lecture. I simply couldn't have you suffer further by wasting an entire teatime in her presence."

He felt his cheeks flush. "That was most uncomfortable," he said gruffly, hoping that Tessa's actions might be because she cared for him. At least a little bit. He added, "Am I really invited to tea—or will I walk into the foyer and walk back out a moment later?"

Tessa's eyes danced with mischief. "We can't have you doing that," she proclaimed. "Your carriage needs to be in front of my uncle's townhouse at least a good hour. Come along. You might as well be given tea while you wait."

Spencer took her hand and tucked it through the crook of his arm. As they mounted the stairs to head to the drawing room, he decided it had been a very good day.

CHAPTER SEVENTEEN

E XCITEMENT FILLED TESSA.
       Tonight was the opening ball of the Season. She was now dressed for the event which would take place at Lord and Lady Healey's townhouse several blocks away from her uncle's.

She wore one of her favorite new ball gowns, an elegant, sophisticated silhouette in a pale shade of blue, so pale it was the color of ice. The color served to bring out the intense blue of her eyes. Abra had dressed Tessa's hair high on her head, allowing wisps of curls to frame the sides of her face. Fortunately, she had a pearl necklace which would draw attention away from the low scoop of the gown's neckline. The piece had been a gift from her parents on her eighteenth birthday in anticipation of her come-out, which was to have occurred several months later.

The come-out would finally take place tonight and eagerness caused her belly to flutter in anticipation. She glanced into the mirror and wished she could tug the neckline of the gown up a bit. It revealed the top curve of her breasts, something she was not used to showing off. Adalyn had laughed off Tessa's complaints at Madame Chevalier's shop. Even Madame herself told Tessa that she had a lovely figure and her beautiful breasts were meant to be seen and admired.

"You want a husband, *n'est-ce pas*, Lady Tessa?" the modiste had asked. "If so, you must display your assets. You are a clever young woman but men will not want to hear talk. They will want to see. At least at first. When you find several you like and who are attracted to you physically, then you may talk with them and find the one who will capture your heart."

Madame's advice made sense. Tessa just didn't want any man to think of her only in a physical manner. Adalyn had told her a good majority of the bachelors on hand tonight wouldn't bother to make much conversation with her at all. They would attend the event to see who was now available on the Marriage Mart and if any of these ladies interested them. Physical beauty was the first thing those men would consider, according to Adalyn, though some might first focus on the size of her dowry and then her looks. Only if both interested a gentlemen would he then make an effort to get to know her.

Tessa had thought that appalling. Of course, she realized Adalyn looked at the entire process with a bit of cynicism. Years ago, she had been as idealistic as Tessa. She would need to temper her expectations, especially since she was making her come-out at a much older age than the others tonight. She wondered if she truly would find a husband this Season or if she would be like Adalyn and Louisa and return again and again without finding her soul mate.

She had finally gotten out of Adalyn that she was looking for love. Her cousin admitted that she had immensely enjoyed each of the past several Seasons but knew it was time to grow more serious, hinting this might be the Season she would finally choose a husband. As far as Louisa went, she had recently shared with Tessa that her father didn't really wish for her to wed. That she was too valuable as his hostess. He had encouraged Louisa to wait until the war with Bonaparte had ended before she became serious about finding a husband.

Tessa thought that ridiculous, especially since the war with France had dragged on for so many years already. If Louisa waited, she might find herself unwed another twenty years from now. While Louisa wasn't as outspoken as Adalyn, Tessa hoped

Louisa would finally stand up to her father and choose to follow her heart.

A knock sounded at the door and Tessa bid her cousin to enter, knowing it would be Adalyn coming to see if Tessa had finished getting ready.

Adalyn's smile told Tessa everything that she needed to know. "You look lovely," her cousin praised. "I don't believe I have ever seen a more beautiful girl making her come-out."

"Well, I am not exactly a girl anymore, am I?" Tessa said lightly. "At eighteen, I would have been that girl. Five years have passed, though, Adalyn. Much has happened which changed me. I am not that young, idealistic woman. But I do believe it is for the best. I would not have wanted to wed and then been unable to tend to Mama and Papa during their long illnesses. My allegiance, naturally, would have been with my new husband. This way, I am getting the best of both worlds. I was a dutiful daughter who cared for my parents as their health declined and I was with them to their final days. That time will always be precious to me.

"However, I believe I am stronger for the experience. I don't have stars in my eyes. I believe I will be able to search for a husband using my newfound maturity. I think girls at eighteen making their debut into Polite Society focus on how handsome their suitors are, while their families look to the man's wealth, title, and social connections. I, at my advanced age, am interested in none of those things. I want a companion who shares common interests with me. Despite what you have told me about the *ton*'s practices, I want a husband whose pledge of fidelity will last throughout our entire marriage. And I want a man who is not only eager to have children but will love them unconditionally."

She ignored the thoughts of Lord Middlefield telling her how he would adore his children.

And how he would love his wife with passion.

"You say nothing of love for yourself, Tessa," Adalyn pointed out.

"I know you have admitted to me you are looking for love,

Adalyn, but I don't really need it. Mama and Papa did not have it and their marriage was a good one. They had a mutual respect for one another. That is all I ask."

"I hope you will find everything you are looking for, Tessa—and even more. You deserve the best of everything."

"And you don't?" she asked.

"I have shared with you how much I have enjoyed not being tied down to a man. So many females my age have two—even three—children by now. I will admit I have been selfish and taken this time as mine. I have gotten to do everything I wanted and met a great many men over these last several Seasons. You also know that I am looking for love." She paused. "I suppose I am afraid I will not find it."

Adalyn's air of sadness hurt Tessa. She wanted everything good for her cousin and though she had thought Louisa might suit with a certain earl, she believed Adalyn would be an even better match—so she asked, "What of Lord Middlefield?"

Adalyn looked at her in surprise. "What of Lord Middlefield?"

"I think you and he might suit," Tessa suggested, wanting to plant that seed within Adalyn as the Season began.

Adalyn shook her head. "No. Middlefield has made his feelings clear. It is you—or no one."

Tessa bit her lip. "I don't like hearing that," she said. "While I am not as adverse to Lord Middlefield as I once was, I don't believe he is the man for me. I still believe him too cocky for his own good."

Adalyn gazed at her steadily. "I believe Lord Middlefield has deep feelings for you, Tessa. You need to give him a chance."

Her cousin moved to the mirror and glimpsed at herself and back to Tessa. "Shall we go downstairs?" she asked. "Papa expects me to be late but he knows you are always on time."

Tessa chuckled. "It is in my nature. Papa stressed to me that others' time was important and I should never infringe upon it."

They left her bedchamber, arm in arm, and headed to the staircase. As they descended and drew near the foyer, she heard voices.

A familiar voice.

Lord Middlefield's voice.

Turning to Adalyn, she gripped her arm and halted their progress. "What is Lord Middlefield doing here?"

Her cousin shrugged. "He may very well be going with us in the carriage tonight to the Healeys' ball. Sometimes, we do travel to an event with one of our neighbors. You will see how crowded it gets once we near the Healeys' townhouse. It is not unusual for our coachman to be forced to park a few blocks away while we walk the remaining distance. Papa long ago suggested that we sometimes ride with others."

Adalyn's nose wrinkled and she said, "Twice last year, we went to an event with Miss Allen and her parents. I hope not to do that the entire Season and have already told Papa of my wishes."

Adalyn tugged on Tessa's arm to pull her down the remaining stairs. Tessa wondered if it wasn't her cousin who had asked for Lord Middlefield to accompany them tonight to the ball. It wouldn't surprise her. Adalyn had subtly championed him during the past week though they had not seen the earl since their outing to the British Museum.

As they reached the bottom of the staircase, Lord Middlefield looked up. Their gazes met, his intense, and then he smiled at her. That brilliant, heartrending smile that made her knees wobble like marmalade. She resolved to resist his charms.

If such a thing might even be possible.

"Ah, the two loveliest young ladies who will attend Lord Healey's ball," her uncle said, bestowing a kind smile upon them. "You both look magnificent, don't they, Middlefield?"

The earl nodded. "I do believe Lady Adalyn and Lady Tessa will be the belles of tonight's ball," he said.

"Here I am!" her aunt called out gaily as she descended the stairs. "I did not know I would be the last to arrive." And then she looked to Tessa. "Of course, Tessa dear, you are always so very punctual. I wish Adalyn and I could be more like you."

"Shall we go?" Uncle Uxbridge asked and their party moved outside to the waiting carriage.

The footman handed her up and then Adalyn and they sat on one of the benches as her aunt and uncle entered the vehicle and sat opposite them. Tessa knew what would happen next as Lord Middlefield climbed inside and took a seat between her and Adalyn.

Her aunt and uncle talked of people who would be at to-night's ball, mentioning most of the guests who had attended the party in Lord Middlefield's honor. Tessa averted her glance, looking out the window, and seeing all the activity on the London streets as they drew near their destination. It was true that the street was congested and carriages lined the way, forcing them to walk two blocks to their destination.

They alighted from the carriage and Lord Middlefield offered his arm to both Tessa and Adalyn and they entered the Healeys' townhouse.

Tessa was caught up in all the excitement as she looked across the receiving line. The women were bedecked in jewels and beautiful gowns and the men were all attired in black evening wear. Of course, none seemed to look as handsome as Lord Middlefield did. They chatted with the people in front of them in line and then those behind them, Adalyn making the introductions since she seemed to know everyone in Polite Society.

Just before they reached their host and hostess, Tessa finally looked Lord Middlefield in the face and said, "Are you as nervous about tonight as I am?"

He nodded. "I have marched into battle with bullets flying all about me and yet the terror I feel now is nothing compared to that."

She saw he wasn't teasing with her. "You are an earl," she said firmly. "A war hero and veteran. You could take on the *ton* blindfolded and come out victorious."

He smiled wryly. "You always know just what to say, my

lady. You have bolstered my spirits considerably."

By now, they had reached Lord and Lady Healey and Adalyn graciously made the introductions. Once her aunt and uncle had also greeted their hosts, the five of them moved toward the ballroom. Tessa's nerves fluttered within her and she gripped Lord Middlefield's arm in support. He smiled down gently at her.

After they entered the ballroom, a footman handed both Adalyn and Tessa a programme. She was eager to dance tonight since she had always enjoyed doing so during the two years before she retired to nurses her parents. Of course, the waltz had not been danced at those country assemblies and Tessa had not learned the steps of the dance for her first come-out, which had never occurred. Thankfully, Adalyn had realized that omission and a dance master had been summoned during the last week to teach Tessa the dance.

She found the steps easy to master but the closeness with where her partner stood made her a bit uncomfortable. She wondered if anyone would ask her to dance the waltz tonight and how she would fare if they did so.

"I must mark down Lord Ellington for the first dance," she remarked. "He promised me he would return from the country by the time the opening ball occurred and had asked for me to reserve the opening number for him."

Tessa sensed Lord Middlefield watching as she scribbled Lord Ellington's name down.

"Might I also ask for a dance, Lady Tessa?" the earl asked formerly.

Not wanting to be churlish, she nodded. "Of course, my lord. I would be happy for us to engage in a number."

He wrote down his name and then excused himself.

Tessa watched him stride across the ballroom. So tall. So broad. So devastatingly handsome. She wondered if she might be wrong in not bothering to consider him as a suitor.

All at once, they were surrounded by gentlemen. Many, many men. Adalyn laughed and coquettishly batted her eyelashes at them as she introduced Tessa. Her cousin had warned her of a few gentlemen who might approach her. Men who truly weren't gentleman at all, but rather, rakehells. As different bachelors signed her dance card, she made certain not to allow any of those rogues to do the same. Adalyn had taught Tessa a few phrases to deflect these few exceptions and she used them with ease, glad that she was no innocent miss straight from the schoolroom who wouldn't have been able to manage as well.

Once her programme was filled, she and Adalyn continued speaking to several people. Louisa joined them, looking wonderful in a pale pink gown. Adalyn kept them moving and they visited two different groups of women. Louisa even told Tessa it would be good for her to make female friends beyond her cousins.

Though the names blurred, Tessa did like a few of the women she met and hoped to pursue a friendship with some of them.

The musicians began tuning their instruments, signaling the ball was about to open. Adalyn's partner came to claim her and her cousin told Tessa to have fun tonight. Moments later, Lord Ellington joined her. The earl's nose looked slightly swollen and the shadow of a fading bruise rested along his jaw. Otherwise, he appeared as handsome as ever.

"Ah, Lady Tessa," he said, his gaze sweeping across her admiringly. "You are a vision in this blue. I am the luckiest man at the ball to be able to claim you for this first dance. I assume you kept it open for me."

"You asked and I did so, my lord," she told him, suddenly disappointed in him for offering to spar with Lord Middlefield without informing the earl what a talented boxer he was. Though Ellington was handsome, what did that say about his character? She had told Adalyn that is what she was interested in yet had been dazzled by Lord Ellington's good looks.

His eyes gleamed and he said, "I suppose you have no other vacancies on your programme."

"I do not," Tessa told him, glad that her programme had been filled since Louisa had shared that dancing with a man more than once in a single evening allowed the *ton* to know you considered that gentleman to be a serious suitor.

"I suppose that is Lady Adalyn's doing. She is certainly looking after you," Lord Ellington noted. "Here, let me escort you to the dance floor."

He offered his arm and they moved toward where the lines were forming for the first dance. Relief filled her, knowing it would be a country dance. She wondered when the waltz would be played this evening and who her partner might be for that number.

As they made their way toward the middle, Lord Ellington said, "I do apologize for missing our trip to the park. Pressing business, you know," he added.

Tessa knew the earl fibbed to her but she never would have called him out on it. She supposed he had been humiliated enough by his defeat at the hands of Lord Middlefield. She had heard talk of the bout at different places they had gone during the past week and even seen an item in the newspaper regarding the incident. She was certain Lord Ellington had not missed seeing it, especially being holed up while his bruises healed.

Tessa lost herself in the dance, feeling the utter freedom it brought. The long years of being in the sickroom and her mourning period melted away as she went from partner to partner, enjoying herself immensely. Each time, her partner returned her to Adalyn and Louisa. Tessa supposed Adalyn had instructed them to do so and after every dance, Adalyn asked, "How was it? How was he?"

Tessa had repeatedly said it was hard to judge a man while dancing, moving about the floor so quickly, conversation almost impossible. However, several had asked to call upon her tomorrow, including Lord Ellington. At first, the earl had pressed for her to go driving with him in his phaeton tomorrow afternoon. Tessa knew not to accept his invitation, however. Adalyn had drilled into her that the day after a ball was when suitors came calling and she must always be home and available for those set hours. If a man asked her to drive in the park, she should only agree to do so after tea since the fashionable hour to be seen was from five to six.

Disappointingly, Lord Ellington had not asked for them to drive then but rather go at two o'clock. Tessa had refused him without giving a reason. At least he had asked to call tomorrow afternoon. She was interested in getting to know him a bit better, not wanting to judge him too quickly. She also wouldn't mind furthering her acquaintance with Lord Wethersby. He had been most pleasant, both at the dinner honoring Lord Middlefield and during their outing to the British Museum. They would dance the final number of the evening.

As she returned to her cousins after the most recent dance, Adalyn informed her, "This next time is the supper dance and you know after you dance it, your partner will be your companion for the supper itself. Would you care to dine with me? Lord Huxley has asked me to be his partner and he is always immense fun." A shadow crossed her face. "Even though I don't think he will settle down until his father passes on and the title is his."

Tessa said, "I will be happy to tell my next partner of your invitation." She glanced down at her card and her heart stopped.

Lord Middlefield was her next partner.

Tessa glanced up and saw him coming through the crowd, looking distinguished and by far the most handsome man in the ballroom tonight.

He reached her and said, "I hope you have enjoyed yourself this evening, my lady. Shall we?"

With that, he led her onto the dance floor. This time, no lines or squares formed. Fear struck her.

This was to be a waltz. She would be waltzing with Lord Middlefield. In his arms. Next to him.

Her mouth grew dry. Jitters overwhelmed her and she trembled.

"Is something wrong?" he asked, concern knitting his brows.

"If you are overtired, we can sit out the dance and allow you to rest."

Tessa shook her head. She was not going to be a coward. She was going to dance the waltz. Despite who her partner was.

Something told her he would dance splendidly.

CHAPTER EIGHTEEN

S PENCER HAD WAITED for this moment all evening.
No. He had waited a lifetime.

He had been agreeable to Lord Uxbridge's suggestion that they go together to the Healeys' ball. Without asking, he knew Lady Adalyn had made the suggestion to her father.

It had been six days since he had seen Tessa. The last time had been at tea after their excursion to the British Museum. He had racked his brain, trying to come up with a way to approach her. Tried to think of somewhere he could invite her. Then he had received a note from Lady Adalyn. Not directly, of course. It came via Bridget, her lady's maid, who had passed it along to Rigsby. His valet had handed it over.

In it, Lady Adalyn explained how busy Tessa would be in the days leading up to the Season, including the dance lessons she was taking in order to know how to waltz. Lady Adalyn wrote that she would continue to drop hints to Tessa, hoping her cousin would favor him with a dance at the opening ball. She begged him to be patient.

Patience had finally paid off.

He'd felt a slight warming from Tessa ever since the outing with Miss Allen and the others. How Tessa had been amused by Miss Allen's pursuit of him. She had even rescued him from having to take tea with the younger woman.

Spencer had seen Miss Allen earlier this evening, a bevy of men surrounding her. She was all smiles. He knew, though, beneath her exterior lay a vengeful woman. He hoped Tessa would watch out for Miss Allen. In the meantime, he did what he could and avoided being anywhere near her.

He had done what was expected. Danced with half a dozen young debutantes. Thank goodness most of the dances were so physically demanding that they lent themselves to little—or no—conversation. The waltz, however, was quite different. It was thrilling, to be sure, but also intimate. He would be able to hold Tessa in his arms and even speak to her if he wished.

Hearing the musicians were about to commence, Spencer took Tessa's right hand and clasped it in his left. He stepped closer and placed his right hand firmly on her back as she brought her free hand to rest on his shoulder. Her lavender scent invaded his senses as he felt the warmth of her body heat near him. It took every ounce of restraint he possessed not to yank her to him and kiss her in front of all Polite Society.

The music began and Spencer began leading Tessa. He had taken a few dance lessons when he'd arrived in London, knowing his skills were rusty and not knowing the steps of the waltz at all. The three-count had come easily to him and he liked how lightly he needed to step, rising on his toes and landing softly on the ball of his foot. Tessa, too, was light on her feet, landing softly and elegantly with each step.

They rose together with each count and fell between those counts, their steps confident as they smoothly glided about the ballroom. She was a dream to maneuver, and he began guiding her in the circular motion his dance master had recommended if Spencer managed to land a skilled partner. They turned effortlessly every third step, gliding fluidly across the ballroom floor.

He didn't speak. He didn't want to interrupt the flow of their dance. Besides, it was the supper dance and he would lead her into supper and remain with her during that break in the dancing. It would allow plenty of time to talk with her.

Spencer wanted to spend the rest of his life with this woman.

The dance came to its conclusion and he halted their steps, holding on to Tessa for a long moment after the music ceased. Her flushed cheeks made her even more attractive than usual and her bright, blue eyes sparkled.

Releasing her, he possessively captured her hand and placed it on his forearm as they shuffled along with the mass to the supper room.

"That was magical. Why, I felt as if we were floating across the room," she said with unabashed enthusiasm.

"You are a graceful dancer," he told her. "I could not imagine a more delightful partner for the waltz."

Her cheeks turned even redder and she glanced away a moment before looking back at him.

"Adalyn said she is supping with a Lord Huxley tonight and said we were invited to join them."

Concern for Lady Adalyn filled him. Spencer had encountered Huxley when he returned to Gentleman Jack's academy two days after his bout with Ellington, overhearing part of a ribald conversation the viscount had with his sparring partner in the dressing room. Huxley was most definitely a scoundrel and might take advantage of Lady Adalyn.

"What's wrong?" Tessa asked, reading his mood.

"I am acquainted with Lord Huxley's reputation. If Lady Adalyn is looking for a husband, I can assure her that the viscount has no interest in being one at this point in his life. She should be warned about him"

"Oh, dear," she said. "Adalyn is getting more serious about marriage. She told me she has had her fun and is ready to settle down."

"Then it won't be with Huxley," he told her. "But Lady Adalyn is an excellent judge of character. She will discover this on her own."

"You think her a good judge of character?

"I do. Why?"

She fought a smile. "Because she has recommended you to me the entire past week."

He flashed her a smile. "You see? I told you so. Lady Adalyn is someone you should listen to wholeheartedly."

Tessa grew serious. "I do think you will make someone a good husband one day, my lord. Just not me."

His heart sank at her words. He had already kissed her twice—and it had felt as if the heavens had moved.

What would it take to win this woman's heart?

"I agree that I will make a fine husband. You should continue to consider yourself in the running to become my countess."

She stopped, allowing others to pass them. "Why? Why are you so insistent on the two of us being matched?"

He thought a long moment. "If I could answer that, I would. I won't speak glibly to you, Tessa. I merely know that my heart has spoken to me. I think yours has also spoken to you but you aren't listening to it at the moment."

She looked at him triumphantly. "See, there you go again. Telling me what you think my heart is saying. You are quite presumptuous, Lord Middlefield. Overconfident. Smug. You think you know what is best for me whereas I believe that is a decision I alone should make."

She began walking again.

Spencer said, "I wonder why you have such a skill in twisting my words? Until I met you, no one ever accused me of being arrogant or overbearing."

"Because all of your friends are men," she said quickly. "You haven't been around many women, I'd venture. No sisters. No females at school, university, or in the army. As an officer, you were used to ordering people about, telling them what to do—and they did it. Polite Society is far different, my lord. Of course, not all the women you meet tonight or during the Season will express their opinions to you. I am fairly certain you can find any number of women to boss about. Ones who will obey you without question. Well, that isn't me, Lord Middlefield. Papa raised me to have a mind of my own."

"So, you will not be an obedient wife?" he challenged.

"No, I suspect I will," she admitted. "But my husband and I will be so like-minded that it won't seem as if I am obeying. Giving in to his whims. We will have mutual interests and mutual respect. I will want to please him. I assure you, we will get along famously."

This time, he halted their progress. Glancing around, he saw they were alone, the others ahead of them out of hearing distance.

"I thought we got along famously when we kissed."

Her cheeks heated with color. "You shouldn't be mentioning that," she said, flustered. "You definitely shouldn't—"

"Shouldn't what, Tessa? Kiss you again? Here?"

Her eyes widened as she blushed to her roots. "You wouldn't dare."

"No, I wouldn't," he agreed. "If we were seen, then it would be expected that we wed."

Confusion filled her face. "But I thought you wanted to wed me."

"I do. But I want you to come to me willingly, Tessa. To me—and my bed. I would never force your hand. I have enough self-discipline to keep from kissing you in public and forcing your hand. Barely."

He knew he looked at her wolfishly and didn't try to hide his attraction to her.

"I see." She swallowed. "You are too blunt, Lord Middlefield. Your manners could use a bit of polish."

"If you wed me, we could practice working on those manners, Tessa."

"I have no intention of wedding you, my lord, but I will comment on your manners now. I am Lady Tessa. You are Lord Middlefield. That is—"

"My name is Spencer," he interrupted, something he believed it important that she knew it. If she knew it, she might start thinking of him as Spencer and not the Earl of Middlefield.

Her lips parted as if she wished to say something further, then she clamped down as if afraid he might bend and kiss her.

"We should go find Adalyn," she said firmly.

TESSA THOUGHT LORD Middlefield impossible.

And so devastatingly attractive.

She tried to clear her mind of such dangerous thoughts. She had decided he was not for her.

Hadn't she?

Of course, she had. He was not good husband material.

Even if he did want an abundance of children. Children he said he would love and cherish. Children he would make certain got all the attention they deserved.

And a wife he would please.

She sensed her cheeks heating again.

I want you to come willingly to me, Tessa. To me—and my bed.

Thoughts of being in bed with him made her face burn. She wished she had a fan. She should have brought one. Adalyn had taught her a few ways to flirt with a fan. She would bring one next time. And flirt outrageously with a huge number of men.

Except for Spencer. No, drat it. Lord Middlefield.

Why had he told her his Christian name?

She glanced up at him as he led her across the supper room and saw that they were headed toward Adalyn and whom Tessa assumed to be Lord Huxley. He was blond, rather tall, and she guessed in his mid-twenties. As they joined the pair, Lord Huxley gave her a roguish smile.

"I already know you are Lady Tessa," he said, his eyes sweeping over her admiringly.

She sensed Spencer tense and glanced up at him, seeing his green eyes glittering in animosity. Seeking to defuse the situation, Tessa squeezed her escort's arm. His gaze met hers and he visibly relaxed.

She turned back to Lord Huxley. "Yes, I am Lady Tessa and this is the Earl of Middlefield."

"Middlefield?" Lord Huxley said, suddenly losing all interest in Tessa. "The one who soundly beat Ellington at Gentleman Jack's?" He offered his hand. "Why, it is an honor to meet you, my lord."

She watched Spencer—no, Lord Middlefield—take the offered hand and shake it.

"Please, have a seat," Adalyn said calmly.

As the four of them sat, Lord Huxley said, "Tell me about it. I have heard from others who were there."

"There is nothing to tell, my lord. Lord Ellington is quite skilled. I merely had a good day and caught the earl off-guard."

"Heard you broke his nose. That blood gushed everywhere," Lord Huxley said enthusiastically.

Spencer glowered at the man, his look silencing Lord Huxley. She had thought him not only physically powerful but saw now how even a look from him could intimidate another.

Yet she had never felt intimidated by him in the least. He had never turned such a look upon her. Only ones of interest.

And desire.

She warmed, feeling his gaze upon her now.

"Shall I bring you something back from the buffet or would you rather accompany me, my lady?" he asked.

"I would like to go and see it. Remember, I have never been to a ball before, much less a supper. Louisa tells me the food looks stupendous and is overflowing."

He took her hand and placed it upon his sleeve. "If you will excuse us, Lady Adalyn. My lord."

"Certainly," her cousin said. "By the time you return, I will have brought Lord Huxley to heel. He will be meek as a lamb and not bother you further, Lord Middlefield."

"I would appreciate that."

Spencer led Tessa toward the buffet. Tessa said, "Lord Huxley made you uncomfortable."

"He did. There is no sense rubbing it in about poor Ellington. He has suffered enough, both physically and in reputation. It's certain that everyone who was afraid to box with him before will want to do so now and he will grow weary from the number of challenges he will face."

"You sound very sympathetic toward him."

"Only up to a point."

"What point?" she asked curiously.

"My sympathy stops when it concerns Lord Ellington's interest in you."

"Oh!"

They had reached the buffet and she knew their conversation should remain private. Tessa turned her attention to the food at hand, marveling at the amount and variety. Soon, her plate was filled and they returned to the table.

Lord Huxley looked a bit contrite as they sat. He rose and helped Adalyn to her feet.

"We are going to partake in the buffet now," her cousin told them and they left.

She sampled a few savory dishes and then went straight to the sweets, saying, "They look almost too pretty to eat but I will not allow that to stop me."

"Back to Ellington," Spencer said.

Tessa wished she could stop thinking of him as Spencer but the damage had been done. He looked as a Spencer should though she had known none before tonight.

"He is good-looking and oozes self-confidence. I know he will try to court you. Be wary of him, Tessa."

"Lady Tessa," she prompted.

"Lady Tessa," he said evenly, giving her a devastating smile. "I have asked around a bit and he is not for you."

She finished chewing her bite and then said, "I would love to know why you think so, my lord."

"Spencer," he urged, ignoring her eyeroll. "Ellington is a bit of a rogue. I doubt he has begun contemplating settling down, much less thinking about children. You need someone more mature than he is."

"He is older than you. I believe thirty or so."

"Maturity does not come with age but with experience," he countered. "Lord Ellington has led an easy, soft life while I have been on my own much of mine and away at war." He paused, growing serious. "War allows a man to realize what is important, Tessa. For me, that is a wife and our family."

Oh, he was saying all the right things to worm his way into her heart yet Tessa still resisted him. Part of her wanted to believe him. Trust him. But she still worried that he was too much for her. He was very much a man, imposing and demanding. Even his very posture told of his strength and sheer physicality. She had thought she wanted a kind, affable man such as her father.

And found herself wanting this man instead.

Her admission flustered her and she glanced away, looking across the room.

"There are so many people here tonight," she remarked.

He reached and covered her hand that rested in her lap. Her eyes flew to meet his. Fortunately, they were in a corner and she doubted anyone could see that he held it.

"There is only one person here tonight that I find worth knowing. Worth spending time with. That is you, Tessa. You."

She found herself wavering and looked at him, helpless to speak.

"May I call upon you tomorrow afternoon?"

She nodded.

"And might we go riding in Hyde Park afterward?"

"Yes," she whispered.

His hand, so large and warm, squeezed hers. "Good," he pronounced.

Tessa decided she had to kiss him a third time. This time, she would refuse to be swept away by the kiss. She would analyze it—and decide if Spencer truly was husband material.

CHAPTER NINETEEN

T ESSA SLEPT LATER than she normally did, missing her daily early morning walk and breakfast with her uncle. Because of that, she rang for Abra and asked her maid to bring breakfast to the bedchamber instead. Although she would miss taking the morning meal with her uncle, with the Season now beginning, it might make more sense for her to eat alone in the future. She did not want the staff to go to extra trouble and thought she would speak to Cook about providing a tray as was done for Adalyn and her mother, at least on the mornings after a ball. She still hoped to get up and walk for a bit of exercise and to clear her head on the mornings after events that did not last until the wee hours of the morning, such as tonight's musicale.

Abra returned with the tray and set it across Tessa's lap. She had remained in bed, a luxury she normally did not partake in. Usually when she awoke each day, she rose and met the day head on. The Season was already changing her daily habits with its late nights. For a moment, she longed for the quiet of the country.

Abra kept Tessa company as she ate, asking her all about last night's ball. Tessa told the servant about the many gorgeous gowns and jewels she had seen, as well as describing the lavish buffet and some of the items she had eaten.

"It all sounds amazing, my lady," Abra commented. "But what of the gentlemen there? Did you dance much?"

"I did. Thanks to Adalyn and Louisa, to some extent, my cousins made certain that my dance card was filled." She paused and then smiled as she added, "I even danced the waltz."

"The waltz?" Abra asked. "I have heard it to be a most unusual dance. What's it like? Why is it so different?"

Tessa thought back to being in Spencer's strong arms.

"I was used to dancing country dances at assemblies I attended before my parents fell ill," Tessa explained. "Have you ever danced, Abra?"

"No, my lady. Sometimes, someone who had had a bit too much to drink at the pub would stand and try to dance some kind of jig but I have never seen or danced myself."

Tessa explained the configuration of the quadrille and some other dances. How you had a partner but moved around the room, engaging with many others during the dance.

"The waltz is like none of these," she said. "Here, I will demonstrate."

Tessa removed the tray from her lap and set it aside. She tossed back the bedclothes and stood, motioning for Abra to come nearer.

"Hold your hand as thus," she said, making Abra the female and Tessa the male who would lead.

She clasped Abra's hand and placed her hand on the maid's back, telling the servant to put her free hand on Tessa's shoulder.

"Oh, my! Abra proclaimed. "We certainly are close."

"The steps go as thus," Tessa explained and began showing the maid, walking Abra through them.

After a few minutes, Abra understood the basics of the waltz and Tessa began to hum a tune. The pair danced about the bedchamber until giggles overtook Abra and she stepped away from Tessa, laughing.

"My, that is something else, my lady," the maid declared. "How often do they dance this number?" she asked.

"Louisa told me it is played once or twice during an evening at a *ton* ball," Tessa shared. "Last night, it was the dance known as the supper dance. Whoever your partner is for it, you dance the number with him and then he leads you into supper. It also was the final dance of the evening."

Abra pressed. "So, who did you dance these two waltzes with? And how did they make you feel?"

"The supper dance was with Lord Middlefield, while the last dance my partner was Lord Wethersby."

Abra's eyes widened. "So, you knew your two dance partners at least. It might have been awkward having only met a gentleman for the first time."

Tessa had thought the same thing. And while she had enjoyed dancing with Lord Wethersby, when she looked back on the evening of her first ball, her memories would always be of Spencer and their waltz.

"I should dress for the day," she said briskly, setting aside ideas of the man she wanted and yet was still reluctant to allow as her suitor. "Choose a day dress for me if you would. A flattering one because I am to receive many callers this afternoon."

Abra's eyes lit with interest. "Might Lord Middlefield be one of these callers?" she inquired. "You did not answer my previous question, my lady. How was your dance with Lord Middlefield?"

"It was marvelous," she admitted. "Lord Middlefield is light on his feet and moved me about the ballroom floor with ease. I felt lighter than air. As if he and I danced upon a cloud."

Her maid gave her a knowing look. "It sounds as if you might be giving Lord Middlefield consideration after all."

Tessa nodded. "Perhaps I judged him a bit too hastily," she admitted, wavering. "I have determined to reconsider my previous position on his suit." Her words startled her because she hadn't known she had decided to until she spoke them aloud.

Abra clapped in delight. "I am very happy to hear that, my lady. If anyone should have cause to dislike the earl, you know it would be me. I don't, though—and I don't think you should either."

"Lord Middlefield has said a few things to me that make me

believe he might be different from my first impression."

"Well, he is as handsome as sin," Abra declared, "and an earl, to boot. That would be enough for me. Do you know how much land he owns?" the maid asked. "Or anything about how much money he has?"

"I don't. I don't care to know any of that. I am more interested in his character."

Abra nodded sagely. "You're a special one, my lady," the servant declared. "I doubt many women in society would think as you do."

The servant moved toward the wardrobe. "I think today we should choose the pale yellow, don't you?"

Tessa nodded absent-mindedly, her thoughts centering once again on Spencer. She continued thinking about him the rest of the morning. Adalyn came to Tessa's bedchamber and encouraged her to come downstairs to the drawing room to see what was there.

The moment Tessa entered, her nostrils were invaded by the sweet smell emanating from the many bouquets scattered about the room.

"Some are for me," Adalyn pointed out. "The large majority are for you, however," her cousin stated. "It seems you made quite an impression on a good number of gentlemen."

She walked about the room, looking at the various bouquets, seeing cards attached to them. She read each one, trying to picture the gentleman who had sent it as she did so. It did not surprise her that the largest arrangement came from Lord Ellington. While he interested her, she did not believe he had the depth that Spencer possessed. She also recalled Spencer's warning of Lord Ellington being a rogue and found herself souring on him.

After viewing all the flowers in the room, she realized Spencer had not sent any. She tried to swallow the pang of disappointment. Then she realized he might not even know it was custom to send a bouquet to a lady in order to show his interest in her. He had no mother or sisters who could have spoken of the practice to him. He had never attended a single *ton* event. All his friends were still away at war. Sympathy filled her, thinking how alone he truly was.

Their callers arrived in batches, some there to visit her while others came to see Adalyn. Before they arrived, Tessa had asked her cousin if any one gentleman stood out from the crowd last night. Adalyn had shaken her head and turned away. Tessa desperately hoped Adalyn could find happiness with the right man, hopefully this Season. For a moment, she questioned herself, once again thinking Adalyn might make a better match for Spencer than she did.

Spencer arrived at the tail end of calling hours. She had feared he wouldn't come at all and instead wait until it was time to drive through Hyde Park together. After the butler announced his arrival, Tessa watched him enter the drawing room, his eyes sweeping over it. A dull flush settled on his cheeks as he realized the faux pas he had made. Quickly, he turned and exited the room.

Excusing herself, Tessa went after him. She hurried down the long corridor, trying to catch up to him, but his long stride had him reach the staircase long before she did. She bunched her skirts in her hands, raising them some, and began to run after him. She reached the staircase and hurried down the first flight, seeing him turn in front of her.

"Spencer!" she called out, aware she used his first name and not his title.

He paused on the landing, looking over his shoulder, and gave her a crooked smile. He waited as she scampered down the flight of stairs, pausing on the last step, looking him directly in the eyes.

"Why are you leaving?" she asked. "Please tell me it is not over some silly flower arrangement."

His eyes darkened. "Or lack of a bouquet?" he asked. "I had no idea it was the expected practice to send flowers. I know now and was leaving to remedy that fact."

Her heart quickened. His words revealed he had not called on any other woman that afternoon, else he would have seen bouquets when he had arrived there.

Boldly, she reached for his hand and took it. As always, being near and even touching him, flooded her with warmth.

"Please, return to the drawing room with me," she begged. "I don't need flowers from you." She swallowed, her gaze direct. "I only need you," she whispered, and then added, "your company, that is."

He gave her one of his rare smiles, which always seemed to touch her heart.

"If you insist," he said.

She turned to go but he held her hand tightly, pulling her back until she faced him.

"Thank you," he said softly. "For coming after me. For pretending you aren't disappointed that I was too ill-mannered to realize I was supposed to send you flowers."

Tessa gazed into his eyes, losing herself in their green depths. "I meant what I said," she said firmly. "Your company is more than enough for me." She gave him a smile. "I look forward to our drive in the park this afternoon. I hope you will stay and take tea with us. It would be foolish for you to leave and return home, simply to return an hour later."

His thumb stroked the underside of her wrist, causing Tessa to catch her breath. She felt her lips tingle, wanting to kiss him right here. It took all her self-discipline not to fling herself at him.

"Come along," she said brightly, her voice trembling.

Spencer released her hand and accompanied her back to the drawing room. They joined the two gentlemen she had abandoned and she thanked Adalyn for keeping them entertained during her absence. At the moment, Tessa could not remember either of their names. All her thoughts centered on Spencer and what his touch did to her.

The two callers made their departure, leaving Spencer the only visitor in the drawing room. Tessa looked to her aunt, who had been sitting in a corner of the room with her needlework, acting as chaperone for both Adalyn and Tessa.

"I have asked Lord Middlefield to stay for tea if that is all right with you, Aunt," she said. "We are to drive in the park afterward and I thought it would be convenient if he remained."

Her aunt set aside the needlepoint and rose, giving Spencer a warm smile. "We would be delighted to entertain you at tea, my lord. It should arrive any moment—as well as Uxbridge. I know he will be glad to see you."

At that moment, her uncle entered the drawing room. He sniffed once in disgust and joined them.

Looking at Spencer, her uncle said, "I hide in my study afternoons during the Season," he explained. "I dislike the smell of all these flowers and I dislike all these young bucks invading my home even more."

Adalyn went and slipped her arm through her father's. "Oh, Papa, you say this every year."

"If you would wed, then all these visitors could be at your house with you and your husband," he said gruffly. "And my home would be my own once more."

"Wouldn't you miss me, Papa?"

"You could always come visit. I hope you will do so often, my child, once you are wed and gone."

Tessa saw the sadness on her cousin's face and wanted to dispel it. Adalyn was one of the kindest people she knew. She couldn't understand why Adalyn couldn't seem to find a husband. Knowing her cousin wanted a love match and would settle for nothing less, she prayed it would happen soon.

The teacart arrived and her uncle pointed out all his favorites to Spencer, insisting that he try each one. It pleased Tessa that he humored Uncle Uxbridge, another point in Spencer's favor. She somehow doubted Lord Ellington would be as patient with the older man.

"It is time the two of you leave," her aunt said. "Else the park will be so full you won't even be able to drive your carriage through it."

"My phaeton, actually," Spencer said.

"We are to ride in a phaeton?" Tessa asked.

He grinned. "I found that I actually owned one. Took it out yesterday to get a feel for it. If you are willing to place your hands in those of a novice, we can use it. If not, my curricle is available to us."

She would never tell him he did everything well merely to keep his ego in check, believing he would handle the vehicle as superbly as he seemed to do everything else.

"If you experience any difficulties, I will take the reins," she proclaimed.

Everyone laughed and Spencer rose, offering her his hand. She placed hers in his, her heart skipping a beat as she did so.

"Will we see you at tonight's musicale, my lord?" Adalyn asked. "At Lord and Lady Rexford's?"

Spencer looked down at her. "Are you planning to attend?"

Tessa nodded.

"I will be there," he confirmed. "Shall we depart, Lady Tessa?"

Leading her downstairs, she saw Abra awaited with Tessa's bonnet and reticule.

"I brought a shawl, my lady, but the afternoon's warmed up and I don't think you'll need it."

"I'll take it all the same," she told the maid. "I would better be prepared than cold."

As she turned, she caught Spencer eyeing her and she grew warm all over.

"On second thought, you are right, Abra. I think I will leave the shawl behind."

After all, she would be seated next to the earl, who seemed to radiate heat like a furnace.

Abra placed the bonnet on Tessa's head and she tied the ribbons in place before accepting her reticule.

"Lead the way, my lord," she told Spencer.

They left the townhouse and she saw the gleaming phaeton standing next to the pavement. An elegant pair of solid black horses were attached to it. It surprised her how large the wheels were and how very little of the actual carriage there was.

"This is rather grand," she commented.

"And rather fun," he told her, climbing up into the vehicle and turning back to her.

He bent and grasped her waist, lifting her with ease as he placed her on the seat. Joining her, she heard the blood pounding in her ears as she realized how close their contact would be. Her entire side was nestled against his, the intimacy daunting.

And very appealing.

Spencer took up the reins and clucked his tongue and the pair of horses began trotting away.

"This is a long way from the ground," she commented. "And those wheels are incredible in size."

"The higher perch makes for bigger wheels. That allows for greater speed. I gather racing phaetons is something common for gentlemen of the *ton*."

"Would your ever race?" she asked him, already worried about his inexperience with the vehicle, though he seemed to be handling it with ease.

"No. I don't see the point in those kinds of competitions. It would be too easy for the phaeton to turn over, injuring the horses."

"Or you," she pointed out.

Spencer glanced to her. "Would that upset you? If I were to be injured?"

She looked away and faced the road ahead. "It would upset me if anyone of my acquaintance were to be injured," she said primly, ignoring his chuckling.

As they reached the park, Tessa saw the line of vehicles trying to enter. Dismay filled her. He seemed in tune with her feelings and slowed the phaeton before pulling it to the side of the street and bringing it to a complete halt.

"Do you not wish to drive through the park? It is the fashionable hour." He paused. "Or would you rather not be seen in my company?"

"No, it isn't that at all," she reassured him. "It is . . . so congested. My idea had been to take in this lovely day in an openaired vehicle and enjoy good conversation as we enjoyed the weather." Her nose crinkled. "With the road so clogged and so many people there, the idea of a drive doesn't appeal to me much anymore."

"You don't wish to be around others?"

Tessa laughed. "I got my fill of being around others in the crowded ballroom last night. As much as I enjoy dancing, there were times I wished I had a bit of elbow room."

"I agree. And with my calendar full of events, I fear getting a moment's respite from crowds will be hard to come by." He paused. "I have another idea, though. One which would help us to enjoy the day and the ride. Do you trust me?"

God help her, she did. "Yes."

A slow smile caused his mouth to turn up. "Then you are in for a treat."

CHAPTER TWENTY

S PENCER BYPASSED THE entrance to Hyde Park, the tension melting away the further they went from the crowds.

As they drove, he said, "I hadn't realized it until I came back to England but I don't like large groups of people." He paused and then added, "I think it is the war. It changed me in ways I am only beginning to realize."

"How so?" Tessa asked.

He glanced down at her and saw she was truly interested.

"Being around others never bothered me much growing up. As a boy in public school, you soon learn there is nothing such as privacy. I did savor returning to Stoneridge, though, whenever I had a holiday. It is located in Kent, which I believe is the loveliest place in all of England. I would roam the estate all day. Being out in nature seemed to renew me."

"I know what you mean," she said. "As much as I liked coming to London with Papa and Mama for a few months each year, I prefer the country. How do you think the war has changed you, Spencer?"

"It certainly hardened me. I had never seen anyone die before I arrived on the Continent. Death became commonplace. I had to steel myself against it." He thought a moment. "It is as if I erected a barrier between what I saw and what I could allow to affect me. I trained men to go into battle. I led them into the firefight. And then I saw their lifeless, broken, bloodied bodies after the conflict ended."

He shuddered. "As their commanding officer, it was my duty to write to the families to inform them of their loved one's death. I cannot tell you the number of times I had to pick up my quill and write the same words, trying to give the receiver of my letter solace and let them know how bravely that soldier had performed. How his death contributed to the war effort and England's eventual victory."

Tessa placed her hand on his arm. "That must have been terrible. Seeing men fall. Having to watch them die. Writing their families. And then doing it over and over again."

"It was quite difficult," he admitted, liking the feel of her hand on his arm.

Especially liking that she left it there.

"The countryside of Spain was beautiful and yet I grew to hate it. We studied maps of the area. Sent out scouts and received their reports. Planned and plotted our next attack. We did the same things, over and over, with very little favorable results."

"Do you believe this war will ever end?" she asked softly.

"Eventually. The casualties will grow too great to continue justifying battles to continue occurring. Or the government will spend too much money and simply run out. It all boils down to the Little Corporal."

"Bonaparte?" she asked.

Spencer nodded. "He is mad. There is no doubt about it. Mad—hungry—for power. He has a vision of all of Europe being in his control. Even beyond. He must be stopped. If he is—if he can be captured or killed—I know we could talk sense into his generals. This has gone on far too long."

He sighed. "I despise loud noises now. Probably from my time on the battlefield and hearing all the cannons firing. I hate being around crowds, as well. Most likely because I couldn't avoid them in the army. It has been very difficult for me to be in London. The streets teeming with people. The barrage of carriages. Even the swell of the *ton* at last night's ball almost overwhelmed me. I look forward to the day I can return to the country."

Left unsaid was he wanted to do so with his bride.

Spencer had sensed a softening in Tessa. He would need to tread carefully so as not to chase her away. She almost seemed within his reach. Perhaps one more kiss might convince her.

He looked to the road ahead and said as they passed it, "That is Tattersalls. They sell the best horseflesh in London. I came here the other day with Lord Wethersby."

"I remember you discussing that plan. Did you buy any horses?"

"No, but I am thinking of doing so."

He thought of a beautiful mare that he had seen, her lines fine and her chestnut coat glossy. The horse would make a fine wedding gift.

"Do you ride?" he asked, ready to satisfy his curiosity.

She chuckled. "You cannot live in the country and not do so. At least, I couldn't. Papa was always out on the estate and I was always with him. I rode from a young age. I gave it up when I nursed my parents although I have since begun riding again ever since I moved in with Uncle Uxbridge."

"Was it hard being turned from your home by the new Lord Paxton?"

Tessa thought a moment and then said, "It was—and it wasn't. I had grown up at Oakley and so it was home. With Papa and Mama gone, however, nothing truly tied me to the estate. My cousin's wife made it perfectly clear it was her home now. She wanted no interference from a daughter of the house. I am fortunate my uncle—Mama's brother—took me in."

Spencer decided he would confront this Lord Paxton on Tessa's behalf.

He turned the carriage north and said, "Since Tattersalls is on the edge of London, I ventured out a bit after Lord Wethersby concluded his business. It was nice to escape the noise and smells of London. I enjoyed it so much that I brought this phaeton here yesterday to indulge in the peace and quiet."

They had only traveled a few minutes from Tattersalls and yet they had quickly left London behind. Wide open spaces appeared to the left and a grove of trees emerged on the right.

Slowing the horses some, he said, "I hope this is more to your liking, Tessa."

Her hand had remained on his arm, wrapped about it just above his elbow. The warmth of her touch permeated his body.

She smiled. "This is much more what a drive should be like. I can hear myself think." She inhaled deeply. "The air already smells sweeter. I truly despise the vile smells of town. How wonderful to find this oasis such a short way from town."

Spencer continued another minute and then steered the phaeton just off the road, coming to a stop next to the woods.

"Would you like to get out and stretch your legs?" he asked.

"That would be delightful," she told him.

Climbing from the high perch first, he then reached up and captured her waist, swinging her down. When her feet came to the ground, he didn't release her. He didn't want to. He wanted to hold this woman forever.

He saw her swallow, her large eyes gazing up at him. Then she wet her lips and desire filled him. He bent and briefly touched his lips to hers, merely grazing them. Wanting more but not sure if he should take it in broad daylight. Though they had seen no one on the road, another carriage or even cart could come by at any moment.

Instead, he took her hand in his, lacing his fingers through hers, and led her the slight distance to the trees. He entered the dense wood, the trees so quick that they filtered out most of the sunlight, and stopped at an enormous oak.

"I want to kiss you again, Tessa," he said, his voice rough and raw.

"I want to kiss you, too, Spencer," she replied, surprising him. "I decided I needed to."

"Why?" he asked.

"To see if you are the one for me."

This time, he was the one who swallowed hard. He knew he had heard her words but they still stunned him, nonetheless. His hands went to her waist again.

"What changed your mind?"

"You," she said softly. "You are not the man I first thought you were. I am afraid I judged you too quickly—and too harshly. You are more thoughtful than I first believed." Smiling, she said, "You are still a bit overbearing but you have grown on me, Spencer. And . . . I quite like how you kiss me."

"You said you needed to kiss me."

She nodded. "I think kissing is an important part of marriage, don't you?"

"I couldn't agree more." He glanced around. "We won't be fearful of being interrupted."

"That should help," she agreed. "I like when you have kissed me. I think you have held back some, though. I want you to kiss me the way you would kiss your wife. I need to see what that would be like. Can you do that?"

"I think I could kiss you all day," he admitted.

"What are you waiting for?"

His mouth slammed down on hers. He had been gentle before and would ease up soon. But now desire filled him. Spencer wanted Tessa to see just how much he did want her. How sparks could fly between a couple.

How they were truly meant to be together.

Forever.

He branded her as his, his tongue sweeping inside her mouth and mating with hers. She answered his call, as hungry for him as he was for her. She tasted like spring—fresh, clean, and warm. His hands tightened on her waist and he maneuvered her until her back rested against the old oak. Her palms had gone to his chest and stroked him, enflaming his need for her. As he kissed her, his thumbs began stroking her ribcage, feeling the tremors that ran through her.

Spencer wanted her. All of her. He wouldn't take her here in the open. But he would show her a taste of what marriage could be.

As he plundered her mouth, his hands moved up to her breasts, kneading them, the pads of his thumbs brushing back and forth against her nipples. They hardened into tight buds and he rolled them between his fingers, tweaking them lightly, hearing her gasp of pleasure.

He broke the kiss and moved his mouth down the long column of her slender throat, finding the pulse point as it fluttered wildly. He nipped her there, wanting to leave his mark on her, then soothing the bite with his tongue. His tongue glided down her throat and to the top of the curve of her breast, tracing the curve as he kneaded the breast. Little sounds came from her, which fanned the flames of his desire.

Spencer used his thumbnails to tease her nipples and then flicked his tongue along one. Tessa gasped. He pushed her gown lower until his tongue reached the nipple, toying with it as he flicked it back and forth. She clutched his shoulders and murmured something as he took the tight bud into his mouth and sucked hard. Her body jerked and trembled and he sucked even harder. He felt her hips move and wanted nothing more than to bury himself within her. But he wouldn't.

He would merely continue the lesson in love.

As he continued devouring her breast, his fingers slid down her hips to her thighs, stroking them. Tessa squirmed now and he abandoned her breast, kissing his way back up to her lips. This time, he sucked on the lower one, then bit into it. She moaned and clutched him. He continued his assault on her mouth as he maneuvered her gown higher, wanting to touch the tender flesh beneath it. Finding her thigh, he glided his fingers up and down it, each time moving closer to his final goal.

He touched her sex and she broke the kiss.

"Oh!"

Spencer gazed at her, seeing her eyes darkened to a deep blue that was almost black.

"Oh, is right, my love."

As he gazed into her eyes, he moved a finger teasingly back and forth across the seam of her sex. Her eyes widened as he pushed a finger inside.

"Oh!" she repeated, blinking rapidly.

He smiled wolfishly. "Oh, again."

When she averted her glance, he said, "No. Look at me."

Her gaze met his again and he began moving his finger, allowing another to join it. He had her pinned against the tree now, his body pressed to hers, his fingers stroking long and deep.

"What are you doing?" she managed to get out.

"Giving you pleasure. Making you come."

"Come?" she asked and sucked in a quick breath.

"It is called orgasm. I plan to give you many of them."

"Oh!"

He grinned.

And found the sweet bud. Though he longed to taste it, he didn't want to frighten her with too much passion. His fingers would be enough. Spencer rolled his finger against it and began a circular motion. Tessa began moving against him, moaning, then bucking against his hand. He increased the pressure and then the pace, seeing she was close.

"Give in to it," he urged. "Take a leap of faith and jump off that precipice."

She did.

A cry came from her lips and he captured her mouth with his, plunging his tongue deep inside her mouth as she moved against him. He felt her tighten, squeezing his fingers, the tremors pulsating as she bucked against him.

"Yes," he said, breaking the kiss. "Fly, Tessa. Fly!"

Finally, she ceased moving, growing limp. He removed his hand from under her skirts and took her waist again, holding her in place as he ravaged her mouth a final time. Never had Spencer wanted to consume a woman as he did Tessa. She was life itself to him. He had to have her.

And he would.

Breaking the kiss, he studied her and then commanded, "Open your eyes."

She did so, the blue depths blazing even as she wore a dazed expression.

"You are mine now, Tessa. No one else's."

She nodded.

"I want you to say it."

"I am yours," she told him. "And you are mine." Her hands came up and framed his face. "We are each other's."

Spencer liked that. "We belong to one another. We will wed."

She smiled wryly. "There you go. Telling me what to do again. You should at least ask me, Spencer."

"I would do anything to please you," he said earnestly.

Dropping to one knee, he took her hands in his and gazed up into the face of the woman he loved.

Yes, loved.

He didn't know when it had happened. He wouldn't question how. Spencer only knew that he loved Tessa Foster fiercely and would go to the ends of the earth for her.

"Tessa, I love you. I won't hide that fact from you."

Her jaw dropped.

"I want to marry you. I want you to be my countess. I want to make a family with you. I want to go to sleep with you in my arms and awaken and find you still there. I want to grow old with you. And, God, I want to kiss you every minute of every day."

She beamed at him. "I love you, Spencer. I didn't know I did until just now. But I know my love is true and everlasting."

"Be mine, Tessa. Be my wife and my life. Will you do that?"

"Yes. A thousand times yes!"

Spencer sprang to his feet.

And kissed her again.

CHAPTER TWENTY-ONE

A S SPENCER'S STRONG hands clasped Tessa about her waist, she felt a warm surge ripple through her. He placed her upon the phaeton's seat and joined her there, taking up the reins. He flicked his wrists and the horses came to life, starting up. He maneuvered them so that they faced the opposite direction and they returned the way they had come, back toward Tattersalls and then London itself.

So many feelings filled her. Feelings for the man beside her and for what he had done to and for her. She hadn't dreamed she could feel the way she did as he had touched her so intimately.

"Will it all be so wonderful?" she asked.

Spencer looked down at her and Tessa saw love for her shining in his eyes. Had it always been there and she had missed seeing it or, like her, had Spencer just discovered the depth of his feelings when they had kissed?

"It will only get better," he promised. "You got but a small taste today of what physical love can be," he said. "The fact that we add emotional love to the mix will make the physical ties between us grow even stronger over time."

"How do you know this?" she asked. And then hesitantly added, "Have you ever been in love before?"

"Never," he assured her. "And I never thought I would be in love. That I would find something so ethereal.

"Until I found you."

A glow filled her, spreading throughout her until it reached even the tips of her fingers and toes.

He continued, "You have much to learn about lovemaking, Tessa. Kissing is a huge part of it."

"Well, I certainly enjoy kissing. Especially kissing you," she added, laughing. "I have never kissed any man before you and now I know I never will." She placed her hand on his arm. "I mean that, Spencer. The depth of my feelings for you already surprises me. But my heart tells me it will only grow over time."

She saw the gleam in his eyes as he said, "I have only begun to kiss you, Tessa. I have only kissed you a few places. I plan to kiss you everywhere." He paused, his gaze intense. "And I do mean everywhere."

She felt her cheeks reddening, thinking of places she would like him to kiss. To touch.

"I plan to educate you thoroughly," he explained. "I will kiss your eyelids. Your elbows. Your belly, where you will carry our babes. I will kiss you gently. With fervor. With more passion than you can imagine now—but you will know what I speak of soon."

He waggled his eyebrows and added, "And I plan to taste you everywhere."

"Everywhere?" she squeaked, her thoughts turning wicked.

"Everywhere," he said resolutely. "Kissing will be a huge part of our lives. It may even take up a majority of our days."

Her cheeks now burned but she boldly asked, "Will I be able to also kiss you everywhere?"

Spencer laughed rich and hearty, a sound she enjoyed hearing now and knew she would love to grow to love over the years.

"You are inquisitive. I'll give you that," he said. "And if your curiosity extends to my naked body, then you may have at it, my love. Through exploration, we will each find what pleases the other. Just like today when I discovered a few things that please you."

Tessa grew hot all over, thinking of his fingers inside her, moving, stroking, pleasuring her. "I am eager for you to educate me, my earl," she told him flirtatiously, and slipped her arm possessively through his.

They drove the remainder of the way to Mayfair in silence, happiness blanketing her. When they arrived at the Uxbridge townhouse, she told him, "You must come inside. We must tell Adalyn and my aunt and uncle of our betrothal."

"You don't think they will believe it to be too soon?" he asked, suddenly lacking in confidence, which touched her.

"They will be thrilled for us," she assured him. "All they and my parents ever wanted for me was to find happiness with a good man. I have done so with you, Spencer. I cannot imagine any man who could make me as deliriously happy as you have."

"I feel the same way about you, Tessa," he said solemnly. "You are my present and my future. If you are ready, let us go share our good news."

She had him drive the phaeton back to his townhouse and leave it there. Together, they crossed the square to her uncle's townhouse and were greeted by Rainey.

"Where are Lord and Lady Uxbridge?" she asked the butler.

"Lord Uxbridge is in his study, my lady, while Lady Uxbridge and Lady Adalyn are in their bedchambers."

"Thank you," she said, looking to Spencer. "Why don't you go find Uncle Uxbridge and tell him we need to speak with him? Bring him to the library if you would."

Spencer caught her elbow as she turned away and pulled her back toward him. "I will."

"What?" she asked. "Why are you looking at me like that?"

"Because it is the first time we are parting since becoming engaged. I am loath to separate from you."

She laughed, thinking him quite romantic. "You are most amusing. Now go. I will fetch my aunt and Adalyn."

This time as Tessa turned, Spencer caught her wrist and pulled her to him again. But he didn't merely study her. He bent and brushed his lips softly against hers in a sweet, lingering kiss.

When he released her, she didn't even bother to glance about and see if any of the servants had seen them kiss or not. She didn't care.

She was in love.

Tessa danced up the stairs, going first to her aunt's rooms and knocking upon the door. When she was bidden to enter, she did and told her aunt she had something of great importance to discuss with her in the library.

Her aunt bit back a smile. "I would guess at your news but I see you want to share it with all of us at the same time."

Tessa nodded. "You understand me well. You always have. Why don't you go to the library, Tessa? I will fetch Adalyn and we will be there shortly. If you go to her now, she will get it out of you."

"I am certain you are correct." She chuckled. "Very well, I will see you downstairs."

Entering the library, she saw her uncle already present with Spencer and crossed to them.

"Do I need to send for champagne?" Uncle Uxbridge asked, his eyes full of mischief.

"It wouldn't hurt," she said loftily. "I think a glass of champagne would be just the thing."

Her uncle rang and Rainey appeared.

"Champagne for five, Rainey. As soon as possible."

The butler smiled broadly at Tessa and said, "Right away, my lord," quickly exiting the room.

Adalyn entered with her mother in tow and said, "What is going on? Bridget was trying a new hairstyle out on me for this evening but Mama insisted I come to the library with her immediately." Her cousin's eyes flicked from Tessa to Spencer and back to Tessa again. She gasped. "Don't tell me. You are—"

"Engaged," Tessa provided. "And very happy about it," she added.

Hearty congratulations occurred and, soon after, Rainey appeared with the champagne.

Her uncle raised his glass and said, "Your parents would have been so pleased at this news, Tessa, just as your aunt and I are happy, as well. You are a daughter to us and I hope you will do me the honor of allowing me to escort you down the aisle whenever the time comes."

She glanced to Spencer. "We haven't even talked about dates," she said anxiously. "What are your thoughts?"

Spencer took her hands in his and squeezed them. "My thoughts are to find out how and when I might be able to purchase a special license."

Everyone laughed and Tessa said, "So, you want to marry quickly?"

"It would be my desire to do so but I will not deny you the Season you never had, much less a wedding you have always dreamed of."

"I don't really care about the Season anymore," she admitted. "All I care about is becoming your wife. I have never dreamed of a large *ton* wedding and, in fact, I would prefer it be much smaller. Perhaps we might have it here and the wedding breakfast, as well."

She looked to her aunt. "Would that be agreeable with you?"

Her aunt beamed. "We are happy to host your wedding, my dear." She looked up at Spencer and said, "If you could give us a week, my lord. It takes time to bake a cake and prepare other foods for the wedding breakfast. I will need to know your favorites to serve. I already know Tessa's preferences."

Glancing back to Tessa, her aunt added, "We must think of the dress which can serve as your wedding gown. A week is too soon to have a new one made up but you have several you may choose from that you had created for the Season."

Adalyn said, "Oh, I know exactly which one Tessa should wear."

"Which one?" she asked.

Her cousin shook her head adamantly. "Not in front of his lordship. It is to remain a surprise. But I know he will admire you in it."

Tessa glanced to Spencer. The look on his face told her he would admire in—or out of—any gown chosen and she blushed profusely.

Uncle Uxbridge asked, "When would you like us to announce your betrothal? Of course, we will place the announcement in the newspapers."

"It might be nice to do so at tonight's musicale," Adalyn suggested. "It will be a smaller, more select group in attendance. They would feel privileged to hear of the first betrothal and wedding to occur this Season." Then she told Tessa, "I will write up the wedding announcement for you and get it to the papers tomorrow. It will be printed in the following day's editions. Is that agreeable?"

"Whatever you wish to do, Adalyn," Tessa said. "I am fairly ignorant of how Polite Society manages these kinds of things."

"Will you remain in London for the rest of the Season?" her cousin asked Spencer. "Or will you leave on your honeymoon instead?"

Spencer said, "I believe we should stay at least another month. I want to give Tessa the opportunity of attending several societal affairs. I also would like the chance to accompany her to the opera and perhaps a play or two. Then we can leave town."

He looked to her. "Is that acceptable to you?"

"That would be lovely," she told him. "It will give me enough of a taste of the Season and then we can escape London for Stoneridge."

"No honeymoon?" he asked.

"Being at Stoneridge will be honeymoon enough," she said emphatically even as her cheeks pinkened with thoughts of their wedding night.

Adalyn clapped her hands. "Oh! It is a love match," she declared. "Who would have thought so?"

"I should leave and allow you to dress for this evening's event," Spencer said. He took her hands and lifted them, pressing a tender kiss upon her knuckles.

Tessa thought of him saying he would kiss her in many places and decided this was the start of that.

After Spencer left, Adalyn took Tessa's hand. "Come. I want to show you which gown I believe you should wear on your wedding day. Next week!" she squealed.

The two cousins hurried up the stairs, Tessa's heart as light as her feet.

In a week, she would become Spencer's wife.

CHAPTER TWENTY-TWO

T ESSA DRESSED WITH care, knowing she would be an object of interest tonight once her betrothal was announced. She had shared her news with Abra, who already had learned of the engagement, thanks to the gossip which had spread throughout the kitchens after Rainey had said Lord Uxbridge called for champagne to celebrate.

"I believe you should wear the sky blue gown tonight, my lady," Abra recommended. "You look well in any shade of blue, but particularly this one."

"As always, I put myself in your hands, Abra."

Tessa gazed into the mirror after dressing, watching Abra style her hair very simply this evening. Once more, she called for her pearls, wanting her parents to be with her tonight in the sharing of this happy news with others. She only wished they could have met Spencer and seen how happy she now was.

Adalyn arrived and told her that it was time to leave for the musicale. When they arrived in the foyer, Tessa saw Spencer present. Her heartbeat sped up merely at the sight of him.

He came to her and took her hands in his. "Ready for to-night?" he asked.

"I am ready for tonight—and every night that follows," she told him boldly.

A slow smile spread across his face and he tucked her hand

into his arm, escorting her to the waiting carriage. Inside, she sat next to him, relishing the warmth of him against her. For the life of her, she couldn't remember why she had objected to him and his suit so much. Though it hadn't happened that long ago, the day they met when he came to her rescue seemed a very long time ago.

They arrived at Lord and Lady Rexford's townhouse. As she descended from the carriage with Spencer's help, Tessa noticed though there were many carriages about, it was considerably less crowded than the previous night's ball.

Her fiancé led her to the entrance and said, "I think we are both relieved there won't be a mass of people waiting within."

"I am grateful for that," she replied. "It also reassures me that we are like-minded."

He grinned. "So like-minded that I will be at Doctors' Commons first thing tomorrow morning in order to purchase our special license."

Just hearing those words brought a thrill to her. Once again, she thought how in a week's time she would be Spencer's wife. The Countess of Middlefield. A married lady.

There was no receiving line and they went directly into the ballroom, where a series of chairs had been placed in rows. Scanning them, she thought there would be about four to five dozen people present for tonight's concert, given by a known Italian opera singer. People milled about the ballroom, some with cups of punch in hand, and Spencer asked if she might want some.

"Not now," she told him. "Louisa tells me there will be a break in the evening's entertainment in order to give the guest time to rest her voice. Perhaps then I might care for something."

"Then I will leave you in your cousin's hands."

"Where are you going?" she questioned.

"I want to give you time to socialize with others," he said. "I will do the same."

As he moved away, Tessa felt a sense of pride in his appearance.

This man was hers. All hers. And she was his.

Adalyn said, "I see Louisa. Shall we join her?"

Tessa agreed and they went to where her cousin stood with a few others.

Pulling Louisa aside, Tessa said, "I have news to share with you. I want you to hear it before others do."

Louisa's eyes lit with interest. "Might it concern a certain earl? And an announcement?" she asked.

Tessa laughed. "It does," she confirmed.

Louisa clasped Tessa's hands, squeezing them tightly. "I am delighted, Tessa," her cousin told her. "I liked Lord Middlefield from the start. I think you have made a fine choice."

"I believe the same," she answered.

Louisa drew her back to the circle she had been standing with, one in which Adalyn had joined, and Louisa introduced Tessa to those she did not already know. As she stood listening to the conversation, her eyes roamed the ballroom, finding Spencer. He must have been doing the same because his gaze connected with hers and he smiled.

She glanced away and saw her father's brother, now Lord Paxton, looking at her steadily, his wife by his side. He nodded coolly and turned away.

Lady Paxton did not acknowledge Tessa at all.

Adalyn leaned toward Tessa and said, "Let's go meet a few others."

The pair moved away and Tessa found herself talking with a few women from the previous evening. Then she sensed a presence at her elbow and turned.

Lord Ellington stood before her. He bowed and then took her hand, kissing it, and holding it too long for comfort. Tessa eased it from his grasp.

"I am delighted to see you here tonight, Lady Tessa," Lord Ellington said. "It seems a month of Sundays since I have last looked upon your fair face."

Tessa now saw him for what he was, a rogue who scattered meaningless compliments. "I saw you this afternoon, my lord. When you came calling upon my cousin and me."

"Did you enjoy the bouquet I sent, my lady?" he asked.

"It was very pretty," she told him.

"Pretty?" he asked, incredulous. "I believe it was the most outstanding of all your flower arrangements. Certainly, the largest."

"Yes, I would agree with that," she said. "It was quite kind of you to send it to me."

Tessa saw that guests had begun moving to their chairs and she said, "If you will excuse me, my lord?"

"Why, I thought we might sit together this evening, my lady," Lord Ellington said smoothly, taking her hand and placing it on his forearm.

"I have already promised Lord Middlefield that I will sit with him for the musicale," she said, removing her hand from his sleeve.

The earl frowned. Then he brightened and said, "Well, you have two sides, my lady. Middlefield can sit on one. I plan to sit on the other."

With that, he reclaimed her hand, this time tucking it possessively in the crook of his arm, and leading her toward the seats.

His emboldened action, after Tessa politely turning down his request to sit with him, bothered her greatly. As they moved toward the seating, she spied Spencer hurrying to meet up with them.

Lord Ellington indicated a row. "Does this suit you, my lady?"

Before she could answer, Spencer arrived and said, "Lady Tessa does not require your presence any longer, Ellington. She has promised to sit with me for tonight's performance."

Lord Ellington's brow furrowed. "The lady told me that very thing," he informed Spencer. "I told her she has two sides. You are welcomed to one but I am definitely taking the other."

With that, Lord Ellington guided Tessa into a row and she

sat, glancing back worriedly at Spencer. His jaw was tight as he moved down the line of chairs and joined them.

By now, she had pulled her hand from the earl's arm and folded her hands demurely in her lap. She sensed the hostility in the air and prayed these two would not come to blows again over her.

Lord Rexford appeared, greeting his guests, and announcing the soprano who was to sing this evening.

The opera singer took her place, joined by a pianist and violinist. The woman was truly gifted but Tessa heard little of what she sang, concerned about how Lord Ellington would react to the betrothal announcement.

Then she decided she wasn't going to let Lord Ellington's reaction infringe upon her evening. This was her first musicale. Her uncle would announce her engagement this evening. She would be marrying a man she loved. Nothing was going to dampen her spirits.

As anticipated, after an hour of entertaining Lord Rexford's guests, the opera singer took her leave, to enthusiastic applause.

Lord and Lady Rexford appeared at the font of the gathering and invited their guests to come and partake in a light supper, noting the entertainment would continue in an hour's time.

Spencer rose and offered his hand to Tessa, who took it. They moved from their seats, Lord Ellington on their heels.

"And whom might you be supping with tonight, Lady Tessa?" Lord Ellington challenged.

Not wanting Spencer to answer for her, she said, "My aunt and uncle and my cousins, my lord. I will see you when the concert continues."

She squeezed Spencer's arm and he moved her away.

"He's not going to be happy once the announcement is made," her fiancé noted.

She glanced up at him and said, "I don't care about Lord Ellington's mood. I am interested in our happiness alone." She gave Spencer a smile.

He returned it and led her to what had been designated as the supper room, leading her to the table where her uncle and aunt sat.

As Tessa took a seat, Uncle Uxbridge said, "I have spoken to Lord Rexford and he is more than happy to have me announce your betrothal at the end of supper this evening."

Instead of the buffet from the previous night, footmen appeared and placed plates in front of them, with another footman coming by to fill their wine glasses. Tessa soon was caught up in the conversation at the table, though she ignored the stares of Lord Ellington. She sensed his eyes on her during the entire supper and did not want to draw attention to this fact, although she believed Spencer was more than aware of it.

Lord Rexford, who sat at the table next to theirs, stood, glass in hand, and tapped a spoon upon it. The sound signaled for those in the room to cease speaking.

Lord Rexford smiled broadly and said, "I am delighted to introduce to you my good friend, Lord Uxbridge. He has an announcement of importance to make."

Tessa watched as her uncle rose, all eyes upon him.

"I am fortunate to have both a brother and a sister," he began. "The three of us were always close. Though my beloved sister has passed away, I am blessed to have her only child, Lady Tessa Foster, as my niece. Tonight, I am delighted to announce Lady Tessa's betrothal to the Earl of Middlefield."

Uncle Uxbridge raised his glass and toasted, "To the happy couple!"

The entire room took up their wine glasses and echoed his words. She sensed every eye on her and Spencer as the room began buzzing.

Spencer leaned close and in her ear said, "We will be deluged with well-wishers now."

His lips grazed her lobe as he spoke and she could only think of this being one of those many places she wanted him to kiss her.

"Shall we go and face the others, my love?" he asked, helping

Tessa to her feet.

They moved about the supper room, greeted by all with happy wishes upon their betrothal. A few asked about the wedding and when it would be held. All she committed to was telling others that it would be soon. To her, their wedding would be a private affair, with no details for consumption by the *ton*.

Lord Rexford began ushering his guests back to the ballroom for the last of the musicale and as they moved in that direction, their paths crossed with her uncle and his wife. Tessa recalled Lady Paxton's last words to her and decided being polite but brief with this woman would have its advantages.

A brief silence ensued and then Lord Paxton said to Spencer, "I offer you my heartiest congratulations, Lord Middlefield. You, as well, dear Tessa."

Tessa felt Spencer tense and he said quickly, "You are Lord and Lady Paxton?"

Her uncle nodded, while Lady Paxton oozed hostility.

Then Spencer said, "You wanted nothing to do with Tessa. You tossed her from her home. You did not care for her welfare. As far as I am concerned, you do not exist."

He led Tessa away, but not before she saw the started O formed by Lady Paxton's mouth.

"I cannot believe you said that to them."

Spencer looked down at her. "Are you upset by my actions/"

"On the contrary, I applaud them. You wanted to be my champion from the first moment we met—and I believe you will continue to champion me as long as I draw a breath." She gazed at him lovingly. "And I adore you for it."

He smiled sheepishly and then said, "If we were not in public, I would kiss you. Hard Frequently. And," with a gleam in his eyes, "not always on the mouth.'

She shivered in delight. "I anticipate I will enjoy those kisses," she said, batting her eyelashes seductively at him.

Spencer laughed heartily as he led her back to their original seats. It surprised her when Lord Ellington joined them again. She thought he might have had the decency to leave them in peace.

The earl took his seat next to her and gave them both a friendly smile. "You are a sly devil, Middlefield," Lord Ellington said. "You moved rather quickly, taking the most eligible woman off the Marriage Mart. I suppose I have learned a valuable lesson in this." He paused, gazing intently at Tessa. "And that is when I know I want something, I should move with all haste to possess it."

Lord Ellington settled back into his chair and added, "I hope we can all remain friendly."

Tessa had not been friends with him and Spencer certainly had not been friends with Lord Ellington but she was pleased that it seemed there was no animosity on his part.

"I am glad you have received our news so well," she told him.

"When might you wed?" the earl asked. "Will you be the first couple of the Season to marry at St. George's?"

Spencer quickly said, "We will marry by special license next week."

"I see," said Lord Ellington. He smiled broadly again. "My congratulations on both your engagement and marriage."

By now, the soprano had returned to the room and Tessa gave her attention to the opera singer. She had been so worried about Lord Ellington's reaction and now realized she never should have been. She was merely one of many women the earl had paid attention to, not only this Season but in others Seasons. Something told her that he hadn't been as interested in her as he claimed. Instead, he had only thrived on the competition between him and Spencer, brief as it was. Her feminine intuition told Tessa that Lord Ellington would quickly move on to other conquests.

The musicale ended and Lord Ellington bid them a good evening. She and Spencer met up with Adalyn and then her aunt and uncle and returned to the carriage.

As the others entered the vehicle, he quietly said, "I ask that you have nothing more to do with Lord Ellington. It is not jealousy on my part, Tessa, but instinct tells me that he is not to be trusted."

Knowing his instincts had been keenly honed during his years of battle, she readily agreed. As she settled into the carriage, she promised herself to hold no more conversations with Lord Ellington in the days leading up to her wedding. In fact, she thought about skipping a few of the events she had already agreed to attend in order to have adequate time to prepare for her wedding day.

Tessa slipped her arm through Spencer's and leaned her head against his shoulder as the horses carried them home, contentment filling her.

When the carriage arrived, she was reluctant to release him. An idea occurred to her, one so naughty that she probably shouldn't voice it.

She decided to anyway.

As her aunt and uncle and Adalyn bid Spencer goodnight and moved toward the townhouse, Tessa held back.

"I want you," she said breathlessly. "Tonight."

Spencer's look of confusion was priceless.

"Do you mean . . . what I think you mean?" he finally sputtered.

"Yes," she said, her smile widening. "I want my earl to begin my education tonight."

"I don't see how—"

"I will sneak you up to my bedchamber," she said casually, as if she did this sort of thing on a nightly basis. "Come to the window of Uncle Uxbridge's study in half an hour. I will unlock it and grant you entrance."

"But how—"

Tessa placed her gloved fingers against his lips. "No more worrying. Now, go," she ordered.

He grinned at her, kissing her fingers. "At least let me walk you to the door. Hopefully, that will be the only time I see your footman tonight."

He did so, pausing as the door swung open. "Goodnight, Tessa," he said, brushing his lips against her cheek, and then making his farewell.

Tessa's heart raced, knowing Spencer would soon be in her bed.

CHAPTER TWENTY-THREE

ESSA PRACTICALLY SKIPPED up the stairs, wondering how she had been so brave and bold but knowing in her heart it was what she wanted. They would be wed in less than a week. What would a few days matter if they started their adventures in love ahead of the ceremony?

Abra greeted Tessa when she entered her bedchamber. While the maid undressed Tessa, she told Abra a little about the musicale, trying not to betray her excitement. Abra helped her slip into her night rail and Tessa called for her dressing gown.

"You aren't going straight to bed, my lady?" the servant asked, confused.

"I am not tired and think I will read for a few minutes," she fibbed. "Perhaps that will help me to grow sleepy. And don't think I have forgotten about our reading lessons," she added. "Lord Middlefield and I will remain in town for a month after our wedding before making our way to Stoneridge, his country seat. If you are still willing to come with me, we will begin your literacy lessons there."

"I will never leave you, my lady," Abra swore. "I don't expect you'll ever be rid of me. Trying to rob you turned out to be the best day of my life."

Abra threw her arms about Tessa spontaneously and then quickly pulled away.

"Sorry, my lady. I know I'm not to do that sort of thing."

Tessa petted the servant's hair. "You may do so anytime you wish, Abra. That day changed both our lives," she said, thinking how it was when she met Spencer. "I am always ready to celebrate it."

Abra grinned. "Goodnight, my lady."

The maid took her leave and Tessa paced about the bedchamber, seeing that the bed had already been turned back. She stopped and stared at it a moment, thinking of what would take place in it soon. A shiver ran through her, eagerness filling her, knowing how ready she was for Spencer to teach her about lovemaking.

She continued moving about restlessly for a few more minutes before opening her door and slipping into the corridor. Making her way to the stairs, her bare feet made not a sound as she scampered down them two flights and then went down the hallway to the back stairs. Hopefully, no servants would be moving up and down them now that the house had settled for the night. She had to avoid the main staircase because it emptied into the foyer and a footman would be on duty all night at the door in case an emergency arose.

Creeping through the kitchens and down another corridor, she came to her uncle's study and entered it. Tessa went to the large casement window and pulled open the drapes before unlatching the window and swinging it open.

Spencer was already there.

He hoisted a booted foot over the windowsill and climbed inside, closing the widow behind him. Taking two steps toward her, he enfolded her in his arms, his warmth reassuring. Her cheek rested against his chest and she heard the steady beat of his heart increasing. They stood together for a long moment before he tilted up her chin, lowering his mouth to hers for a sweet kiss.

"Are you ready to go upstairs?" he whispered.

"Yes," she told him and took his hand, lacing her fingers through his.

Guiding him from her uncle's study, she pulled him along, clinging to the shadows until they reached the servants' staircase. Then Spencer surprised her, sweeping her off her feet and carrying her up the flights of stairs.

She directed him to her bedchamber and they entered it, with him closing the door behind them. Still holding Tessa in his arms, he crossed the large room and set her on her feet next to the bed. His large hands framed her face as he gazed at her lovingly.

"Are you certain this is what you want?" he asked. "It is a bit unorthodox. I am perfectly willing to wait a week."

"I'm not willing to," she told him. "I love you. We plan to be together forever." Tessa paused. "I am ready for our forever to begin now."

The heat burning in his green eyes told her how much he wanted her. His lips claimed hers as his arms came about her, bringing her against the hard wall of muscle that was his chest. The kiss became more demanding. More urgent. Every part of her came alive as Spencer hungrily devoured her. She opened to him and his tongue swept inside, mating with hers. She inhaled the spice of his cologne as her palms stroked his face, a slight stubble now on his cheeks at this late hour.

His lips whispered across her cheek and to her ear, nibbling the lobe. He whispered things to her that caused her skin to prickle, telling her where he would touch her. Heat pooled between her legs and a throbbing there began dominating her thoughts.

Slowly, even as he continued to kiss her, Spencer found the knotted tie and undid it, pushing open her dressing gown. His hands went to her back, moving up and down sensually. Tessa found herself pressing against him, wanting to get even closer. His hands slid around to her front and began kneading her breasts. They seemed to swell as he did so.

He moved to her shoulders and eased her dressing gown from them, pulling it down her arms. It fell away, pooling at her feet as that throbbing dominated her thoughts. Then his fingers slid under the thin straps of her night rail, slipping them from her shoulders. Somehow, he worked the top of the night rail down to her waist, baring her breasts to him. His mouth went to one, his teeth grazing the nipple, causing a rush of hot desire to flood her. His tongue flicked back and forth and then circled the bud, which tightened. He took it into his mouth, suckling her, the pressure so pleasurable that she felt the dampness between her legs now.

Spencer finally moved to her other breast and worshipped it the same way, with teeth and tongue and hands. By now, Tessa panted with want and need. He knelt, his tongue traveling down her belly until it reached her night rail. He pushed the garment over her hips, allowing his tongue to continue downward. Need rippled through her as she pushed her fingers into his hair.

He stopped just shy of her nether curls and rose again.

"I need to feel your satin skin against mine," he said, his voice raw and rough.

Lifting her in his arms again, he placed her on the bed and stepped back. Quickly, he divested himself of the loose coat he wore and yanked his shirt over his head. She marveled at his physique—a broad, muscled chest dusted with a light matting of dark hair that disappeared into his pants. He turned and sat on the bed, struggling to remove his Hessians but determined to do so. One they were gone, he stood again and removed his trousers, stepping from them. His legs were long and also muscled, his calves so beautiful that she almost cried.

Spencer climbed onto the bed and scooped her into his arms, his mouth coming down hard on hers, taking control. He kissed her with an urgency that she instinctively understood, though she had no idea how things would culminate. Her mother had never explained marital relations to her. Tessa was curious—and ready—for what lay ahead.

His hands began roaming her body and she did the same, wanting to know the feel of him. She tweaked his flat nipples, knowing how she had enjoyed his touch on hers. He growled in response, apparently enjoying the attention there. Then his hands glided along the curve of her hips and parted her thighs. He positioned himself between her legs, kissing her inner thighs as she pulsated.

Slipping a finger inside her, he said, "You are wet for me, Tessa. That means you want me as much as I want you."

He stroked her deeply. Her hips began to rise with each stroke. The same feeling from previously built within her. Anticipation flooded her, knowing what would come.

This time was different, though.

Spencer said, "I want to taste you."

Immediately, Tessa knew what he meant. She was mortified. Intrigued. Aroused. She trusted him, though, and would do whatever he asked of her.

His hands pushed her legs further apart, baring everything now. Instead of embarrassment, desire flooded her, knowing he saw the very essence of her. His fingers parted her folds as his head lowered between her legs. She felt the tip of his tongue, gliding along her sex, teasing her unmercifully.

Then it plunged inside her, startling her, heightening her awareness of everything. She found her fingers tangled in his hair again, holding him closer to her as he licked and sucked and nipped. She began whimpering. Rising to meet him. Moaning like some wanton.

When he found her bud, she tensed and then panted as his tongue swirled about it, stroking it maddeningly. The pressure mounted and she flung herself over the precipice, dizzying colors dancing before her eyes as waves of pleasures washed over her. She felt as if every bone in her body had melted away as she lay there afterward, spent and motionless.

Spencer began working his way back up her body in a series of kisses from her core to her mouth. When he kissed her again, he moved until he hovered above her. Lifting his mouth, he said, "The first time there will be pain. Never again."

Before she could think on his words, she sensed his member at the entrance to her core and he pushed quickly inside her. A moment of hurt occurred and her nails dug into his shoulders.

He didn't move, though, and she understood that he was letting her body become used to him inside her, stretching her, filling her.

"Better now?" he asked softly.

"Yes."

"Good."

Slowly, he began to move, slipping away from her and then plunging in again. The friction went from pleasant to electrifying. Her hips rose to meet his thrusts, every nerve in her body firing now. Their dance slowed and sped up before the pace became frenetic. She moved with him as one and as his seed spilled inside her, they both cried out their pleasure.

Gradually, she began to come back to earth, aware of Spencer's weight driving her into the mattress. He started to move from her and she clung to him.

"Don't go," she told him.

"I don't want to crush you." He rolled to his side and wrapped his massive arms about her, holding her close. The sound of his heartbeat thundered against her ear as they lay together, their bodies cooling.

Finally, he kissed her again, long and lingering, and then released her. He sat up, throwing his legs over the side of the bed and stood. Tessa watched him dress, thinking how wonderful the experience had been and how they truly were each other's now and forever.

Spencer went and retrieved a basin and washcloth. He bathed her, explaining he had ruptured her maidenhead and there was a bit of blood. He ministered to her so lovingly, it gave her a glimpse of how their lives would be. How giving he was and she knew he would always treat her like a queen.

"Come, let us get you back into your night rail. Abra will suspect something if she comes to awaken her mistress and finds her with no clothes on," he teased.

Tessa stood and allowed him to dress her. She remembered

to pick up her dressing gown and place it across the foot of the bed, where she usually left it.

Spencer tucked her back into bed again, smoothing her hair and then kissing her.

"I hate to leave you," he said.

"I hate it, too," she replied.

"Do you have any regrets?"

"None," she said fiercely. "I wish we could wed today and do all of this over again."

He chuckled, his palm cradling her cheek. "We will. First, I must purchase the special license this morning. I will do so when Doctors' Commons opens."

"Do we have to wait?" she asked.

He kissed her brow. "We do. Your aunt wants everything to be perfect for you." He grinned. "It doesn't mean I cannot come visit you again."

She took his hand and kissed his palm. "I wish we didn't have to go to the ball tonight."

"We do. By then, news of our betrothal will have spread and there will be many who wish to congratulate us."

"But it won't be over until so late. You probably won't be able to come to me tonight."

He kissed her, hard and swift, and then said, "We can worry about that later. Get a few hours of sleep now, my previous love."

Spencer went to her door and she blew him a kiss. He pretended to catch it and place it in his pocket.

Tessa burrowed into her pillow, her body sated, her lips still burning.

And fell into a deep, peaceful sleep.

CHAPTER TWENTY-FOUR

S PENCER ROSE, HAVING only slept a couple of hours after his late night visit to Tessa. He was grateful that last night's musicale had ended much earlier than the previous evening's ball had, giving him the opportunity to spend that magical time with his fiancée. Already, he despised the late hours of the Season. Being a former military man, he was used to rising well before the sun did so. He knew from having grown up in the country that country hours were quite different from city ones. He couldn't wait to return there. With Tessa.

As his wife.

As he dressed for his usual early morning ride, Spencer couldn't keep the grin off his face. He closed his eyes, returning to the moment when he had joined with Tessa. He could still smell the scent of lavender that clung to him. Feel her silky hair and satin skin. Taste her essence.

Her spontaneous invitation to her bed last night had shocked him. He had thought her a perfect lady and still thought she was. But he knew now that she had a sensual side to her nature, one he couldn't wait to further explore. Though she had been a virgin, Tessa hadn't shied away from anything in the lovemaking process. She hadn't seemed self-conscious about her own naked body and had looked upon his with curiosity.

And desire.

Spencer knew with experience that Tessa would grow bolder as they learned what satisfied the other. He eagerly awaited their next encounter. It still astounded him that he had won her heart and she would soon become his countess. He couldn't wait to start his life with her. He never dreamed of marriage when he had been a soldier, much less thinking he would marry for love. His life had changed radically in the past year. He was now an earl. A man betrothed to a woman probably too good for him, but happy that she loved him, nonetheless.

Spencer slipped from the house, which had yet to stir, and headed for the mews. He greeted Pilgrim, stroking his nose and then saddling the horse. As was his custom, he rode from Mayfair toward Hyde Park and would ride Rotten Row in the early morning peace. He did not see Tessa out for her daily morning walk as he went, doubting she would keep to that during the Season. He knew he had exhausted her last night and hoped she would get the rest she deserved.

But he did hope they would keep to a very different form of early morning exercise once they were wed. One which would bring them great joy—and eventually children. Why, Tessa might now be carrying his babe after last night's coupling. Thoughts of waking up next to her for a lifetime had him almost turning Pilgrim back to Mayfair. He resisted the urge, knowing he couldn't call at this early an hour, much less make his way to her bedchamber and love her completely and thoroughly.

As he approached the entrance to the park, he remembered her saying she did enjoy riding. Once he left Doctors' Commons with the special license, he would go to Tattersalls and purchase that beautiful chestnut mare for her that he had seen. It would serve as a wedding present. Riding gave him such joy and it was something he knew they could share together. Spencer pictured them teaching their children to ride and had to blink back the tears which began to fill his eyes.

All he wanted in life was Tessa and the family they would create. It seemed impossible that a dream he had never dreamed suddenly existed for him—and would now come true.

He pushed Pilgrim now, giving the horse his head as they rode through the park and toward Rotten Row. The place stood deserted and the hoofbeats of his horse echoed loudly in the silence. As he turned along the row, it startled him to see a carriage in the midst of the path. Quickly, he pulled up on the reins, bringing Pilgrim to a halt in order not to crash into the vehicle. He hadn't the foggiest clue why it would be standing here, blocking the path.

Seeing a coachman in the driver's seat, he called out, "What the devil, man?"

The door to the coach swung open and a dark-clad gentleman climbed from it. He turned and Spencer recognized something about the man's profile.

Ellington . . .

The earl approached. Wariness filled Spencer. His focus was fixed on the earl, so much that he did not hear anyone behind him until it was too late.

Without warning, someone gripped his arm and jerked him from his horse.

Spencer fell to the ground, the air whooshing from him, as strong hands grabbed both his arms and yanked him to his feet. He whipped his head from side to side, finding two large men holding him as he tried to catch his breath again. He pulled on his arms, trying to free himself, missing the fact that Ellington now stood in front of him.

A sudden blow to his gut startled him. His knees buckled. Only the fact that the men had hold of him kept him on his feet. As he struggled against them, still fighting to get enough air into his lungs, he saw Ellington's predatory smile.

Spencer went cold inside.

"It's a good thing I know all about your movements, Middlefield," the earl began, his eyes lazily looking Spencer up and down.

Again, a quick blow from nowhere stunned him. He

wheezed, battling to get a breath.

"You humiliated me," his enemy continued. "It's rare to find a man who will stand up and spar with me because of my reputation as being the finest boxer among the gentlemen of the *ton*. I usually have to match my fists and wits against a professional."

Spencer figured it was time for Ellington to strike him again. He tightened his belly and chest and while the punch hurt, it didn't daze him as before.

"Everyone wants a go at me," Ellington continued. "All because they think I am now beatable. Because of you."

Two more punches occurred, both again in his gut.

The earl paused and looked at his fists, which Spencer saw had leather strips wrapped around them for protection. He twisted, trying to break free, but his captors held fast.

So he viciously kicked Ellington in his crown jewels.

The earl shrieked, staggering back. He collapsed to the ground, folding himself small, as if Spencer could do him further harm.

As Ellington lay there, Spencer slammed his heel into the knee of the man on his right. It buckled but the man, whom Spencer believed to be a professional pugilist, held fast. To counter his attack, both men twisted Spencer's arms behind his back now. They held him so tight that he was afraid if he struggled overmuch, he would only break both arms, leaving him helpless. Ceasing his struggles, he concentrated on Ellington.

The earl finally rose, a bit unsteady on his feet. Then he launched himself at Spencer, delivering a series of blows everywhere. Jabs to his face. Cross punches. Uppercuts. He tried to turn his face when he could and stiffen his chest but Ellington managed a good deal of damage. Spencer knew a few ribs had to be broken, along with his nose, blood pouring down his front. He ached mightily.

Ellington withdrew, shaking his hands. Even with the protection of the gloves, the man's hands had to be hurting from the punishing blows he had used to connect to Spencer's face and torso.

All the fight had gone out of Spencer. He dangled from the men's hold on him, barely able to lift his head as Ellington came near again. When it fell, Ellington grabbed a fistful of Spencer's hair and raised his head.

Ellington's fury was evident as he spoke, spittle flying from his mouth.

"You are a no one. You had no right to swoop in and claim Lady Tessa. She will be mine. Not yours. *Mine.*"

With that declaration, Ellington smashed his fist into Spencer's face, anger delivering the blow. His sight grew dim and he collapsed totally, only held up by the two ruffians on either side of him. Spencer fought to remain conscious, worried what might happen if he passed out.

"Finish him off," Ellington commanded. "I want him beaten to death. Make him feel every blow. Do it quickly, though. Daylight will break soon."

"Can we have his horse?"

"Yes. And anything he carries on him. You know where to meet tonight. You will receive the remainder of your payment then."

With that, Ellington stalked off, climbing into his carriage.

One man released Spencer and he wanted to fight back but the other captor pinned his arms behind his back. Blows rained down upon him and he grew weak, even as he heard a shriek in the distance.

His head dropped. He gasped, taking a breath from his mouth, his nose too clogged with blood to allow air through.

His last conscious thought was of Tessa.

TESSA AWOKE, A bit sore but feeling more alive than she ever had. *All because of Spencer.*

She decided if being wanton meant she pleased her husband-to-be, then she would remain wanton for all time. She rose, stretching her hands high over her head, her thoughts turning to wicked things she wished to try with him tonight.

Or not. Another ball was scheduled to take place this evening. If it were anything like the last one, they wouldn't even dine until midnight and then the dancing would continue afterward. Last time, it had been after three when she had arrived home. Perhaps she could claim a headache and skip the event altogether, spending hours with Spencer in her bed.

Grinning, she dressed quickly, wanting to walk since she had missed doing so yesterday. Just before she left her bedchamber, Abra appeared, shaking her head.

"I thought you'd get it into your head to get up and walk this morning, my lady. It's a good thing I came to check on you else you would've left without me."

The maid paused, studying her a moment. "You seem in awfully good spirits."

Guilt caused Tessa's cheeks to flush. "Why do you say that? I haven't even said a word until now."

Abra took a step forward and sniffed. "You've been kissing Lord Middlefield." The servant paused. "Or doing more than kissing him. I can smell him on you."

"Can you truly?" she asked worriedly.

"A bit. We'll have you wash up before your breakfast. Lord Uxbridge won't suspect a thing. Never you worry, my lady. Come, let us get in the walk you are so insistent upon taking."

The two went down the stairs and out the front door, greeting the footman still on duty from last night. As they stepped onto the pavement, Tessa heard the echo of hooves sounding and quickly looked to her right, catching sight of Spencer riding from the square.

"I hate that I missed him," she said and then brightened. "We can go to Hyde Park. I am certain that is where he's gone to ride. We might catch him there or even on his way back."

"And what might you wish to do if we do catch up to his lordship?" Abra asked, a sly smile turning up the corners of her mouth.

"Why, kiss him, of course!"

Tessa began laughing and Abra joined in.

"Oh, it does seem you have it bad, my lady."

She giggled, feeling girlish and lighthearted. "I do, don't I? Come Abra, let's go."

They set off at a brisk pace toward Hyde Park, which was only blocks away. While she knew Spencer would arrive long before they did, she hoped to see him on his return from the park, if only for a few minutes.

They left the streets of London and entered the eastern side of the park. It looked incredibly different at this time of day, deserted as opposed to how congested it had been when she was last here with Spencer.

"Do you know where his lordship rides?" Abra asked.

"I believe Rotten Row. Do you know where that is, Abra?"

"I do, my lady. It's along the south side." A sheepish grin graced the maid's face. "I might have even nicked a bob or two there."

"Those days are far behind you, Abra," Tessa proclaimed. "You are now an elegant lady's maid, soon to be lady's maid to the Countess of Middlefield."

"That sounds so grand, my lady. Aren't you glad I tried to rob you and Lord Middlefield came to your aid that morning?"

"I am," Tessa admitted. "But no more brandishing of knives, please."

When Abra looked guilty, Tessa asked, "Do you carry your knife with you now?"

Abra nodded. "I don't carry it about the house, my lady, but when we go places, like these walks, I have it on me. It's second nature, I suppose. I'd rather be safe than sorry."

Tessa couldn't blame Abra or fault her thinking. The girl had led a rough life and the streets of London proved dangerous to many, especially the downtrodden and unfortunate. She had the blessings of good birth with her father's name, as would her children with Spencer.

Smiling brightly at the maid, Tessa said, "That is quite all right. I am glad you are prepared on both our behalves."

She saw her words pleased the servant. They continued deeper into the deserted park, making good time. Soon, the broad track that was Rotten Row came into view.

She saw a carriage in the middle of the row, which seemed incredibly odd to her. Her heart began beating wildly as she saw two men holding another in the distance, while a third savagely beat the restrained man. Then the man stopped and spoke to the pair before he abruptly left, moving toward the carriage. Once he entered it, the vehicle quickly took off, leaving behind the two men to brutalize their captive.

Tessa wasn't having any of it. She pulled on Abra's arm and began trotting toward the danger, her heart telling her she must stop it. She even shrieked loudly, hoping that would warn off the men engaged in their criminal act. She glanced at Abra, who knelt quickly, then rose with her blade in hand.

"We must help that poor man," she declared and Abra nodded, her face grave.

The two women closed the distance between them and the trio. As they drew closer, she noticed the riderless horse standing to the side. Tessa recognized it.

It was Spencer's horse.

Uncontrollable rage filled her as she realized her beloved was the man who had been attacked. She grabbed Abra's wrist, swiping the dagger from the servant's hand, and charged toward the men.

She quickly took in the scene, seeing the two large brutes. One held Spencer, whose face had been beaten so severely that he was barely recognizable.

"Get away from him!" Tessa shouted.

The man who was about to strike Spencer lowered his fist.

"Stay out of it, Woman," he growled.

Then Abra spoke up. "You're Horton," she accused. Looking to the man holding Spencer, she cried, "And you're Lewis."

Surprise filled the first man's face at being recognized as the second man who held Spencer appeared worried.

The first demanded, "What's it to you?"

Tessa, anger swimming through her veins, brandished the knife at Horton and said, "Move away from him now. The man you attack is my betrothed. If you dare strike him again, I will use this knife to cut off your bollocks and cram them down your throat. Then I will slit your throat and yank them out and stomp on them."

"She means it, Horton," the one called Lewis said nervously.

She glared at Horton and said, "You have chosen the wrong person to cross. Leave at once. Leave London. Change your names. Run for your lives. My two uncles are powerful peers, one highly placed in the War Office. He has at his disposal dozens of men who will track you down and see you hang at Newgate if you don't do as I say."

Lewis, who still held Spencer, released him. Spencer crumpled to the ground but Tessa couldn't minister to him yet. She had to see these men and their threat gone.

Her gaze steady, she said, "Before you go, tell me—was that Lord Ellington who began this?"

Both men looked frightened. Lewis nodded and quickly revealed, "Yes, my lady. We are to meet him tonight to receive the rest of our payment."

"Tell me when and where this meeting is to take place—and exactly what you were being paid to do to my fiancé."

Horton nodded and provided her with the information.

Holding the knife steady in her hand, she ordered, "Go. Don't make me change my mind else I will lead the party that tracks you down. My justice would be swifter and far more painful than any granted by law."

The men hurried away and as they did, Tessa handed the

knife to Abra and dropped to her knees, a numbing cold sweeping through her body. She lifted Spencer's head and cradled it in her lap. The fight had left her now and tears swam in her eyes as she saw the swelling and bruises already beginning to appear.

She looked up at Abra and said, "Hurry back to my uncle's and have them send for a doctor," she ordered crisply. "Then have a carriage sent with several footmen to help convey his lordship back home."

Abra nodded, placing the dagger next to Tessa on the ground. "You can count on me, my lady," the servant said. "But I'm leaving the weapon with you. Just in case."

Abra took off running and Tessa knew her maid would not let her down. She turned back to Spencer, smoothing his hair, her tears flowing freely now. His eyes remained closed and, for a moment, she feared he might have been beaten to death. She ripped off her gloves and touched her fingers to his throat, finding his pulse beating slowly but erratically. Relief swept through her.

Suddenly, his eyes opened and he smiled crookedly at her. "My Boudica," he whispered. "Always . . . charging in . . . saving . . . others."

Love for this man swelled within her and she told him, "Don't you dare die on me, Spencer. We are meant to live a lifetime together. In love. I forbid you to die."

Her beloved gazed up at her and once more whispered, "My . . . Boudica."

His eyes closed, his breathing still shallow. She supposed he had broken ribs which made each breath painful and difficult.

As Tessa waited for help to arrive, she swore to have her vengeance upon Lord Ellington.

CHAPTER TWENTY-FIVE

T ESSA SAW HER uncle's carriage finally approach, not understanding why it had taken so long to arrive. She glanced down at Spencer, whose eyes were still closed.

"Help is here, my dearest," she said, her fingers lightly smoothing his brow.

"Mmm."

That one sound was the only one he had made since he had last spoken. She had found she couldn't speak to him. Her throat had been almost swollen shut with emotion, tears silently falling down her cheeks. She silently prayed over and over that he not be taken from her. That God would allow them to be married and grow old together. She desperately needed these prayers answered.

Without Spencer, she couldn't go on.

The carriage rolled to a halt near her. Two footmen sat with the driver and jumped from their perch as two others who had ridden along the back also climbed down. The door swung open and Uncle Uxbridge appeared, still in his nightclothes, a banyan thrown over them. His hair was askew and worry filled his face.

He came straight toward her and knelt, placing his hand upon her shoulder. Strength from him seemed to flow into her, calming her.

"Abra told us everything," he said. "I waited for Dr. Presley to arrive so he could come with us and supervise moving Lord Middlefield."

His words explained the delay though, in truth, it was still very early. No riders had yet appeared in Rotten Row. Tessa hoped they could be gone before anyone did arrive. She wanted no gossip about this event.

Because she wanted Lord Ellington to be taken by surprise.

Dr. Presley appeared and also knelt, taking Spencer's wrist and frowning. He set Spencer's hand back down and Tessa took it as the physician lightly poked and prodded.

"The carriage floor has numerous blankets piled upon it, Lady Tessa," Dr. Presley told her. "Lord Middlefield is a large man and we could not place him prone along the seat."

The doctor rose and gave the footmen instructions. A large blanket was brought and spread out on the ground next to Spencer. Then the four servants lifted him as he groaned, placing him on the blanket. They took up the four corners and used it as a sling, carrying Spencer to the carriage.

"How is he?" she asked worriedly once her fiancé was out of earshot.

"He has taken a severe beating. If you had not come across him when you did, I doubt he would have lived."

"But he will live," she insisted.

Dr. Presley shrugged. "I believe so but I make no promises, my lady. Sometimes there are injuries inside the body which we cannot see. Let us hope Lord Middlefield has none of those."

"He was having difficulty breathing. I think his ribs must be broken. Or at least some of them."

"I will know more when I can examine him more thoroughly."

Uncle Uxbridge helped her to her feet and Tessa instructed one of the footmen to ride Pilgrim back to Spencer's townhouse. Then she climbed inside the carriage and sat on the floor, once more cradling Spencer's head in her lap. She placed her hand on his. His fingers moved and she twined hers through his, fighting to hold back the tears. They would do no good and only worry him if he saw them.

The carriage returned to Mayfair and the footmen, as gently as they could, removed the injured Spencer from the carriage and carried him to his bedchamber. Tessa wished they would have taken him to the Uxbridge townhouse where she could minister to him around the clock, but it would only hurt him more if they tried to move him again. Already, he had lost consciousness due to the pain. She wouldn't put him through anything unnecessary. She stood beside his bed now, her fingers still holding his.

Marsh, his butler, and Mrs. Marsh, the housekeeper, hovered as they awaited instructions from Dr. Presley. Other servants also slipped into the room, horror in their eyes.

A stout man came and said, "I am Rigsby, Lord Middlefield's valet. Everyone out except for the doctor and Lady Tessa. Wait in the hall, Marsh. And Mrs. Marsh. I will relay what the doctor needs. His lordship needs quiet."

The gaggle of servants filed from the room and Rigsby closed the door.

Dr. Presley looked to her. "My lady, you must also leave. I must cut his clothes away in order to tend to him."

Before she could protest, Rigsby intervened. "His lordship loves Lady Tessa with all his heart. He needs her here. She will stay," he said, his face stern, daring the physician to thwart him.

"This is highly unorthodox," Dr. Presley protested.

"Lord Middlefield is betrothed to Lady Tessa," the valet explained. "He was to purchase a special license this morning. If she sees a little more of him than she should, it won't matter. He will do better with her here. I guarantee it."

Spencer's fingers slightly tightened on hers. "Stay," he croaked.

Dr. Presley cleared his throat. "Very well. Lady Tessa may stay, my lord."

She thought Spencer tried to smile but it was too hard to tell with his face so swollen.

Rigsby removed his employer's boots and cut away his clothing. Sitting Spencer up and trying to remove each piece would have been too much. As the pieces came off, she winced, seeing his battered torso and limbs.

For modesty's sake, once all his clothing had been removed and set aside, Rigsby raised a bedsheet to Spencer's waist.

Dr. Presley then examined Spencer thoroughly, his hands gentle. He spoke as he worked, giving a running commentary to keep Tessa and Rigsby informed.

"His lordship's body has been battered severely. I have detected three ribs which are broken or cracked and another two which are deeply bruised. It is possible Lord Middlefield also has a concussion from the many hard blows he received to his head."

"What does that mean?" she asked quietly.

"A number of things. He could suffer from blurred vision and headaches. Memory loss. A ringing in his ears. A type of brain fog. Chronic pain. He could have trouble focusing. It could lead to balance issues."

"What can we do?" Tessa asked, hoping she kept the desperation from her voice.

"Rest is vital," Dr. Presley explained. "He should remain in bed for at least two to three days. His brain, as well as his body, must rest in order to heal. No reading or lengthy discussions. No physical activity of any kind. Quiet is encouraged. Do not ask questions of him. If he asks something, answer him but no conversations that go on beyond a few sentences."

"What about the rest of him, Doctor? His body?" Rigsby asked.

"Several things can be done for his lordship. First and foremost, though many find them disgusting, are using leeches. They are highly effective in removing bruises almost instantly and completely. I will do so now."

The physician opened a large satchel on a nearby chair and removed a jar. Tessa shivered as Dr. Presley opened the lid and carefully picked up a live leech. He set the leech directly upon

Spencer's chest and repeated the process several times until more than a dozen leeches fed off him. True to his word, after several minutes, the bruising lessened and as the leeches grew full, Dr. Presley removed them and replaced them in the jar.

"Arnica will help reduce Lord Middlefield's pain and increase circulation in the area around his bruising."

He instructed Rigsby how to create a gel by mixing arnica with water and told the valet to rub the gel created directly onto the affected areas.

"Do not cover it with anything," Dr. Presley stated. "The only exception will be once it is applied, we will wrap linen bandages about Lord Middlefield's torso. It may help his ribs by limiting his movement."

"How often should the arnica be applied?" Tessa asked.

"A few times a day until all bruising is gone," the physician told her. "I will also tell Mrs. Marsh about steeping Saint John's wort in warm water for twenty minutes. It will help in the swelling and is also a natural pain reliever. His lordship should take a single sip of this mixture daily until no bruising remains."

She glanced down and saw Spencer's brow furrowed in pain.

"His breathing is very shallow. I am worried about that," she admitted.

"His lordship must do breathing exercises," Dr. Presley said. "Shallow breaths risks pneumonia developing. He must learn to fight through the pain and take big, deep breaths. I shall write down for you when to begin and how often."

"Before you leave?" she asked anxiously.

"Yes, I can stop in Lord Middlefield's study and do so, my lady."

"Thank you, Dr. Presley. For everything."

Tessa asked Rigsby to show the doctor to Spencer's study and stay with him until the breathing instructions were committed to paper.

"I'll bring them to you straightaway, my lady. And see that Mrs. Marsh steeps the Saint John's wort."

The two men left the bedchamber and she was now alone with Spencer. She moved to sit upon the bed, taking his big hand in both of hers and bringing it to her lips. She kissed it tenderly.

"I hurt," he said.

"Did you hear everything Dr. Presley said?" she asked.

"Most of it. Don't talk much. Rest."

"That's right, my love." Tessa bent and softly kissed his cheek.

"I will be thinking, though," he said. "About what to do to Ellington."

She stiffened. "No, you won't. You are to leave your mind a blank and concentrate on nothing. Besides, I have already told Uncle Uxbridge Lord Ellington is responsible."

What she didn't tell Spencer was that she had also asked her uncle to send for her Uncle Edgar. Since Tessa knew the time and place Lord Ellington was supposed to meet his ruffians, she wanted him confronted then and there.

"Good," Spencer murmured. "Should . . . have known . . . my Boudica . . . would take care . . ."

He stopped speaking and Tessa saw he had fallen asleep.

She sat stroking his arm lightly until Rigsby returned with a page.

"Here you are, my lady. Nothing too difficult. Though I suspect his lordship might be a difficult patient."

She smiled as the valet handed her the page. Reading through, she saw Spencer was to do three seconds of deep breathing in order to expand his ribcage, followed by three more seconds of relaxed breathing. That was to be followed by a few huffs of short breaths, with a light cough thrown in. Once again, another three seconds of relaxed breathing would follow.

"The doctor said do it in this order," Rigsby explained. "And to repeat the cycle three to five times. We are to do this multiple times a day."

"It will hurt," she agreed. "And he's certain to get cranky."

The valet smiled. "That he is, my lady. But you will be here to calm his temper."

"I can tell you are a valued and trusted servant, Rigsby."

"I have only served Lord Middlefield for a short while. I have done my best to whip him into shape. He needed quite a bit of work." The valet paused. "I believe between the two of us, we will see that his lordship lives up to his potential."

"Oh, you are going to get along splendidly with Abra," Tessa declared.

"Your lady's maid?"

"You know her?"

Rigsby nodded. "I know of her. I am stepping out with Bridget, you see. Lady Adalyn's lady's maid. She has told me quite a few things about Abra."

"I think Lord Middlefield and I are very fortunate to have you and Abra in our lives, Rigsby." She looked to the bed where Spencer lay sleeping and back at the valet. "I must go home for a bit. I have summoned my uncle, Sir Edgar Goulding, from the War Office. I want his help in bringing Lord Ellington to justice."

Rigsby's quick intake of breath was audible. "Lord Ellington did this? The earl that his lordship trounced at Gentleman Jack's?"

"He did. Along with two thieves from the streets whom I banished from London. But it is Lord Ellington I want to pay for his crime."

The valet shook his head. "It doesn't work like that in Polite Society, my lady."

Tessa didn't like the sound of that. "What do you mean?"

"I mean that a peer would never be brought to justice for a crime."

She became incensed. "But he ordered those two men to beat Spencer to death!"

"It doesn't matter," Rigsby said, shaking his head sadly. "Lord Ellington is an earl."

Tessa stood. "Well, it matters to me." She strode across the room.

"What are you going to do, Lady Tessa?" Rigsby asked.

"Find a way to see that Lord Ellington pays," she said.

CHAPTER TWENTY-SIX

T ESSA DASHED ACROSS the square and Rainey admitted to her uncle's townhouse.

"Where are my uncles?" she demanded.

The butler said, "Everyone is in the library, my lady."

She hurried up the stairs, anger still filling her at what Rigsby had informed her about.

Was it possible Lord Ellington would not be punished for his misdeeds?

She rushed into the drawing room, where she saw both uncles, her cousins, and her aunt waiting anxiously.

Her aunt rose and took Tessa's hands in hers. "My dear, how is Lord Middlefield? And how are you?"

Tessa took a deep breath and tried to compose herself, not wanting her ire to spill out upon her kind, concerned relatives.

"Lord Middlefield's injuries are very serious, Aunt," she said. "We need to sit and talk about what the outcome should be."

The six of them gathered, all eyes upon Tessa, and she said, "Is it true that Lord Ellington will receive no punishment for his actions?"

Uncle Edgar nodded sadly. "The earl is a peer of the realm, Tessa," he began. "Peers don't commit crimes very often and when they do, it is usually against a member of the lowest class and thus ignored by Polite Society."

Fury sparked in her anew. "But this isn't just any crime, Uncle Edgar. Lord Ellington hired two criminals to aid him. They restrained Spencer while Lord Ellington beat him severely. Then the earl gave the men instructions to finish off the task. Uncle, they were told to beat Spencer to death. To leave him in the park, his pockets emptied, as if he had been robbed by footpads. Lord Ellington even told them they might take Spencer's horse and sell it, dividing the profits between them. Surely, he must be brought to task for this.

"It is attempted murder!" she exclaimed.

Uncle Uxbridge cleared his throat. "It is just how things are, Tessa. You will have to accept them."

"What if I have to accept Spencer's death at Ellington's hands?" she asked, outraged. "Spencer is far from being out of the woods, Uncle. Dr. Presley has tended to him the best he can but he has told me there could be internal injuries so grave that they could end Spencer's life. And that is not accounting for the head injuries he might have suffered from the many blows administered by Lord Ellington's fists.

"I want justice—and I will have it."

"He cannot be arrested, Tessa," Uncle Edgar told her. "The only recourse would be if Lord Middlefield challenged Lord Ellington to a duel. I can't see that happening anytime soon."

For a moment, Tessa toyed with the idea of issuing that challenge herself and then gave it up. She doubted Lord Ellington would accept her challenge and even if he did, she had never fired a gun. It would be utter suicide on her part.

"Then can't *you* do something?" she demanded. "You are a highly placed official in the War Office. You must have the resources to do something. Can't he be stripped of his title? Anything?"

She fell back against her chair, exhausted. The thought of Lord Ellington not having to pay for his crimes appalled her.

Adalyn spoke up. "There are ways to make Lord Ellington suffer," she said. "One way would be financially." She paused.

Her gaze connecting with Tessa's. "The other would be to ruin him socially."

Tessa understood immediately what Adalyn referred to.

The cut direct.

It was a form of social rebuke. A judgment from the *ton* upon one who had curried immense disfavor with society.

It would be a start. A small one, but at this point, Tessa would take any victory she could.

She sat up again and clasped Adalyn's hands. "How do we go about it?"

Adalyn said, "Leave it to me and Louisa. Our fathers, as well. Between us and our social connections, we can see that it makes a difference, beginning with tonight's ball at the Blasingames'."

Tessa looked to her uncles and said, "Lord Ellington will be in attendance at tonight's ball. I know this because the two men he hired to help him murder Spencer are to meet him two blocks from there."

"Why are they meeting him?" Louisa asked.

"The earl was supposed to complete payment to them for the death of Spencer," Tessa said flatly. "In exchange for learning the circumstances, I told these men to leave London and never return. They are guilty of a crime but the bulk of the guilt lies at Lord Ellington's doorstep."

She looked at the group surrounding her and said, "Social ruin will be the first step. We will work on financial ruin after that. I must return to Spencer now."

Tessa rose and Adalyn asked, "Will you attend tonight's ball, Cousin?"

"No, I don't want to leave Spencer's side."

Adalyn took Tessa's hand and said, "I think you should be there to witness Lord Ellington's social downfall."

She replied, "Then I will come home and dress shortly before the ball is to begin and accompany you there." She squeezed Adalyn's hand. "Thank you for what you are doing."

"I promise that Lord Ellington will be totally humiliated

tonight when he arrives," her cousin said.

Tessa left her uncle's townhouse and crossed slowly back to Spencer's residence. Hopefully, it would be their home one day. She hoped beyond hope that Spencer would recover from his severe injuries. Even if he didn't and he wasn't the man from before, Tessa knew she would remain by his side. Knowing Spencer was to have purchased a special license today, she wondered if that might be something one of her uncles could arrange for instead. She planned to wed Spencer as soon as possible.

Marsh admitted her and she returned to the sickroom, where Rigsby sat by his master's side.

The valet told her, "I was able to get him to sip from the Saint John's wort mixture Dr. Presley recommended. It is incredibly powerful and his lordship is to drink from it only once a day. Dr. Presley also sent a message that he will return mid-afternoon to check on his lordship."

Tessa pulled up a chair to the bed and slipped her hand around Spencer's.

"Very well," she said and settled in for the vigil.

⇥⟫⟪⇤

TESSA LEFT SPENCER'S townhouse in better spirits. Dr. Presley's visit, coupled with Spencer being awake and alert for a few hours, had raised her spirits immeasurably. Spencer had apologized for not being able to purchase the special license and she had told him not to worry because it had been taken care of. That seemed to soothe him. He had then told Rigsby that the valet must go to Tattersalls at once.

The servant had looked at her and whispered Spencer might be delirious.

Spencer overheard it, which Tessa took as a good sign, and said, "No, I was to buy my bride a wedding present there."

He explained about a chestnut mare he had wanted to give her and begged Rigsby to leave at once and arrange for its purchase and delivery.

Rigsby left at once for Tattersalls and Tessa kept her vigil at Spencer's bedside until the servant returned. Finally, Spencer fell into a deep sleep and she explained briefly to Rigsby the beginning of Lord Ellington's downfall, which would occur at tonight's ball.

"Go, my lady," the valet urged. "I will stay at his lordship's side. You need to see this humiliation."

Tessa returned to Uncle Uxbridge's townhouse and found Abra anxiously waiting. The moment Tessa entered her bedchamber, Abra threw her arms about her mistress.

"Oh, my lady, I am so sorry. Lord Middlefield is the best of men."

"I must look my very best tonight, Abra," she told the servant.

As Abra prepared Tessa for the evening, she briefly explained what was in store for Lord Ellington.

"I don't think it's near enough, my lady," Abra declared. "It's unfair. Totally unfair that a peer doesn't suffer any consequences for wrongdoing." A gleam entered her eyes. "Perhaps Lord Ellington might meet up with an unexpected footpad."

Tessa shook her head violently. "No, Abra. You are not to attack the earl in any way. If you were caught, you would be the one swinging from a gibbet. I can't have that."

She left her bedchamber and descended the stairs, where she found her aunt and uncle waiting for her.

"Where is Adalyn?" she asked.

"She has gone ahead," Uncle Uxbridge told her. "We will meet up with her there."

Tessa was silent as the carriage took her to Lord and Lady Blasingames' townhouse. Nerves filled her at what was to come. She wondered if Adalyn, Louisa, and her uncles had been able to pull off the miracle she needed tonight.

Just before they disembarked from the carriage, Tessa asked, "Is there any way you or Uncle Edgar could arrange for the purchase of a special license so that Spencer and I might wed as soon as possible?"

Her uncle frowned in concentration and then said, "I don't know if that is a possibility but Edgar and I will go to the Archbishop of Canterbury himself tomorrow. Edgar has known the archbishop for many years. If it is legal for us to obtain it for Lord Middlefield, we will do so."

As Tessa climbed from the carriage, she decided a wedding and its breakfast were no longer important. Only Spencer was. She wanted to be his wife—and in case she carried his child now—she wanted that child to be legitimate, especially if an heir.

They entered the townhouse and joined the receiving line, where she received congratulations on her betrothal from those nearby. When they reached their host and hostess, they, too, were effusive in giving their best wishes to her and Spencer's upcoming nuptials.

"And where is Lord Middlefield this evening?" Lord Blasingame asked.

She smiled politely. "My betrothed was unable to attend, my lord. He sends his regrets."

Entering the ballroom with her aunt and uncle, the butler announced their arrival. Immediately, she spied Adalyn and Louisa and made her way toward her cousins.

Adalyn said, "It has all been arranged. We have called in every favor we could."

Tessa said, "I can't thank you enough, Adalyn."

Louisa asked, "How is Lord Middlefield now?"

"Dr. Presley saw some improvement this afternoon," she shared. "I have asked your father and Uncle Edgar to explore the possibility of receiving a special license, even though Spencer cannot apply for it himself. I wish us to wed immediately."

Adalyn nodded. "I agree. It will not be the wedding you had anticipated but you will have a lifetime with the man of your dreams." She gazed intently at Tessa and said, "You *will* have that a lifetime with him, Tessa. I promise."

Though Tessa knew her cousin could not make promises like that, it still reassured her.

Louisa said, "Please excuse me. I see someone else I must speak with who can help in tonight's endeavor."

"I want you to wait over here," Adalyn told Tessa as Louisa left, leading Tessa near the entrance where Lord Ellington would appear. "Stand here," her cousin ordered, "so you will be partially hidden by the potted plant. Once Ellington makes his way through the ballroom, follow him. Revel in what you see. If you wish, confront him in front of the crowd. That would be most effective if the truth came from your lips in front of everyone present."

Tessa nodded. "Thank you again."

Adalyn left her side and Tessa's eyes went to the doorway. A good two dozen parties were announced and the ballroom swelled to full capacity before she spied Lord Ellington in the entrance.

The butler announced him and the buzz of conversation, which had filled the room, immediately ceased. All eyes fastened upon the earl as he stepped inside, a jovial smile upon his lips. He started to stop at the first group he encountered, only to find the entire circle of people look him up and down and quickly turn their backs upon him.

Frowning, he continued deeper into the room, only to have everyone whose path he crossed do the same.

By now, Tessa had fallen into step behind him and continued being his shadow until he stopped and gazed across the room.

"Lord Ellington," she called out loudly and the earl wheeled to face her.

The little conversation which had begun again now halted. The ballroom was as silent as a tomb. Every eye in Polite Society watched as she confronted the villain who had almost taken Spencer's life.

"My lady?" Lord Ellington said, his face drained of color.

"I am not and never will be your lady, Lord Ellington," her voice ringing out across the ballroom. "You thought to court me but lost out to a much better man. A man whose boots you are not fit to even lick."

She stepped toward him, her anger controlled but now erupting.

"You have enjoyed an easy, charmed life. You move throughout Polite Society, having friends and wooing beautiful women. You have a reputation as a master pugilist. But you are a sore loser."

"Why, I—"

"Silence!" she commanded, glaring at him. "You pretended to befriend Lord Middlefield and instead wished to see him suffer at your hands during a so-called, friendly sparring match. My fiancé surprised you that day, my lord, and soundly defeated you in front of many gentlemen of the *ton*. You did not handle your loss with grace and aplomb as a gentleman should."

Tessa paused, her eyes narrowing. "Instead, you sought retribution of the worst kind. You hired two criminals to attack Lord Middlefield in Rotten Row. Then you proceeded to have those men restrain him while you rained down blows upon him. He was helpless to defend himself. And then after savagely beating him in such a horrendous manner, you instructed them to complete the job you refused to do.

"You ordered them to beat him to death."

Gasps filled the ballroom. The very air charged with anger, all directed at Lord Ellington.

"I wanted you," the earl pleaded.

"No, you didn't. You convinced yourself you did because Lord Middlefield was interested in me. You wanted what you couldn't have." She gazed at him steadily. "And now you have lost everything you did have. Your reputation will forever be in shreds for having deliberately engineered an attack on and ordering the murder of a fellow peer. No one will invite you to

ALEXA ASTON

their social affairs. No one will wish to be seen in your company.
No man will box with you or pretend to be your friend. No lady
will dance with you. No one will enter into any kind of business
dealings with you.

"You, Lord Ellington, are forever ruined."

He looked at her, no longer confused. Quickly, his eyes dart-
ed about the ballroom to confirm what she had said. Tessa saw
the contempt on the faces of every member of the *ton*.

The earl's gaze returned to her and his face revealed his true
nature as his venomous hate became obvious.

"You bitch," he growled, his hand raising to strike her.

Tessa reacted quickly, glad she stood close enough to him to
slam her knee into his groin, a move Louisa had taught her
cousins years ago. One Tessa had never thought to use.

Until now.

Lord Ellington gasped, his fist falling as he doubled over,
clutching himself.

The entire *ton* also gasped collectively.

Lord Wethersby emerged from the crowd near her, touching
her elbow. "Are you all right, Lady Tessa?" he asked.

"I will be when this filth is removed," she replied.

"Gladly," the viscount said.

Lord Wethersby moved to Lord Ellington and jerked him to
his feet. Several other gentlemen stepped forward, taking hold of
the earl, and the group hustled him from the ballroom.

A cacophony of voices erupted about her, the shock of the
moment now over. As usual, Polite Society needed to gossip
about what they had seen.

Louisa appeared. "You were magnificent, Tessa. I am proud
to be your cousin." She embraced Tessa.

Adalyn joined them and the three cousins tightly clung to one
another.

Then Uncle Edgar touched her shoulder. "I believe it best if
we all leave now, my dear."

Tears freely flowed down her cheeks as she took his arm and

he escorted her from the ballroom. Her aunt and uncle joined them.

"You have given Polite Society something to talk about for years to come," her aunt said, slipping her arm about Tessa's waist. "And you have made women proud. You stood up to that horrible man. Why, you can do anything, Tessa!"

Through her tears, she said, "All I want is to be with Spencer."

CHAPTER TWENTY-SEVEN

S PENCER AWOKE AND kept his eyes closed. The familiar scent of lavender still lingered in the air but Tessa's hand did not hold his, as it had for most of the past week.

Gradually, he opened his eyes, thinking his body ached everywhere. Surprisingly, though, after only three days the bruises were all but gone. Tessa told him it had been thanks to Dr. Presley's leeches and the gel containing arnica that Rigsby had coated across Spencer's body.

After a week, however, his ribs still troubled him and would for a bit longer, according to the physician.

Not enough to prevent him from attending his own wedding. *Or keeping him from bedding his wife.*

Spencer had done everything in his power to be ready for today, which had been designated as their wedding day, even doing the torturous breathing exercises prescribed by Dr. Presley. Actually, they had only been awful the first day. Both Tessa and Rigsby rode roughshod over him, talking him through inhaling deep breaths which forced his ribcage to expand. Almost as painful had been the short huffs and forced cough.

He had repeated the exercises several times a day and found they did help though he would never divulge that to the two tyrants known as his fiancée and valet.

Rigsby entered the room, carrying a breakfast tray. "Ah, good morning, my lord. Ready to slip on the old ball and chain today?"

If he were to be a prisoner, he would choose to be Tessa's prisoner again and again.

She had told him that Lord Ellington wouldn't be bothering them anymore but hadn't given him any details. Those had come from Miss Goulding, who came to visit him a few days after the now-infamous ball at the Blasingames' residence.

Miss Goulding had shooed Tessa away, telling her cousin she would sit a few hours with Spencer while Tessa took a long bath and napped. While Tessa was gone, Lady Adalyn arrived. Together, the two women gave him an elaborate account of the encounter between Tessa and Ellington, even standing and acting out what had occurred. To hear of Ellington's shame and disgrace in front of all of Polite Society had brought a smile to Spencer's face.

That—and knowing his Boudica had gone into battle once more.

For him.

For love.

"Please refrain from thinking that my bride will be my jailer, Rigsby," he told his valet, seeing the smile the servant bit back as he placed the breakfast tray down and helped Spencer sit up.

As he breakfasted, the valet kept up a running dialogue, filled with his usual gossip. Instead of cutting Rigsby off, he listened. It seemed the *ton* had united as a whole behind Tessa and her bravery in calling Ellington out. She was its new darling, despite having gone to no more events since she spent every waking moment by his side.

The two of them had talked things over and decided after today's wedding that they would retire to the country for the remainder of the Season. When he next attended a ball with Tessa as his wife, he wanted to dance the waltz with her in front of everyone, gliding across the dance floor and twirling her about. As it was now, he would have to gingerly make love to her until his ribs healed.

Rigsby put him through the dreaded breathing exercises, which seemed easier today than in days past. Afterward, he soaked in a hot bath and allowed Rigsby to gently bathe him. Dressing proved to be an arduous task but it would be worth it to stand next to Tessa and speak his vows.

He had practiced walking about his bedchamber and now Rigsby gave Spencer a walking stick.

"I'm not an invalid," he muttered but took the stick in hand and it helped him ease down the stairs.

Together, he and his valet crossed the square to Lord Uxbridge's townhouse.

"I'll leave you here, my lord," Rigsby said as they approached the front door. "Bridget'll be waiting for me at the servants' entrance around back. I'll return—"

"Stay as long as you like," Spencer said. "At least for today—and tonight—I will have a new, vastly improved valet to undress me."

Rigsby roared with laughter. "Just another thing Lady Tessa can add to her list of accomplishments. I mean, Lady Middlefield," the valet corrected as he parted from Spencer.

Before Spencer could knock, the door to Lord Uxbridge's townhouse swung open and Rainey, the butler, greeted him, a broad smile on his face.

"Good morning, Lord Middlefield," Rainey said. "May I say you are looking particularly well this day?"

He hoped he looked well enough to wed and merely said, "Thank you, Rainey. Is everything here in good order?"

The butler nodded reassuringly. "All is well, my lord. Thank you for providing Cook with a list of your favorite dishes. You will find them all on the table today for the wedding breakfast."

"Excellent," he replied. "Where is the wedding being held?"

"In the drawing room, my lord. I shall take you there now."

"I know my way by now, Rainey," Spencer said.

Using the walking stick provided by Rigsby, he made his way up the stairs and to the drawing room. He entered and saw a few people already present.

Lord Uxbridge came to meet him. "You are looking well, Middlefield," the earl said. "Are you ready to enter a state of holy matrimony?" he asked, his eyes twinkling.

Panic seized Spencer. "The special license!" he cried. "Did . . . is it—"

"Yes, Edgar was able to obtain it. He is well acquainted with the Archbishop of Canterbury. In fact," Lord Uxbridge said, glancing over his shoulder and back to Spencer, "the archbishop will perform today's ceremony."

His jaw dropped as he looked across the room and saw Sir Edgar Goulding in conversation with the archbishop.

"Come and meet him," Lord Uxbridge urged.

They crossed the room and came to a halt in front of the archbishop.

After being introduced Spencer said, "I had no idea that you would be marrying Tessa and me today, Your Grace. I am most grateful to you—and Sir Edgar—for arranging the special license for me since I was physically unable to do so."

The archbishop nodded. "I was happy to do my old friend a favor," he shared. "I am sorry of what passed between you and Lord Ellington but I hear that your fiancée certainly put the wicked earl in his place. I met your bride yesterday," the archbishop continued, "and she is a most formidable lady."

He smiled. "She is indeed, Your Grace. I am most fortunate to have won her hand—and her heart."

Lady Adalyn and Miss Goulding approached him, with Miss Goulding saying, "Everyone in the *ton* has been asking about you, Lord Middlefield."

"Since we are to be family, would you please consider calling me Spencer?" he asked.

"I would be happy to do so, as long as you refer to me as Louisa."

"And I am Adalyn," the other said. "Neither of us has brothers so I do believe we will adopt you to be an honorary one of ours."

Spencer chuckled. "And I have had no sisters until now. I am blessed not only to be wedding Tessa but to be marrying into this loving family. I thank both of you for your support in helping this wedding occur today, from my pursuit of Tessa through the actual ceremony today."

"I do believe you will make a fine husband to Tessa," Adalyn told him.

Louisa added, "And an even better father."

Lady Uxbridge appeared and said, "It is almost time to begin, Lord Middlefield. Let me show you where to stand."

Spencer followed Tessa's aunt to the large fireplace, where the Archbishop of Canterbury stood facing the room. Lord Wethersby joined him. Spencer had sent a note to the viscount a few days ago, asking him to stand with him at today's ceremony. He liked Wethersby a great deal and hoped the man might be husband material for either Louisa or Adalyn.

He dipped a finger into his pocket and handed Tessa's wedding ring to Wethersby.

"This is yours for safekeeping," he said. "Thank you for agreeing to stand with me today."

Lord Wethersby grinned. "I would stand by you any day, Middlefield. The honor is mine."

Spencer turned and faced the door, waiting for Tessa. Moments later, she arrived and his heart almost exploded with love.

As she came toward him, he noticed she had worn blue, the color he liked to see her in the most. But it wasn't the gown which caught his attention. It was the love shining in her eyes for him, love he knew was reflected in his own.

Lord Uxbridge escorted his niece to her groom, looking like a proud papa as he handed Tessa off. She joined Spencer, slipping her hand through his arm and giving it a squeeze. They gazed at one another for a long moment and both mouthed, *"I love you"* at the same time, causing a warmth to rush through him.

Adalyn and Louisa joined them, standing to Tessa's left and

they all turned toward the archbishop, who began the ceremony.

"Dearly beloved, we are gathered together here in the sight of God . . ."

Spencer took the words to heart, knowing they bound him to Tessa forever.

Then the archbishop instructed him to use his right hand to take Tessa's and said, "Repeat after me, my lord."

Spencer echoed the words, gazing directly in his bride's eyes, seeing hers brim with tears and feeling his do the same.

Then Tessa did the same—but her words startled Spencer.

"I, Tessa Boudica Foster, take thee, Spencer Edward Haddock, to be my wedded husband, to have and to hold from this day forward, for better for worse, for richer for poorer, in sickness and in health, to love, cherish, and to obey, till death us do part, according to God's holy ordinance; and thereto I give thee my troth."

The ceremony continued and after several minutes and numerous prayers, the archbishop pronounced them man and wife.

Spencer faced his bride—now his wife—and bent, brushing his lips against hers in a sweet, soft kiss.

Breaking it, he said only so she could hear, "The words in the ceremony did not go far enough, my love. I want you to know that I plan to make every day a happy one for you. That I will hold you close and cherish your mind, your body, and your spirit. I respect you. Admire you. Worship you. My dreams have come true today because we have become one."

Then Spencer kissed her again, sealing these new vows, his heart bursting with love.

Those present applauded the new couple and Lord Uxbridge invited everyone to come to the wedding breakfast.

Their guests left the drawing room, with Spencer and Tessa bringing up the rear.

As they proceeded downstairs, he said, "I found it interesting that I was actually marrying my Boudica."

She beamed. "I told you Papa had an interest in history. That extended to naming me. Mama didn't care for the name Boudica at all and insisted it serve as my middle name. So I was christened Tessa Boudica Foster and have always gone by Tessa."

He touched a finger to her cheek. "I will always call you Tessa—but I will remember that you have the heart and courage of the incredible Boudica." He stroked her cheek and then mused, "Perhaps I will call you Boudica when I have you in our bed."

Her cheeks flushed and he added, "Boudica was known for her fierceness and devotion. I see both of those in you, my dearest love."

Tessa took his wrist and turned his hand, pressing a kiss into his palm. "I will love you forever, Spencer. My devotion will know no boundaries." She placed his palm so that it rested against her cheek. "My heart is yours."

Spencer kissed his new wife with great tenderness, knowing each day would see their love grow.

EPILOGUE

Stoneridge—August

S PENCER HELPED TESSA into the saddle and mounted Pilgrim. They had been out visiting tenants at Stoneridge all day and were ready to return home for tea. They trotted their horses side-by-side until they reached an open field. Tessa glanced at him, mischief in her eyes, and then she took off.

For a moment, he merely watched her on the chestnut mare that served as her wedding gift. She looked as one with the large beast as they flew across the meadow. Pride swelled within him, seeing how well she handled the horse. How well she handled everything. Tessa had taken to her role as a countess and made numerous improvements in the running of the household. His tenants adored her. When Spencer showed up for a visit without her, they didn't bother to hide their disappointment.

And she would bear their first child come the new year.

Tessa had told him she was with child two weeks ago. He had already suspected as much. Her breasts seemed fuller. Her belly slightly rounded. She had been ill a few mornings, retching into a bowl, and then seemingly fine afterward. By her calculations, it looked as if she would give birth in mid-February. His dreams of a family would now come true.

All because of the woman who held his heart.

Spurring Pilgrim on, he gave chase, arriving at their stables well after she did. He dismounted and tossed his reins to a stable lad and then took her hand, leading her back to the house. They had consulted the local doctor, who said Tessa could ride another two or three weeks and then she should curtail that activity. He had suggested taking up walking for exercise.

"Shall we take tea outside?" she asked, slipping her arm through his. "It's such a lovely day."

"I like that idea."

As they entered the foyer, Spencer told Callender they would have their tea outside.

"Very good, my lord," the butler said.

They cut through the house and went to his study. He opened the French doors and they stepped outside again, where a table with four chairs sat in the shade. Tessa had suggested the arrangement, noting that she and her parents had a similar one at their country house. In the two months since they had arrived, it had become their habit to sit outside during various parts of the day. Sometimes, at breakfast. Other times, after dinner, where they would sip on a glass of wine as they held hands.

The teacart arrived soon after and they dug in, both ravenous after their day out on the estate. Once they had eaten, Spencer took Tessa's hand in his. He leaned toward her and slipped his hand about her nape, drawing her close so he could nibble on her delicious lips.

Lifting his mouth to where it hovered over hers, he asked, "Shall we go upstairs, my Boudica?"

He addressed her this way in moments of intimacy, loving the brave and powerful woman he had wed.

"I thought you would never ask," she said seductively, causing a frisson of desire to ripple through him.

His mouth touched hers again, heat filling him.

Then someone cleared his throat.

Annoyed, Spencer broke the kiss and glanced up. "What is it, Callender?"

"You have a visitor, my lord."

"A visitor?" His annoyance grew. "We aren't expecting anyone. Tell them to go away."

"Spencer," his wife chided. "We should at least find out who it is." She looked to Callender. "Who has come to call?"

"The Duke of Camden, my lady."

Spencer started. His mouth grew dry. Panic filled him. His gaze turned to Tessa.

"Show His Grace in," she told Callender.

The butler left and she squeezed his hand.

"There is only one reason Camden would be here," he said dully. "Ev has been killed in the war." A wave of sadness swept over him, a physical ache. "Though why Camden would come to tell me of his brother's death in person, I haven't a clue."

She cupped his cheek. "Perhaps the duke brings you something from Everett. Something he wanted you to have," she said softly. "Something to remember him by."

He steeled himself. "Ev's brother is detestable. I met him a few times over the years, before he came into the dukedom."

"Well, he is here now. Try to be hospitable."

Spencer saw the French door open and gripped Tessa's hand, tamping down his sorrow, his throat thick with emotion.

Shock filled him as the Duke of Camden walked through the door, a grin on his face.

It was Ev.

About the Author

Award-winning and internationally bestselling author Alexa Aston's historical romances use history as a backdrop to place her characters in extraordinary circumstances, where their intense desire for one another grows into the treasured gift of love.

She is the author of Regency and Medieval romance, including: Dukes of Distinction; Soldiers & Soulmates; The St. Clairs; The King's Cousins; and The Knights of Honor.

A native Texan, Alexa lives with her husband in a Dallas suburb, where she eats her fair share of dark chocolate and plots out stories while she walks every morning. She enjoys a good Netflix binge; travel; seafood; and can't get enough of *Survivor* or *The Crown*.